THE MUSIC OF THE SPHERES

A Countercultural Tragedy

Allister Thompson

For the real-life Teresa to my Simon

CONTEMPORARY MUSIC IS NOT THE MUSIC
OF THE FUTURE NOR THE MUSIC OF THE PAST
BUT SIMPLY MUSIC PRESENT WITH US: THIS
MOMENT, NOW, THIS NOW MOMENT.

—John Cage, *Silence*

AUTHOR'S NOTE

All of the following events in the life of Simon Hastings really did take place, no matter how fantastic they may seem. In this age of rapid technological advancement, trendsetters fast become the stuff of legend to subsequent generations. I knew Simon very well, being a friend and a journalist who has exhaustively documented his career, and I firmly believe that he will eventually be recognized as one of these quasi-mythological figures. I could have written this book as a common biography or in the breezy journalistic style with which you may be familiar from my work. But somehow, as pretentious as it may seem, the grand narrative style of fiction seems the only proper treatment of my subject.

Not since the Persians first used unpleasant musical tones so effectively to unman their foes in their ancient battles with Athens and Sparta has humankind witnessed an explosion of so many odd sounds; new musical styles that challenge the mind and soul, warring for the loyalty of the population in this so-called "information age," in which audio technology is so widespread and available. It was the discordant tones of the Saxon hordes that helped drive William and his invading Normans away from our unfriendly shores during their first invasion in 1070, a more powerful weapon than any gun or bow. The First Great War was partially ended in 1925, not by nuclear weapons but rather by the incessant blasting of hypnotic tritones by British gliders over the spires of Berlin, Dresden, and Milan. The great Russian Gregorovich's compositions gained him such favor in the court of Frederick III the Humpback that it was said the real power in Prussia lay in the composer's quill. All of this, of course, is well known to the educated reader, and it is not my intent here to inflict a lengthy history lecture.

The use of electrical impulses in music-making has revolutionized the world in many ways. Now, in this newly democratic age, we follow new heroes, not only trade union leaders like Tom Mann, who whipped up rage and change with fiddle tunes and miners' ballads, played on giant phonograms, during the Syndicalist meetings of the 1940s, but that very modern figure, the "rock star." Their messages, be they inspiring or vacuous, have gained such a hold on the modern mind that the genre has eclipsed all others in its ability to alter the sometimes easily swayed perspectives of the masses.

Therefore, no threat to social "stability" is presently considered as serious by the repressive governments of the Western world. Hastings and his bands, The Spheres and Astronomy, must be put in their proper place at the forefront of this rebellious new sonic movement.

Most of the story told in these pages was related to me by Hastings himself, shortly before his tragic death one year ago at the age of thirty-six; his message and his music were just then beginning to be embraced as widely and enthusiastically by the music-loving public as they had been by critics and friends such as myself. I well remember the night I left a portable tape recorder running during an evening of wine and cannabis, as Hastings told me this bizarre tale at length (or *ad nauseum*, as I thought at the time). He told me that he was himself working on a draft of the story you are about to read, despite the terrible risks he would undertake by publishing it, but a shackling depression had descended upon him in recent months.

I was at first skeptical of many details and hoped to have the opportunity to corroborate some of the facts before publication, especially since surprisingly few of these events have ever made an appearance in the press. Sadly, due to several months of laziness on my part, his untimely death means he will never see his story in print, but I believe this book will be a fitting memorial to a great man.

You will have to do your best to forgive my occasional flights of fancy and elaboration, but I vigorously insist that the events described herein did occur. I have used Hastings' own notes extensively to recreate the episodes as vividly as possible. Hastings participated in a series of the most dramatic events of our time and yet remained unheralded for his heroism. He was a most remarkable man — and I was there, a *New Musical Tribune* reporter, documenting his career. His work with The Spheres will, I believe, in time become immortal in the annals of the musical arts, a fitting complement to the icons of past ages, the Bachs, Salieris, and Wilsons. I should note that owe a great debt of gratitude to a few people, most notably my wife, Vera, who has had to put up with my obsessions for so long, but also the inimitable Martin Sharpe-Thornton and Teresa Cappadocia for inspiration and encouragement. Last but not least, my editor, Alexandra Coffey of Peregrine Books, for shepherding this book to its completion and for possessing the courage to push for the publication of a book guaranteed to cause great controversy. We have had to rush through the editorial process to counter the rumored publication of a rival version of this story by one of my colleagues who claims to have obtained many (but surely not all) of the facts through German sources.

So, without further ado, here is the story of Simon Hastings in the time of our indomitable counterculture and some of the most important circumstances of our age.

—Rodney Blair, Edinburgh, July 1973

ONE

A soft gurgling drifted through Simon Hastings' spacious loft flat as a murky brown liquid seeped from a small bottle, through a plastic tube capped with a needle, and into a swelling vein on his right forearm. The tubing, like the drug itself, was grade-A, sterilized, and government-approved. When the bottle had drained completely, he pulled out the tube with a satisfied grunt.

The air in his flat was thick, weighed down with the must of days and months of cigarette smoke, a fitting complement to the ponderously slow, reverby blues playing on the stereo, the new collaboration between James Hendricks and Klaus Stockhausen, "Drones for Electric Guitar and Treated Magnetic Tape." The monochromatic drony sounds perfectly matched the mood in the flat. Wispy clouds filtered greenish harvest moonlight through the massive uncurtained windows as Hastings picked up his jade and chromium electric guitar, manufactured to his personal tastes and specifications by the world's most esteemed luthier, Sven Hagstrom of Sweden. Hastings proceeded to ferociously jump up and down and high-kick, running around the room with the guitar for several minutes, emitting the occasional yelp, moan, or falsetto note.

The year was 1968, now remembered as a critically important time in the culture of our age, the apex of the development of various subcultures just then starting to gain recognition by the commercial "mainstream." It was a particularly exciting time to be playing rock and roll in New York City, the capital of the Colony of Virginia. Freed by technology and a relatively novel state of democracy from the oppressive class control of aristocrats, landowners, and lordly tycoons and their tight control over what was presented as art and entertainment, youth culture in England, Europe, and Virginia had exploded in the 1960s in waves of dissonant sound and color. The fortuitous legalization and regulation of almost every narcotic and hallucinogenic known to humankind by a new breed of lawmaker hadn't hurt this development. The sale of recreational pharmaceuticals was now tightly monitored worldwide and was considered an excellent way to keep the population docile, tranquil, and happy, although the multinationals that manufactured such compounds could be considered to possess more actual, palpable power than the governments charged with regulating them.

The burgeoning counterculture was considered a necessary evil by the new corporate establishment, an unwitting cash cow consuming products made at the behest of straight-laced businesspeople who wouldn't dare to touch the stuff themselves.

The colorfully named Cognitive Vibe Enhancer 3, which Hastings had been injecting, was a compound sold by KässelPharma GmbH of Augsburg, the largest producer of recreational pharmaceuticals in the world, just ahead of Colombian Cartels Inc. and United Chinese Chemical. This drug, which had been copied by several generic manufacturers with mixed results, imparted a sense of misty well-being to the user's psyche; those familiar with its effects will recall the amplification of one's perception of another person's behavior. Frowns were perceived as smiles, smiles as beams, and laughter as joy beyond expression; negative feelings were almost completely blocked while the drug was in the user's system. It was also physically nonaddictive, like most of the new pharmaceuticals placed on the market in the last decade. Addictive substances, with the exception of cigarettes and alcohol, had been officially illegal throughout the Empire since the 1940s. Despite the fact that the CEO of KässelPharma at the time of this story, Helga Schmidt, was reputed to harbor disturbingly reactionary views on how society should properly be run, extremely "square" to say the least, the company's products were the stimulants of choice for hipsters worldwide.

Finishing his bizarre warm-up, Hastings wiped the sweat from his forehead with a hairy wrist, breathing heavily but feeling much better. He was in his early thirties and airily unashamed of his relatively advanced rock and roll/countercultural age, still with jet-black, perfectly straight hair and still remarkably thin considering his high alcohol intake. He was dressed in a clingy shirt swirling with bright colors and skin-tight black jeans. This had been his stage uniform of late. Though he was not technically the star and focus of the band, being only lead guitar and not the singer, after all, and he really didn't spend all that much time preening in front of mirrors, Hastings sometimes fancied himself a rather Romantic character.

"Better shove off," he declared to the walls in his precise South London accent with a sweeping gesture. "Me chariot awaits."

Placing the Hagstrom in its case, he cursed the roadies in advance for the leads, guitar stands, vintage guitars, etc., that were sure to go missing in the course of another wild evening. Such was the price of rock and roll excess. Stepping out of the lift, he raised his coat collar against the pea-soup fog that rose in a phosphorescent haze from the polluted waters of the Hudson. Though he could only see clearly for about twenty feet in any direction, he managed to hail a garishly striped cab and gazed vacantly out at the deserted streets with their abandoned, gape-windowed storefronts, occasionally glimpsing dazed, drug-induced expressions that mirrored his own on the faces of the few pedestrians.

The C-Enhancer was really kicking in quickly this time; a good thing, since the early fall weather had him feeling a little bit more melancholy than usual. Melancholy was a good Romantic coat to wear, but not when it started to become more real than an affectation. The cabbie was driving a little too fast (he had seemed to recognize his minor celebrity fare and was presumably trying to impress), and soon the spired skyline of Holborn, home of Elysian

Fields, the colonial center of the new musical underground, loomed into view.

Hastings and his band, The Spheres, were on the verge of becoming genuine rock stars, despite or perhaps because of their extremely radical, out-there psychedelic sounds, but they were still less popular than those old standbys The Beach Bums, The Lonely Hearts Club, and The Jet Set, who had helped lead the rock and roll revolution but who were now considered pretty square by those in search of a fresher high. The psych scene had only really broken through onto the pop charts in the last year or so.

Though The Spheres could probably have sold out the 2,000-seat King George VII Theatre if they chose to attempt it, they preferred to play as often as possible in the more intimate and comfortable setting of Elysian Fields, featuring up-and-coming acts as support. For instance, day one of this particular three-nighter had featured Kamshaft, a dangerous-looking biker band fronted by warty, throaty bassist Lenny Lurch, and the wild, anarchic, always impossibly stoned Pink Gremlins, whose usual gimmick was to destroy the stage as thoroughly as possible at the end of their set. It was quite a release for both band and audience. That had led to the band being blacklisted by most venues, but they had promised to tone down their act for the night so that The Spheres would have a stage to tread on when they were done. This time they had only smashed a couple of holes in the stage with their battleax and thrown a few shot putts out into the audience, with no major injuries. Their girlfriends had gone to bail them out of jail, as ebullient as ever with their creation of another local legend. The Spheres had concluded the evening with a four-hour set of their trademark space-rock as the audience freaked out in unison. Night two would no doubt be just as memorable.

The band featured Hastings on guitar, the always foppishly stylish Martin Sharpe-Thornton on the bass guitar, Ed "The Hammer" Bentham on the drums, and charismatic former astrophysics postgrad Guy Calvert on lead vocals, Mellotron,

Minimoog, VCS3 synthesizer, virginal, and portative pipe organ. The lineup was rounded out by the mysterious Electron Z (no one knew his real name, and he claimed to have forgotten it himself), who created the real hallmark of their sound. He was known for his two-foot pompadour and that fact that he hardly ever seemed to sleep; and when he did, it was often on the sidewalk. Electron Z pounded and scraped blocks of wood and chunks of metal, parts of his own anatomy and other people's, and any other objects that came to hand. The sounds were processed through a microphone and an echo unit, producing outlandish, otherworldly sounds a *Musick Maker* writer had described in an uncharitable moment as "like nothing this planet has ever heard — and hopefully will never have to hear again." The liquid light show was the last touch needed to send any crowd of stoned hippies into a frenzy.

Hastings was jolted out of a reverie by a lurch and the sudden screech of the taxi's brakes. A group of teenagers in pork-pie hats and breeches had run out in front of the car and were attacking it with cricket bats. Hastings could see the sodium glow glinting menacingly off their red contact lenses and designer gas masks, but their bats were having little effect on the Plexiglas hull of the cab. *Another bad trip for the yobs*, he thought. *They never can handle their medicine.* Acts of random violence were on the rise; the peace-and-love message seemed to be falling on deaf ears in the desolate inner-city neighborhoods, which were blighted to say the least. The police force tended to concentrate on keeping the suburbs as safe and isolated as possible, leaving the city to rot or thrive unchecked. In fact, the authorities in general seemed quite happy to have the lower classes exterminate themselves.

The popular theory in the media was that these acts of unaccountable savagery were encouraged by the side effects of cheap knock-off or homemade copies of drugs like the rather expensive Cognitive Vibe Enhancer series and No-Catch Cocaine, which were widely used by those with the dough to buy them for their more powerful effects. It vaguely occurred to Hastings that perhaps the drugs causing all this trouble might not be the knock-offs at all, but he lazily discarded that train of thought.

The cabbie finally lost patience with the situation and revved up, knocking over one of the attackers and leaving the rest to comically shake their fists in the exhaust cloud. They were soon left behind in the fog.

Tonight's show, the finale of the series, featured a fascinating bill. First up would be The Asparagus Stalks, a group of white Hindu vegetarians who propounded their creed via the new hard rock genre, a style of music highlighted by an overpowering use of distortion. They chanted Hari Krishna-style over a bed of punishingly repetitive guitar riffs that slowly wore down the mind's resistance, creating a meditative state. They would be followed by something very different, the extremely controversial and generally hostile Muttonchop Killers, whose Midwestern frontman, Ned Loogeant, vociferously spouted tirades promoting the hunting of small mammals with bow-and-arrow and condemning vegetarian "limp-wristers" and "communists." No one could decide whether the whole act was a crude performance-art satire of the average man or whether Loogeant really was as much of a redneck as he seemed, and Loogeant wasn't letting on. He was given the benefit of the doubt by most of his acquaintances because of the sheer peculiar magnetism of his act, but Hastings had never really cared for him.

A crowd was already thronging the neon-bathed entrance of Elysian Fields, which was located in an old fish-packing plant. It was an ugly box of a building. Wreathed in the greenish mist and pot smoke, the leather-jacketed and bell-bottomed young people gathered around the doorway looked like ghosts released from a murky hell. They had even started a couple of bonfires to keep warm in the unseasonably cold early fall temperatures. Hastings smiled; this had easily been one of the band's most successful stands since moving to New York from London. Television appearances had helped raise their profile in the colonies to the point where they were verging on stardom. The recent appearance on *Virginian Concerthall* had been of particular benefit; Guy had sounded off with pretentious certitude in the interview portion about the youth movement's hatred of the mannered musical classicism of their parents' generation. Guy had no doubts whatsoever about his self-proclaimed position as the spokesman/prophet of this new generation. The band members had decided to wear some extremely colorful Chinese silks for the occasion.

The short-back-and-sides, tweet-clad interviewer, Philip Crump-Henderson, one of the pillars of the Empire's intellectual establishment, had shown a great deal of snide condescension toward The Spheres' musical efforts.

"Mr. Calvert, I will come directly to the point, and I must ask you whether you really believe that this thing you call your music, which to the trained and sensitive ear seems to be nothing but a deafeningly loud static, with one or two recognizable chords popping up out of that horrible mire now and again, is as artistically and spiritually satisfying as the timeless work of, say, a Salieri, Gregorovich, or a Humperdinck? Some might say, including perhaps myself, that the claims of the new pop groups to artistic legitimacy are not only unfounded, but actually laughable." He leaned back in his seat with an appropriately derisory chuckle, twitching his dyed mustache, adjusting his cravat, and looking very satisfied.

Guy, however, lived for this sort of argument and for the shock caused by the erudition coming from his scruffy exterior. "The world of classical composers," he replied, sucking demurely on a Silk Cut, "reflects accurately the purpose for which it was created, purposes which are thankfully now becoming obsolete. The pieces composed by your beloved Humperdinck were largely commissioned by rich patrons, the aristocracy, to provide courtly entertainment for the fellow members of the oppressor class. They weren't even likely intended to be great works of art, so it's ironically amusing to observe the veneration that people like you show them. Meanwhile, the vast majority of humanity lived short and brutish lives outside the gates. This upper-class music has no soul, no artistry. It was created with neither love nor passion.

"It's only time, Mr. Crump, that has afforded this music its fame. That's why bloated old windbags like yourself worship at the altar of a time when people like yourself, or at least you imagine so, had the rest of us under control, although I personally doubt you have a single drop of aristocratic blood in your veins."

Crump made a spluttering noise, but Guy talked right over him. "Now, *our* music is a direct, emphatic rejection of values such as yours and an embrace of freedom and beauty. It requires a completely new mindset to appreciate. It's no surprise at all that you and I can't agree on the artistic merit of my works." He sat back, fluttered his long eyelashes, and smiled.

The Spheres were not invited back to *Virginian Concerthall.*

The cab pulled around the rear of the club, where Hastings tipped the driver handsomely and autographed his hot dog wrapper. Jerzy, the band's hulking Polish roadie/bodyguard, was guarding the back door. With a swagger in his step, Hastings entered the murky depths of Elysian Fields.

TWO

Aside from a one-sided brawl between some of The Asparagus Stalks and Muttonchop Killers, resulting in a couple of puffy lips and black eyes, the early sound checks were uneventful, and all was ready for the evening's extravaganza. While Jerzy laboriously tuned up the guitars and laid out the items that Electron Z would strike throughout the set, the lighting crew tested their gear and made sure that nothing would be set alight. The Spheres relaxed at a corner table. Asparagus Stalks plus a twelve-hippie-girl entourage, all dressed in white robes, were meditating en masse in another corner, trying to regain their composure; The Spheres respectfully ignored them. A faint, chanted "om" floated across the room every now and then.

The C-Enhancer had settled quite nicely into Hastings' consciousness. He viewed the room through a rosy veil, and he could feel his synapses crackling with pleasurable thoughts. Puffing on a massive spliff, he laughed loudly at each and every joke that came to his ears. Guy had already managed to inject several different substances into his pockmarked left arm, but he had run out of juice early and was starting to get grumpy.

"Yewd betta lay off her a woile anyways, Guy," The Hammer advised with sleepy concern. "We don't need yer goin' wonky onstage agin, mate." His six-foot-five frame was crammed under the table, and his deep-set eyes were hidden under his huge, frizzy mop of red hair. The Hammer preferred to stick to good, old-fashioned ale, being conservative in many respects — except where music and sex were concerned. In those areas he could be uncomfortably radical. The portion of the table in front of him was filled with empty pint glasses.

"Edmund, would you kindly go and fuck yourself?" Guy disposed of his last needle with a flourish. "Christ, you'd think the stuff was still addictive, eh? Well, someone will come along with a fix soon enough, I daresay. One of our 'fans'!"

Even when speaking disparagingly, Guy Calvert could make a person feel very special. Though his charm and charisma were most certainly affected, the rock and roll masses of Virginia had thus far taken quite well to his exaggerated persona; he was the hero of the moment, the intellectual leader of a cultural revolution. The Wilson brothers could never compete with an image like Guy's. His golden blond hair and trim beard were pinned to the bedroom walls of thousands of "delinquent" teenage girls who took the free-love message to heart. And almost anyone could see that under the top layer of bravado a very serious, concerned person held sway. The only chink in the armor in which he had enclosed himself was the fact that without a steady diet of new and unusual chemicals in his system, Guy became completely uninspired and couldn't write or perform at all. Not all dependencies were physical in nature, after all.

"Suit yerself. Yer me fuckin' meal ticket, after all, ain't ye? Oi wouldn't want to lose me plum situation." The Hammer was unusually surly tonight, even for him, Hastings thought as he guffawed lustily as this exhibition of rudeness.

"Now, now, lads, let's relax here," Marty drawled. He was dressed in his usual full aviator's uniform, complete with goggles. Marty was the band's moderator, as well as #2 finalist in *Four-String Enthusiast*'s annual bass poll, just behind Jacques Bruce of La Crème. "We're here to blow minds, not our cool. As long as Simon comes down from his lovely cloud sometime this week," he added pointedly.

They all stared at Hastings, who was trying to pull himself together. Maybe he should have turned down that last hit. "Don't … orry … bt … me," he managed to force out. His mumble was greeted by roars of laughter.

"Excuse us, please, we're trying to astral project over here, all right? Can we get some peace and quiet?" shouted an Asparagus Stalk from across the room, attempting to sound forceful, which only made The Spheres laugh louder. Hastings, who hadn't even heard the complaint, had no idea what he was laughing at, but he practically fell out of his chair.

"My apologies, my brothers and sisters," Guy said gravely. "We would never interfere with your search for the direct path to bliss here in this slimy back room, would we, chaps?" His bandmates shook their heads, suppressing giggles.

The tension was broken by the arrival of Billy Prestwick, the manager of both bands. His electric wheelchair burst suddenly through the back door. Waving cheerily at the Stalks, Prestwick zoomed over to The Spheres' table. "Taunting those poor buggers again, are we?" he screeched in his astonishingly high, gravelly voice, gesturing grandly. "I prefer that all the horses in my stable prance together. Go navel-gaze for a while with them, Hammer, make 'em happy." Hastings started laughing again. "What the hell's the matter with this one? Too much of the good stuff today, eh?"

Billy put an arm around Hastings in a fatherly manner. "Don't make us set you up with a downer, boyo. Won't be much of a gig for you then." He scratched his goatee and oversized sideburns. Despite being confined to this chair, Billy was a perpetual whirlwind of energy, truly the Svengali of the New York scene. The rumor around town was that he had once been a policeman before his injury, but it was unsubstantiated.

Raised voices at the other end of the room saved Hastings from having to attempt a reply and be subject to further ridicule. A small, olive-skinned man with longish, greasy black hair and dressed in a white zoot suit was arguing with Jerzy, trying to gain entrance to the room. He certainly didn't look like the average hippie punter. The man was carrying a large rucksack. Billy wheeled over to check out the situation.

"Listen, my friend, I only want to offer my wares to these

nice gentlemen. I've got only the best licensed Colombian pharmaceuticals." His esses were sibilant, and he drew out the word "pharmaceuticals" for an uncomfortably long time. There was something persuasive in his Latin accent.

Jerzy loomed menacingly over him, the veins of his forehead popping and his crew cut bristling. "I don't care what you selling, scumbag. No one comes in here before doors open, you got that? Scram!"

But Guy's ears had pricked up, having caught the magic p-word. "I say, bring the chap on over here, Billy! Let's see what he's got!" he called, his eyes sparkling.

"As you like, Dionysius! Off you go, then," Billy said to the little man. "More fuel for the fire, eh, boys? What a night this will be!"

The Asparagus Stalks had by now left the room in a huff, and the light and sound crew had finished their testing and gone to dinner, so The Spheres were the only potential customers in the room. The little man slid over to their table.

"You'll like what I have here, my friends! The latest new products from South America, only recently approved by the authorities and ready for testing by connoisseurs! Brought to you at only slightly higher prices." He unfastened his bag and began to pull out sachets and bottles. Guy gaily rubbed his hands in anticipation, but the rest of the band looked skeptical.

The labels did look official — all Colombian Cartels products.

"Oi don't fink this is a very good idear," The Hammer rumbled. "You can get perfectly good stuff at the bar when it opens, or at the chemist's. We don't know if this stuff is the real deal, or where 'e got it."

The dealer shifted his weight a little at this but otherwise remained deadpan. But the rest of the band rolled their eyes at The Hammer's characteristic hand-wringing; Guy actually seemed irritated, a rather rare occurrence.

"For God's sake, man, haven't got any bloody spirit in you? It's not like the chap's going to poison us, is it? Wouldn't be good for business. I don't have time to run to the chemist's, and the pharmaceutical bar won't be open for ages. Do you want to see how I'll perform with empty veins?"

"Bloody drummers, all the same," Marty put in tiredly. Hastings' head was starting to clear a bit, and he too regarded the drugs spread out on the table with interest. Electron Z, who had little regard for drugs, conversation, and human company in general, had wandered over to the stage to reinspect his props and shape his pompadour.

Muttering something about it being their own fucking lives, The Hammer stormed off to the booze bar in the front room to get another bitter, and the rest of the band began examining the wares.

"What's this?" Guy had picked up vial of attractive golden liquid. "Haven't seen this one before."

"Ah, that is the very finest new product of the Colombian Cartels group: Cortezuma #1," the dapper salesman pronounced with a flourish. "Guaranteed to produce a beautiful high, accompanied not only by feelings of elation but also great strength. Like cocaine, but much, much better." His sibilants really were very … reptilian, Hastings thought. "And those tablets you hold in your hand there, sir," gesturing at Marty, "are a crystallized peyote product, a recipe borrowed from the Navajo. An ancient recipe for a modern age."

"Smashing!" cried Guy. "Navajo! I'll take two of each. Any for you, Billy, Simon, Marty?"

"None for me," Billy said. "I've got a lot of people to talk to, all on your behalf, of course, and I've got to be on my best behavior. You chaps'd best get backstage. The doors'll be opening soon. Take your little pills and potions with you."

"I'll pass too," Hastings said, adding, "thanks, anyway," with his usual politeness. His mum, God rest her, had raised him to be nice. "Still coming down from the CVE, and I don't go for mixing." Truth be told, something was nagging at him, telling him not to partake, but he was still feeling too muddled to analyze the feeling.

"Suit yourself, love," Marty said, handing a few bills to the dealer, who was still wearing his smile but had fixed his rat-like eyes on Hastings with disturbing intensity. "Something new and special for after the show."

"It was a pleasure serving you, gentlemen. Until next time." He gave Hastings another odd, hateful look and then slithered across the room and out the door, followed by Jerzy's suspicious gaze.

"All right, lads, let's go back. Immediately! Do what you need to do there! Come on, Hammer." Billy led the procession backstage to the green room, The Hammer trailing reluctantly with a pint of bitter in each hand.

*

By nine thirty, the room was packed to the rafters, and the doormen were turning away unhappy punters. The leading lights of the scene were all hanging out by the bar: Ricky California was there, known as the "White Hendricks," and Buckley and Drake, the star folk duo. Lenny Lurch was hanging out in a corner with Twink the mad drummer, Ludwig Froese of synth band Orange Soma, Rick Taggert of The Kidney Stones, and a few beat poets. Exotic-looking short-haired girls with sparkles on their faces and spliffs in their fingers and preening long-haired men engaged in idle banter while The Pretty Things' latest LP blared over the loudspeakers. The alcohol bar was doing a roaring trade, as was the now-open pharmaceutical counter. There was barely room to move in Elysian Fields, a massive rectangular space, the back wall of which was taken up entirely by the mixing set-up and lighting equipment, with even a few newfangled lasers awaiting their deployment.

Backstage, Guy was already scaling the heights of drug-induced ecstasy, and his bandmates were becoming a little concerned that he had prematurely shot his proverbial load. He was talking rapidly, tripping over his own words, had already managed to insult Ned Loogeant's rabid (supposed) right-wing views several times (never a good idea if you liked your teeth), and was presently involved in a somewhat nonsensical philosophical discourse with Frank Smith, a.k.a. Baba Yogi, leader of The Asparagus Stalks. Hastings sat quietly with Electron Z and Marty at the minibar, injecting a quick hit of No-Catch Cocaine from the legitimate pharma bar to try to restore his energy by set time.

"Listen, old chap," Guy declaimed heartily, "I am totally simpatico with your musical and spiritual goals, much more so than those of that Neanderthal over here." He gestured at Loogeant, who glared back. "The purpose of music isn't to enrage people in some superficially cathartic way — it's to peel back the layers of untruth and materialism in which we cloak ourselves, thus revealing the naked truth of what we are. Only then can we feel true empathy."

Baba Yogi bowed slightly. "Thank you, my son."

"Frankie, don't 'my son' me. I know you're only twenty-five. You're younger than me!" Guy threw an arm around the baba and raised his bottle to the ceiling. "Ah, if only we could truly mirror the beauty we see when we gaze into the night sky, eh? I'm serious! To capture the essence of the infinite ... the immortal significance of the universe in a couple of chords and a few verses of doggerel. To connect with, to contact that something..." He trailed off for a few seconds and became sober. "Do you feel it sometimes? That you're nothing, but that state of nothingness is so beautiful, so perfect, and that you're channeling the beyond, that you've been chosen to mirror this infinite perfection?"

"All the time," Baba Frank said placidly, his hands folded across his bosom.

"Bollocks!" yelled The Hammer. He was already completely soused and was deliberately hanging out with the Muttonchop Killers faction.

Hastings smiled. He was not unappreciative of mysticism and often attempted to take refuge in its mild but muddy waters, but he was a natural cynic, unable feel the same naïve enthusiasm as Guy. Hastings suffered from a kind of permanent existentialist morbidity that affected his life every day. Until he understood how and why he, a mere collection of atoms, could perceive the fact of his own existence but not its meaning, he would never be happy. Guy snidely called this "adolescent melancholy," but hell, it had made for a few good lyrics.

Guy continued to stare up at the plastic yellow stars glued haphazardly to the cobwebbed ceiling. "I feel that tonight is going to be very special, Simon, Marty ... I think we're going to break through. I can make these people fly! The drugs aren't enough. We have to provide the release through our music! This could be the night I've always waited for. Mind you, I always say that, don't I? We have to — ow!"

Billy Prestwick's wheelchair had come flying up a ramp built especially for his use and slammed into Guy's backside, knocking him over. The Hammer and Loogeant both broke out into raucous laughter.

"Sorry, chum!" Billy screamed with delight as Baba Frank lent Guy a hand up. "Let's round up the Stalks and get going here!" He grabbed Frank by the hood of his robe. "This could be your big break tonight, Frankie! Everybody who's anybody is here. Get out there and kick arse in the name of Shiva or whoever the hell it is you worship! They're waiting!"

Jerzy bustled by, wheezing under the weight of a massive metal statue of a garlanded Ganesh, the Stalks' only stage prop. He returned a few seconds later with a jug of cold milk that would be ritually served to the god throughout the set.

"Baba Yogi is my name, if you please," Frank answered calmly but with ever so slight an edge of irritation, wiping ash from Billy's cigar from his sleeve. "All will be as Brahma commands — success or failure." He gravely motioned to his following, who had been quietly smoking spliffs in a corner and nursing their wounds and feelings, as far away from the Muttonchop Killers as possible. The other three musicians and the six hippie girls (who danced and waved sticks of incense and fed the milk to Ganesh) followed him as he strode through the beaded curtains onstage to scattered applause.

"Bloody wet blankets, that lot," Billy muttered.

The Spheres
Astronomy
(Aureola Records)
Starred review in *NMT*, June 5, 1968
by Rodney Blair

Well, the long-awaited sophomore effort from The Spheres lads is here, and it's been well worth the wait. The band's debut shocked the rock world with its innovative use of electronic sounds and synthesizers and its refusal to conform to any sort of rock and roll tradition. On this second effort, the sound is preserved, but there has been more care lavished on the vocals and lyrics, much to the benefit of lead singer Guy Calvert, who possesses one of the most distinct voices on the contemporary music scene. The stellar axework of Simon Hastings also shines, dripping with reverb and echo, buoyed by the rock-solid rhythm section. The only criticism I can offer is that there is very little rhythmic variety to be found in the songs, which are all very long and seem mainly designed to induce a trance-like state in the listener. This is a hallmark of the new psychedelic rock, and we'd better get used to it, since it doesn't look like it's going away any time soon. It's certainly visceral, majestic, and exciting.

Highlights of this record include the haunting "Judgment Day" and the ecologically themed "Barren Planet." The songs explore lyrical territory thought to be the exclusive domain of poets, leaving the lad-meets-lass themes of conventional pop far behind. The band's maturity on this second album is impressive and will solidify its place as one of the finest bands in the world today. A tour of the British Isles is planned for the fall.

THREE

A squeal of ear-splitting feedback exploded from Baba Yogi's Hiwatt amplifier, and then the drummer started up a thunderous tribal pattern as the band launched into its first number, "The Elephant God Lives Within You." The dancers whirled around the stage, tossing flower petals into the bemused audience as Frank played the same simple riff over and over on his multicolored Stratocaster. His normally reserved, tranquil demeanor had disappeared, and he jumped around like a madman in a sort of Dervish-like trance, grinning like a killer. The combination of the frantically spiritual visuals and rather gritty heavy music certainly set the audience momentarily back on its heels, but the crowd soon began to come around and was gyrating as ferociously as the hippie girl dancers, who were now waving pungent sticks of incense that filled the room with a sickly-sweet scent. The Asparagus Stalks thumped their way through a set of mostly one-to three-chord, drony numbers with a heavy bottom end, but with Baba Yogi's high-pitched voice wailing over everything else in faintly Eastern-sounding scales. As always, they ended with their signature chant, "The Cow Is Your Friend," all ten voices in unison like a monastic prayer:

The cow is your friend,
And so is the bird,
Eat him not or you will rot,
On the wheel of endless rebirth.

Love all as one, one as all,
Love the flowers and leafy trees,

Love them well, enjoy their smell
Heaven is in all you see.

By this point their bizarre display had completely won over the easy-to-please punters, some of whom had taken the messages to heart and were busy attempting the full lotus position on the sticky floor.

"The blessings of the gods be upon you! Thank you, New York! All right! Rock n' roll! Yeaaahhhhh!" Frank screamed deafeningly into the mic, shook sweat out of his matted hair like a wet dog, and led his troops offstage to adoring cheers.

"Bravo, Frankie! You did us proud!" Billy wheeled enthusiastically to embrace his second-most-favorite protégé.

"Vishnu truly smiled on our performance tonight, my brother. We'll move some units now for sure! I mean, it was a very moving evening." Frank had yet to reconstruct his usual holy façade.

"You've bloody well made your name! This evening is going to be legendary!" Billy was in a state of rapture, no doubt envisioning a glorious future for himself managing the two biggest rock bands in the world.

The Asparagus Stalks headed toward the back of the room to receive the praise of The Spheres; much to his own surprise, Hastings had enjoyed the set immensely. But the back-slapping was rudely interrupted by the arrival of the Muttonchop Killers, who burst in backstage wearing their all-black-leather stage regalia, tough-looking jackets and army helmets. Loogeant knocked Baba Frank over as he swaggered by. "Outta my way, you mystic pussy! We're gonna make sure these space cadets will never wanna go on after us again. C'mon, boys!"

Leering, he brushed aside the stringy brown hair that hung over his gaunt, intense face and rushed toward the stage. Loogeant must have weighed all of a hundred pounds, but his appearance belied an energy and strength born of pure anger. He seemed to hate everything equally, but he remained to most an oddly fascinating figure. There were rumors he was a heroin addict at the age of nine, back in the early days when addictive drugs had become easy to obtain on the underground market.

"Sometimes I wonder why we started hanging about with that fellow," Guy said disgustedly as he helped Frank to his feet.

"They didn't frighten away all of the groupies, did they?" Marty peered forlornly out the back door into the alley but saw no one.

"Everyone knows the groupies come around at the *end* of the show, Marty," Hastings said, patting him on the back. "Don't worry, we'll get you some." Hastings had a steady if unpredictable girlfriend who claimed she'd taken off to climb a mountain in the Andes. In addition to his generally impeccable manners, he was also a bit "old-fashioned" in his attitudes toward sex and relationships. Naturally, he kept this a secret so as not to ruin the band's image.

Once again, the set commenced with a deafening screech of feedback, this time from Loogeant's head-high stack of speaker cabinets. Then the band kicked in, playing something resembling a boogie rhythm, three fuzzy guitars straining the woofers and thundering on the same riff as the players jumped up and down and aimed kicks at the astonished faces in the crowd. The effect was sloppy but powerful and chaotic; the drummer had a bad habit of speeding up and slowing down throughout the songs. This was one of the Muttonchop Killers' first larger-venue gigs in New York since moving from the poverty-stricken former steel town of Wolfeville, a metropolis in the parish of Pontiac in the county of Michigan. No one in New York had ever heard anything like this band; the closest thing they had was Louis Freed and the Cashmere Overlords, an art-rock group that eschewed all melody in favor of sheets of noise.

When Ned Loogeant started to yell (which he did at the top of his lungs), several people in the audience covered their ears in shock:

I'll kill yer mama,
I'll kill yer dad,
And if he's lucky
Yer best friend Chad,
Goddamned commie scum,
Gonna burn yer fuckin' house down,
Kill ya with yer own gun.
How'd ya like that, Comrade?

Kill, kill, kill the Reds!

"Provocative!" Billy proclaimed. "Satirical agitprop!"

"Rot," Hastings mumbled.

"Well, oi loike it," The Hammer said. "Maybe oi'll join up wiv them instead."

Guy shot him a glare.

The Muttonchop Killers raced through a very short set of eight or nine numbers, all of which seemed to be in the same key and tempo, with titles like "Vegetarians are Stupid," "Gonna Kill Me Some Hippie," and "Nuke the Peaceniks Now." By the time they finished, the audience was in full outrage, throwing bottles (some broken), many of which struck the band members in the face. Loogeant was bleeding in several places by the time he lurched to the front of the stage, exposed himself to the crowd, poured a bottle of vodka over his head, and then stumbled from the stage. He had found time on the way to throw some punches at a couple of women and display a certain finger several times with a demonic leer.

"Fuckin' excellent. Great crowd! Sorry, fellers," he smirked, "your peace n' love buddies are in a bad mood now."

Marty regarded him coolly as he tuned his enormous Rick Booker bass. "Don't you worry about that. These people will forget you were ever here by time we're done with them."

"Whatever you say, pretty boy. Metal's the way of the future —

no more of this astral shit."

"A lot of steaks, medium rare, and pointless arson by the sounds of it." Hastings chuckled. "We'll take our vision of the future, thanks."

Loogeant flashed his favorite gesture again, but in a genial sort of way, and departed to find the few groupies who might have been impressed by the masculine violence of his show, followed by his glowering, pimply bandmates, who rarely spoke. Jerzy was making some final repairs to the stage while the staff cleaned up the angry audience's debris. A chant of "We want Guy" had gone up. Hastings started tuning his guitar. Guy was looking a bit funny. His face had a greenish tint, and he was crouching with his head in his hands.

"What the matter? Coming down too soon?"

"Not sure, mate — feeling a bit lightheaded and nauseous. Maybe my first case of stage fright, eh?" Guy flashed a watery smile.

"Sure you're all right? Need a fix?" Marty was injecting his pre-gig dose of KässelPharma Ultra-Speed, something of a superstitious ritual for him. The Hammer was chugging down a final pint or two, and Electron Z was not yet on the scene.

"No time for nerves, old son!" Billy bellowed. "Almost time! All the magazines are here to cover the gig. After tonight, you'll be the biggest stars in rock! You'll go Number One back home!"

"Is my Mellotron ready? And the organ?"

"Everything's a go, Guy. You'll be like a god tonight. Ring in the new age!" With that melodramatic outburst, Billy was gone again to chat with the VIPs.

"All right, let's get out there and drive these people out of their minds!" Marty led the charge out onto the stage, followed by Hastings, Guy, and The Hammer, beer in hand. They had long ago stopped worrying about Electron Z; he usually appeared by the end of the first number. The Spheres had some very long numbers.

A roar greeted the sight of handsome Marty Sharpe-Thornton,

elegant Guy Calvert (female voices predominant), brooding Simon Hastings, and the hulking Hammer, who settled in behind his massive double bass drums and started whacking a fast beat in 4/4.

"Nice to see you!" Guy yelled and was rewarded with another chorus of screams.

"Here's some songs for your enjoyment ... I mean enlightenment!" Then the guitar and bass kicked in. Hastings could feel the power surging through his arms as the sound from his amp blasted through him. He was playing the powerful but strangely delicate progression of "Judgment Day," filtered through Echoplex, chorus, and fuzz pedals. The chiming of his guitar and the pulsating bass line filled his head as he gazed with unseeing eyes into the seething mob. But just as Guy started to sing, as his eyes rested on the back wall, Hastings noticed the peculiar Colombian contraband dealer watching the band with that focused, hateful intensity and almost dropped his plectrum. There was something extremely disconcerting about the mysterious man's presence that sent chills down his spine. He shook his head and put it out of his mind as best he could, focusing instead on the lyrics he had written for Guy to sing.

I knew a man who suddenly went insane.
He ran away, out into lonely meadows,
To the lands beyond where the subway ends.

He lay alone, watching the grass grow,
In a field, near a winding river,
Above his head, not a cloud in the sky.

He reflected, but his mind was full of TV,
He screamed aloud, life's become too easy.
I don't want to die; I'm not even living.

Guy still wasn't looking healthy; his face was now dead white, and he was standing at a strange angle. Still, he was ever the trouper, and the usual mania of performance had come upon him. He was completely possessed by the words he sang, his eyes closed and his arms gesticulating wildly. He cut a magnificent figure, that was certain. Just before the end of the second verse, Hastings heard a swirling sound, like a falling bomb in an air raid, and he knew that Electron Z had finally arrived and was manipulating one of his devices to add the final cosmic layer. They launched into the first chorus, which featured an exhilarating ascending chord progression:

Then the sky opened up,
And rained stars down upon him.
The flowers cried,
In the presence of their maker.

As he launched into his guitar solo, Hastings could see people, stoned well out of their trees by this point, whirling in free-form dance or moving slowly and rhythmically to the music, many with their eyes tightly shut but most staring with a fixed intensity at the rapidly changing patterns made by the liquid lights on the screen behind the stage. He played a series of flowing lines to end the solo; by this time, he was so high on the music that he had no thoughts in his head at all. He didn't even notice that Guy hadn't approached the mic to sing the last verse. He was standing nearby, doubled over, his eyes wide and unblinking like a reptile's.

Sensing that Guy wouldn't be able to finish the song, Marty nervously took his place to sing the last chorus, his deep baritone a full octave below Guy's voice. The audience didn't seem to notice anything amiss.

The sky opened up,
And rained fire down upon them,

There was nowhere to hide,
From the passing of the judgment.

As the last chords crashed, Guy suddenly dropped to the floor, writhing. Before rushing over to his prostrate figure, Hastings glanced instinctively to the back of the room. The dealer was watching with evident satisfaction. He pulled plugs from his ears and casually exited the club. Guy twitched one last time, relaxed, and was still. The gig was over.

FOUR

An eerie silence fell over the room as the audience stood gawking for several seconds. Then a someone screamed. This set off a chain reaction of bellowing and shrieking as people rushed the stage to find out what had happened to their hero. The Spheres still stood in a circle, looking down in shock at Guy's now-still form.

"Out of the way, people. I'm a doctor!" a young, bespectacled longhair yelled, pushing his way through the crowd. "Well, when I pass the exams, anyway," he added in a lower tone few heard as he clambered onto the stage, shoving several mini-skirted mourners out of the way.

After a minute of examination, he looked sorrowfully up at Hastings. "This man's quite dead, I'm afraid. No need for an ambulance." He gently closed Guy's eyes.

"Oi don't fuckin' believe it!" The Hammer moaned. *At least he's got the decency to be upset about it,* Hastings thought dully. He was having trouble thinking and felt like the roof was about to collapse on them all.

"Dead! Dead!" some girls echoed, and others took up the cry. The sound was deafening. Billy, always in control, wheeled up to the mic and reached down to pull it to his level, his face bright red and his veins popping.

"All right, people, the show's over! Lights on, please. Clear off, now. Away with you! We have a medical emergency up here. Keep an eye on the media for reports! No refunds! Please evacuate immediately!"

The punters began reluctantly filing out, some weeping as their trip turned really bad, but others grumbled that this had better not be some kind of publicity stunt, because it was not funny at all.

At least ten women had to be dragged out, kicking and screaming. The stage lights were suddenly switched off, leaving the room in a depressing, dingy half light.

"Marty, go call the bloody police — now! Doctor, what happened to him?" said Billy.

"I've got no idea. It could have been an aneurysm or congenital heart defect; any number of conditions can cause sudden death. Had he been to a doctor recently?"

"Not in years, I should imagine," Billy said, tears streaming down his cheeks. The Hammer was also sobbing lustily. "He had no regard for his personal safety — too busy trying to save the world. What will we do without him?"

"It was poison," Hastings said abruptly. He had with sudden clarity remembered the satisfied smirk on the face of the drug dealer as Guy collapsed — and when he had bought the stuff hours before.

"What?" They all turned to him in amazement.

Hastings was still sitting in a daze on the side of the stage, forlornly swinging his legs. "It was the drugs from that Colombian dealer ... he was there watching the gig ... he smiled when Guy collapsed, and then he left."

"Why would anyone want to poison us? And Marty took the same stuff. He's still here. Don't be preposterous, Simon!"

"No, I didn't," said Marty, appearing from backstage. "I was saving the stuff for later. Didn't want to blow the gig by having a bad trip. If only that bastard Guy could have controlled himself ... well, I guess it wouldn't have made a difference in the end. Anyway, the police are on their way, for what it's worth."

"I doubt they'll be willing to do anything," Billy said grimly. "You know their feelings about long-hairs and radicals. Anyway, there's no evidence yet that he was poisoned. Marty, you'd better pass your drugs on to them."

"If they won't analyze them, I will," said the young doctor. They all looked at him. "Guy was a hero of mine."

"Well, there's no use waiting to talk about it ... what are you lads going to do now? I need to get some sort of press release out there." Though tears were rolling down his chubby face, Billy was, shockingly, already getting back to business as usual.

"'Ow can we bloody well talk about that at a toim loike this, you bastard!" The Hammer roared, roused to sudden anger. Billy cringed back in his chair. "Worried about yer bottom line, arsehole?"

"I can tell you one thing, guys," Electron Z suddenly piped up, to everyone's shock. His face was as unreadable as ever, and he spoke in his usual near-whisper. "This is it for me. It's a sign. This has been fun." He got up and headed for the door.

"That's it? Just like that? Where the hell are you gonna go?" Marty called disbelievingly after him.

Electron Z had a faraway look in his eyes. "I've always dreamed of seeing the Arctic and northern lights, so I think I'll head up to Lower Canada for a while. Nice knowing you." Then he was gone. The other four and the almost-doctor remained in silence for a few minutes.

"Well, then there were three, eh?" Marty said with a bitter laugh. "That's the end of us."

"Don't say that! You've still got bass, guitar, and drums. You fellows owe it to Guy to carry on..."

Marty was rolling his pragmatic eyes, and The Hammer was about to interject angrily when two New York City police in khaki uniforms strode nonchalantly through the doors. They wore the martial cut of the uniforms stiffly but proudly, and they looked around them in disgust as they neared. One was tall and heavily built, the other small and slight.

"I'm Officer Stuyvesant, and this is Officer Peeler," said the heavily built cop, rubbing the side of her chiseled jaw. "I understand there's been a fatality on the premises. This the stiff?"

"Yes, there *it* is," Marty said sarcastically, gesturing wearily at the former Guy. The bassist looked silly and uncomfortable standing there in his aviator's outfit; his jaunty cap was askew and his goggles were crooked.

"We'll have to get this corpse taken to the morgue to determine cause of death ... I guess," Stuyvesant said without enthusiasm. "Pretty unhealthy-looking feller, huh?" Both of the officers smirked.

Billy was now incensed, practically springing up out of his wheelchair. "Do you have any fucking idea who this is? What a fucking tragedy this is? You wankers! And what's more, we have very good reason to suspect foul play, right, Simon?"

Hastings told the officers about the evening's events, but they seemed unimpressed. "Look, I sympathize with your loss," Officer Peeler said, looking anything but sympathetic and twitching his wispy mustache, "but if a guy does as many varieties of illegals as your friend here probably did, he's gonna run into something sketchy someday. And I shouldn't need to remind you that the purchase of street drugs can earn you a strict fine, at the very least."

"The man was deliberately poisoned, you fucking idiot!" Billy screamed. "We demand justice!"

"All right, all right, keep your panties on." Stuyvesant sighed. "They'll do a toxin analysis on the body. Then, and only then, they'll decide on whether this should be a murder investigation. We'll go and call for instructions. You crazy long-hairs all stay here. You'll have to answer a few questions."

While the officers were outside calling for an ambulance, Hastings found that he had lost track of time and glanced at his watch. It was one thirty. The second set would have been well under way by now, but that life already seemed years ago, buried under the crushing weight of the sudden end of a dream.

Silence reigned for a few minutes as each man stared forlornly at the sticky, cigarette-butt-strewn floor. Hastings and Marty were clearly trying to clear away the detritus in their brains from what had ended up a decidedly bad trip of their own. The Hammer looked like he was desperately trying not to throw up the contents of his stomach, and Billy was taking great pains to control his sobbing.

"Anyone got a syringe?" the doctor said suddenly.

"Of course we do," Marty said, "but this is hardly the time—"

"I need to take a blood sample." The doctor's eyes were now surprisingly hard for such a meek-looking man. "They won't examine the body, you know. They won't test anything. They'll come back any moment now and tell us there's no room at the morgue ... as you know, these guys don't really like our type. I've seen situations like this before."

Without another word, Marty scavenged in his pockets to produce a small needle. The doctor swiftly jabbed it into Guy's pale forearm, pockmarked with the tiny craters of a thousand hits, and took a full blood sample. This was Guy Calvert's last puncture. The doctor then rummaged through the pockets of Guy's olive drab army jacket and took the drugs he had bought from the sinister Latino. He also took the drugs Marty had bought.

"All right, someone give me a phone number." Hastings wrote his down on a matchbook just as the officers sauntered back into the bar, a brand-new pair of anticipatory smiles plastered on their faces.

"Well, fellers, we seem to have a bit of a problem here. Seems there's been so many murders and overdoses amongst you hippies tonight that there's no room at the morgue," Peeler said cheerfully. "I declare that this unfortunate died of natural causes. We'll have the body removed to the funeral parlor of your choice, but that's the best we can do."

"You fuckers!" Billy was practically frothing at the mouth.

Peeler turned on him with such anger that even Billy fell back in surprise. "Listen, you little fucking cripple! The only poison this asshole died from was the shit he put in his system every fucking day. They can legalize that stuff, they can say it's safe, they can legitimize your godless fucking lifestyle until there's no order left in society at all, but if you expect any support or sympathy from decent people, don't come running to the law. We. Will. Not. Help. You."

He turned abruptly on his heel and strode out of the club. Even big Officer Stuyvesant seemed taken aback by her partner's outburst. She shrugged a slight apology and followed at a casual slouch.

The Hammer bellowed like an enraged bull and commenced destroying the band's equipment, starting with the drums.

*

Hastings peered gloomily out the windows of the cab. The fog was now so thick that the storefronts emerged like creepy doorways to crumbling mausoleums. It was two thirty. He was too tired even to think, which should have been difficult anyway, what with the incessant chatter of the fat, bearded driver, but thoughts forced their way in nonetheless.

The driver clearly hadn't recognized Hastings, but when he had ascertained that his fare was a musician, he started recounting the tragic life of his half-brother, who had played the accordion with a regiment in the Hungarian army back in the thirties and had apparently come to a very sudden end during the East European Nuclear Incidents that had destroyed all traces of the ancient cities of Belgrade, Sofia, and Budapest. Hastings wasn't even listening to the tragic tale, but at least he didn't have to talk.

Marty and The Hammer had guided the now unconscious Billy home in another cab, carrying Guy's corpse in the trunk to save it from the trash heap, a Christian funeral home, or from being dumped in the river. Their cab had nearly run over a couple of reporters, and they had parted company with the young doctor with gratitude. He had promised to call Hastings the next day, the moment he had any test results. The newspapers were no doubt already preparing sensational front-page speculations concerning the bizarre public demise of a rock celebrity. Hastings really had no idea what to do next; the whole night had been such a blur. For once, he wished he hadn't gotten so high.

The band's dream seemed to be over. That dealer, he was sure, had deliberately removed Guy and had been aiming to kill the whole lot of them. On whose behalf was the question. The attitudes of the investigating officers were by no means a reflection of a minority opinion, and Peeler's words contained a grain of truth. Though reform had created an atmosphere in which people like Guy could express themselves reasonably freely, half of the Empire's politicians, sensing public unease, tried aggressively in every session of Parliament to have the old laws of social control reapplied.

The general public, hiding in suburban fortresses with their plastic toys, their 8:00 a.m. to 6:00 p.m. office jobs, and two- to four-child families, hadn't voted for change, and they had never wanted it. No one could have anticipated the reforms begun suddenly by Profumo's Liberal government in the mid-fifties, and most older people, set in their ways by centuries of social certainty, were still having trouble coming to terms with things like free speech, free sex, legalized drugs, and rock music. The only reason the Profumo-ites were still in power was that there was simply no strong political alternative, the only other legal party in the two-pole system being the Tory Fascists, and not many people wanted that extreme. The Queen had also thrown in her lot with the Liberals, and no one dared gainsay her word; after all, she was the head of the army *and* the church.

So it could have been politicians, police, some obsessed moralist wacko or wound-up family man ... maybe Ned Loogeant had done it as a sick joke. Maybe it was an out-of-work symphony conductor. Hastings had to smile bitterly at that thought, remembering Guy's hostility toward classical music. He hadn't quite agreed and rather enjoyed a spot of Debussy or Rameau every now and then. They had fought many times over the topic, with Guy usually winning through sheer force of loquaciousness. Hastings fought back some tears.

The cabbie was sounding a bit choked up as well. "…so my brother, well, like I say, my half brother, you know, he was vaporized in few seconds, like seven million others, my mother and father and sisters and aunts and uncles too. Just crazy, man. No reason why we should kill each other like that."

"I know," Hastings murmured. The cab pulled up in front of his building.

"Well, things have to get better. I have faith," the driver wheezed. "As long as people keep trying to change things. Young people, eh? Like you. My brother didn't want to die for some country, just to live for the drink and women! Good luck to you."

Hastings smiled and gave the man the generous tip, although his own financial future would now be much more uncertain without a career.

Upstairs in his flat, he lay on his bed in the dark, too tired to think and too disturbed to sleep. He gazed through the uncurtained window at the sky, where a few pinprick stars fought to be seen against the fog and light pollution.

You believed in a greater meaning in life, and I didn't, he thought. *Are you finishing the set in some kind of hippie heaven right now, or are you just going to rot? We won't let them forget what we achieved.*

Whatever might come, Simon Hastings was determined to find out who was responsible for the death of Guy Calvert.

From *The Modern City: An Urban Theorist's Travelogue*
by Prof. S.R.J. Kilbey
(Geelong University Press, 1969)

New York is the largest (and most polluted) city in the Virginias, receiving a constant influx of immigrants, not only from the Empire but from around the world, attracted by plentiful jobs and the happy prospect of a consistent food supply. The older communities (Welsh, Danish, etc.) having spread to the newly pioneered areas of this vast continent, the older neighborhoods have been occupied as the thriving ghettos of new immigrants. The climate of New York is increasingly multicultural, and by far the largest neighborhood is Spanish Stockholm. The purchase of the Floridas from the Spanish by the Belgians (well-known for their brutal colonial policies) forced many of the original settlers northward, where they settled in this part of town. The sprawling district has a rather unjust and frankly bigoted reputation for uncleanliness and violence, but an architecture buff will find more fine nineteenth century buildings left intact in this part of the city than in any other, many of them in the famous Malmö style. Despite the disdain with which life in Spanish Stockholm is viewed by members of the Anglo-Saxon community who accuse the inhabitants of all sorts of iniquities, this neighborhood is well worth a visit by the curious in search of livelier, earthier environment.

FIVE

After a deep but poor sleep populated by phantasms of Guy's corpse in progressive stages of decay, Hastings woke unrefreshed at around eight o'clock. The mists had finally parted, and the hot sun was beating through the windows, which he had forgotten to curtain the night before. He missed his girlfriend, Teresa Cappadocia, a fiery Italian-American-British radical who would be as devastated as he was at the news, but she was off in some southern wilderness communing with the local traditions or something, and he had no way of reaching her. Hastings rolled out of bed, groggily lit a Silk Cut, and checked his refrigerator. He had always been the most health-conscious member of the band and generally kept a well-stocked larder.

He settled on a week-old and rapidly deflating orange and a bowl of Dr. Jordan's Hemp Flakes, a dry, papery cereal he hadn't enjoyed and didn't plan to purchase again. When he flipped on the radio to see how the media was reporting Guy's death, Tom and Jerry's latest hit, "The Prizefighter," was playing. "I am going, but my anger still remains," they cooed in their cherubic voices. Despite the excellent harmonies, the song's melancholy tone hit too close to home, so he abruptly turned it off.

Hastings was suddenly possessed by the desire to hear Guy's voice and the music they'd never again make together. He selected their second and last album, *Astronomy*, and put it on the turntable, heedless of where the stylus dropped. One of Guy's more sensitive numbers came on, "The Shining Sea," a very nice song in A minor.

The light takes so long to reach us,

From the distant galaxies.
And all our lives are but seconds long,
These things we'll never see.

But there's a meaning beyond the awe
This smallness that I feel.
And in the light that we create together,
A beauty is revealed.

The only thing we really own
Is the love that we share.
We're just drops in the shining sea.
It knows no joy or despair.

Another unfortunately apt song to mark the occasion of Guy's death, Hastings thought and was about to succumb to another of his dark reveries when the phone jarringly interrupted the beginning of the song's first chorus. It was the young doctor.

"Well, Mr. Hastings, looks like you were right," the physician solemnly intoned.

"Poison?"

"You got it. There were several kinds of toxins in some sort of cocaine-based product that he must have injected."

"I knew it!" Hastings was angrier than he'd ever been in his life.

"There's more. I just dropped by the coroner's office — an old girlfriend of mine happens to answer the phones there. I showed her my test results, and she had some very interesting news." The doctor paused, as if for dramatic effect.

"Yes, yes, get on with it!"

"This very same mixture of chemicals was found in the blood of Hunter Burlington when he was found dead last week. There's no doubt about it, these tests are very accurate. She didn't think anything of it until I showed her Calvert's results. There's no way it's a coincidence."

"So we have a serial murderer or an assassin on our hands. Someone with a bone to pick with radicals."

Hunter Burlington was the leading Virginian countercultural poet. Though he had started his career writing extremely abstract verse, over the last few years his pen had sharpened and his tone had become more overtly political. He had just released his first book of prose essays, *Reflections on the Coming Revolution*. This book featured several essays on rock music and its role in inciting the current unrest in youthful society. Guy had been overjoyed to find a kindred spirit when he read the piece titled "Classical Music: The Capitalist's Tool of Cultural Oppression." Hastings had only met him once but had seen him reading at Cashmere Overlords gigs, and it was after one of these gigs that he had been found dead. There was no way his and Guy's deaths were unrelated.

Everyone had mourned Burlington but assumed his lifestyle had caught up with him.

"Mr. Hastings? You there?"

"Yes, sure. Well, this is very interesting indeed."

"What you gonna do about it now?"

"Make some inquiries of my own. Marty and I know the places where contraband dealers in the city hang out. If the police won't help us, we'll have to solve this ourselves. Thank you for doing this, Mr.—"

"Wilkerson. Phillip Wilkerson. Hey, no problem. If you find out who did this, I'd be glad to wring his goddamned neck for you myself, man."

After he hung up, Hastings stood for several seconds, trying to control his breathing. No drugs today; it was time for action.

*

It was seven o'clock in the evening, and Marty was looking despondent, slumped behind the wheel of his car. "Look, Simon, we've been all over the city. We've been to the Bronx, Oslo Quarter, Little Newcastle, Stepney, we've been uptown, downtown, we've talked to everyone we know, but no one's seen this bloke. I'm as broken up about what's happened as you are, but looking for some criminal we've never heard of in New York's like looking for a needle in a haystack. I just want to go home and think for a while."

"Stop whining, Marty. It doesn't become you. Anyway, we haven't talked to Lou Freed yet. He may have a lead for us. After all, he was Burlington's best mate." Hastings' face was set and hard and had been all day.

"All right. Let's get this over with." Marty's grumbling was really starting to get on Hastings' nerves, although it was somewhat understandable. He didn't look dapper; he and The Hammer hadn't slept at all. Billy had apparently been out like a light all day and was still sleeping when Marty went out for the day. Staying with Guy's corpse in Marty's apartment hadn't been at all good for The Hammer, and he had disappeared at 6:00 a.m. while Marty was finally dozing. Later that morning, Marty had called a funeral home to make arrangements.

Marty pulled his baby-blue Edsel in behind a mist-green model. They were now going to visit the Cashmere Overlords' sound check at Vic's Sioux City, a popular but seedy bar near Spanish Stockholm. They were playing a double bill with a west coast band named The Kaleidoscope. The bar's entrance sported a tall neon sign in the shape of a cowboy roping a steer. A few young black-shirted hooligans lay passed out on the curb, looking grotesquely like dead soldiers in their masks. All school-age children wore masks by law, but legislation hadn't been passed yet for the general population, despite the atrocious air quality. It wasn't as bad yet as Tokyo or Peking (the former had recently been evacuated in its entirety by the latest Shogun after a million deaths), but it was getting there.

The bouncer recognized them and let them in right away. The Overlords' roadies were loading the equipment onto the stage, and the band members, dressed as always in black leather jackets and blue jeans, were lighting up a bong.

"Guys, it's good to see you," Lou Freed said in his low monotone. His face was inscrutable behind wraparound shades. "I can't believe what I heard. Everyone's been depressed all day, man, for real. When's the funeral?"

"No time to chat about that, Lou. We need to talk about something more urgent." Hastings related the story of Guy's death and the tests of the young doctor.

Freed whistled softly. "I've seen a lot of dirty shit in this town, Si, lived here all my life, but nothing like this. We thought Hunter just overdosed on something tainted, since no one ever told us exactly what happened. You think someone's out to get us?" Neither Lou's face nor his tone showed any sign of fear.

"Well, one thing's for sure, we're clearly getting taken a lot more seriously than we ever thought. Someone believes that killing freaks will take the wind out of our sails. But they're wrong."

"They could come after us next. Who's to say they'll use the same method next time?"

Hastings put a hand on Freed's sleeve. "You can help us, Lou. I need to know whether any of your lads saw someone matching this dealer's description the night of that gig. And if anyone knows who he is."

"Well, I didn't, but let me ask the guys."

When the situation was explained, Cain Jones, the band's Welsh violist, nodded slowly, one lank black lock drooping over his forehead.

"You know, something strange did happen, very strange indeed, while you were fetching your pre-gig calzone. We're lighting up some kind of dried plant, see, much like we are today, when we hear a fuss from the door — someone's trying to get in to talk to us, but Jorge over there won't let him in. He wanted to sell us some drugs, said he had some new products, not yet for sale in the Virginian market. Hunter wanted to have a look, but Jorge said the chap had been making trouble in the Hispanic community, that he was some kind of career criminal just in from South America. Jorge's got a lot of underworld connections, you know. A couple of minutes later, Hunter vanished for a while. Didn't say where he'd been."

"Sounds promising," Freed said. "Jorge! We need to talk to you."

The imposing bouncer lumbered over to them, his pockmarked face set in a glare. "What is it, Mr. Freed? Do you need a bigger guest list?" He had only a slight accent.

"Nope, but we need to ask you something. You remember that sleazy drug dealer you kept out of here when we played that gig a couple weeks ago?"

The bouncer's scowl deepened. "Yes, I remember, Mr. Freed."

"We need to know everything you've heard about that dealer. It's very important. We think he's responsible for Hunter's death."

Jorge's face turned sorrowful. "That does not surprise me. I spend, as you know, most of my time in my own community. This man, who is going by the name Enrique Nuñez, though that is probably not his real name, appeared suddenly, hanging out in the cantinas in Spanish Stockholm, spending lots of money, selling strange chemicals, and trying to pick up our women. We are suspicious of outsiders, and he did not make many friends. My cousin Manuel bounces over at El Corazon, over on Göteborg Avenue. This guy comes there at least once every couple of nights, and he usually gets thrown out within half an hour. When he came here, there was no way I was letting him in."

"Bingo," Freed said.

Marty raised an eyebrow at Hastings. "This has to be the same fellow. Jorge, would your friend know where this guy's crashing?"

"Maybe. He has had to listen to this man blabbering about himself for weeks now."

"Well, well," Hastings said. "Not a very careful assassin."

"He probably figured these deaths would never be investigated,"

Freed put in.

"Well, Marty, we know where to go." Hastings and Marty headed for the door.

"Guys!"

They turned around.

"What are you gonna do if you find this guy?"

"I don't know, Lou. But I'm just angry enough to do something foolish."

Jones started to tune his viola, and they were accompanied by a hair-raising screech as they went through the door.

*

The ride to El Corazon was a silent one, with each lost in his own thoughts. Hastings didn't really have an idea of what he would do should he manage to corner Enrique Nuñez. The police obviously weren't going to do anything to help. The fact that Nuñez had been seen at two crime scenes wouldn't mean much to them if they were dead-set on refusing to assist for ideological reasons. Besides, the trail didn't necessarily end with a Colombian drug dealer who possessed no guessable motive. Guy Calvert had been a dealer's best friend, willing to seek thrills from the underground if mainstream pharmaceuticals had become boring. It was even possible there was some twisted mind behind the murders, someone with a hatred for countercultural musical figures.

Hastings sighed and started reading the cover story of the evening *New York Times*, which Marty had bought outside Sid's:

POP STAR COMES TO "SUSPICIOUS" END
There is widespread mourning today in the musical and music-loving communities at the unexpected death of rising star Guy Calvert, lead singer of popular band The Spheres, onstage at the Elysian Fields last night. According to eyewitnesses, the band had not even completed the first song of their first set when Mr.

Calvert collapsed in obvious pain. He was pronounced dead by a doctor at the scene.

The band's manager, William Prestwick, today angrily accused the police of refusing to investigate a death he called "suspicious" and "very likely the result of foul play." The police department have issued a stern denial that there was any need for further investigation, saying that deaths of this kind can be "quite common in a population with an appetite for unregulated pharmaceuticals such as Mr. Calvert is alleged to have possessed."

However, the incident is being taken seriously at City Hall, with Mayor Bill Pitt VII saying today that if there is any truth to Mr. Prestwick's allegations, the investigating officers should be subject to "strong censure."

None of the surviving members of the group could be reached for comment today, leaving the band's future uncertain. According to prominent music journalist Rodney Blair, a well-known supporter of the group, speaking today from his London home, the death has "not only negative implications for the future of pop, but is a tragedy for the cause of social reform across the Empire and the world, for which Mr. Calvert was an eloquent spokesman."

See page C1 for an overview of Mr. Calvert's short career.

"Good old Billy," Hastings said. "If anyone can make people sit up and take notice, it's him. We've left him all alone to deal with it."

It was now fully dark, and a strong fall smell of mixed burning and decaying leaves poured in through the Edsel's open windows. Autumn had always been Hastings' favorite time, although it was not healthy for his already melancholy psyche. Naturally introverted and occasionally morbid by nature, he was romantically attracted to the aura of decay and the cycle of life that permeated the season. Now, however, the city itself, which had been his natural habitat, disgusted him as he looked out through bare branches on its millions of never-sleeping electric eyes. The metropolis squatted on the edge of the ocean like some primordial monster that fed on human carrion. It would take a million years for this ugliness to finally crumble and its rusting skeleton to be covered again by turf. The city was humankind's decrepit monument to their arrogance, and it would long outlive their undeserved mastery of the planet.

The streets were deserted, as they generally were after nightfall, but it wasn't late enough for any of the brutal young gangs to be slinking through the shadowed alleys. The road was, however, thick with Plexiglas-coated cabs and armored private cars. *We rarely even see each other*, Hastings thought. *We hide in our cages, and when we need to travel, we dash fearfully into another, mobile container, each person desperate to maintain some personal space in an overcrowded world, each filled with hate for the others and forever guarding his personal stash of consumer goods, from which he derives his entire sense of identity and worth. Are we dreaming when we think we can influence the way these people live?*

Aloud, he said, "Everything's gone to shit, mate."

"Almost there," Marty answered, his voice muffled by the Dunhill hanging out of his mouth.

Spanish Stockholm was, by contrast, bustling. They felt the change the moment they turned onto Göteborg Road. Neon lights flashed everywhere, and crowds of revelers filled the sidewalks. No one seemed to be alone; they were all in pairs or raucous groups. The air was filled with cheerful shouts and music from the countless busking Mexican and South American folk groups.

"Well, these people at least aren't quite dead yet," Hastings said, continuing his inner dialogue as Marty maneuvered the oversized boat with difficulty into a tiny parking space.

"Huh?"

"Nothing. Just remarking how lively it is here."

"Tell me about it. These people have some fucking dignity, man."

El Corazon sported one of the largest and brightest signs in the neighborhood, a huge yellow neon palm tree with pink fronds. Two tall, burly bouncers in black T-shirts stood impassively and immovably outside the door with their massive arms crossed, seemingly oblivious to the slight nip in the air. As Marty and Hastings approached the club, another doorman appeared, dragging two smaller men out by their collars, one with each arm. The men were cursing loudly in Spanish. The bouncer deposited them roughly on the pavement with a sneer. The two men were both smallish, with slicked-back hair, and they wore the baggy suits in fashion in the Hispanic community.

They got up and looked as though they were about to start fighting again, but the stares of the three bouncers were enough to send them off in opposite directions.

Marty was the first to get his pluck together and approach the three hulking men, who were now chuckling amongst themselves. It made them look a bit more approachable. "Excuse me, sirs, but we're looking for someone who works here."

The men's faces instantly closed off, and the smiles vanished, to be replaced by fierce scowls. One, a man with a big, bushy beard and a gruff voice, answered, "And why would you be looking for someone here, English? What business you got at our club?"

"Um, listen, we're not here to make trouble," Marty said hurriedly, waving his arms in a placatory gesture. "We were sent by Jorge Jimenez from Sid's Sioux City. He said that his cousin Manuel might be able to help us identify a certain South American who's been hanging about here. Is Manuel here tonight?"

"Why do you want to know about this man?" growled the towering, balding, double-chinned bouncer suspiciously. "And who are you?"

"My name is Marty, and this is Simon. Our friend Guy Calvert died last night, and we have reason to believe this character may have been involved. I hear he wasn't too popular around these parts."

The men's faces showed that they recognized Guy's name. The man with the beard became a little more polite. "Well, I would not be surprised at that. We are sorry for your loss. We Mexicans appreciate music in a way that these gringos, these Virginians," he leaned away to spit, "do not. I am Manuel. Come in."

Manuel led them through the dimly lit, crowded, and smoky bar, past a tiny stage on which a salsa band was jammed. Many couples were dancing energetically in the small open space in front of the stage. Hastings could feel the sweat in the air like a fine mist, and it was as hot as a furnace in the room. Manuel led them past the bar, through a kitchen redolent with the odor of strong spices, and into the cramped, stuffy back office. He gestured to two wooden chairs in front of the desk and poured each of them shots of tequila. Hastings noticed with some disgust that a fat insect lay coiled at the bottom of the bottle but tossed his drink back anyway. The warmth that hit his stomach inspired a new optimism.

"We know quite a lot about this man you describe, and we have had our eyes on him for a while. The police ignore the high level of crime in our neighborhood, as you probably know, so we try to keep an eye on things ourselves. This man appeared a few weeks ago and has made trouble everywhere he goes. He goes by Enrique Nuñez, and he boasts that he is a well-respected man in Colombia. Some members of the Colombian community have identified him as a career criminal there, very notorious in organized crime circles, with ties to the corrupt state police system. As you know, the Colombian state is an oligarchy with strict control over the people. There is also a strong underground crime scene, involved mostly with illegal drugs and the South American slave trade."

"Would anyone know how we can get our hands on this chap?"

"It so happens that you are lucky. Fernando, that's the head barman, lives in the rooming house where Nuñez has been staying. His brother owns it. I will bring him here." Manuel picked up the phone and dialed the bar. A short conversation in rapid-fire Spanish followed. They could hear a voice bellowing on the other end over the noise of the bar. "He will be here in a second," Manuel said. "But tell me, what will you do with this man if you can find him, and the police are being so unhelpful?"

"I don't know," Hastings answered, a little annoyed that everyone kept asking that question. There only seemed to be one answer, and it was one he didn't want to confront. That was if the trail really ended with Nuñez.

A tall, thin man with graying hair entered, dressed in a loud tropical-style shirt. His voice was guttural from years of second-hand smoke intake and yelling over the music. "So you want to know about my pal Nuñez?" He perched on the edge of the desk, eager to please. "I may have to disappoint you."

"How so?"

"Because Mr. Nuñez packed up and left this morning. Told me he was going back home, that things weren't going well here, and I can tell you I was glad to see the back of him."

"He's gone?" Hastings could feel his optimism crashing and burning. The warm, fuzzy feeling from the tequila vanished.

"That's what he told me, although he could have been lying, I suppose. He was nothing but trouble, bringing whores upstairs and, from some of the sounds, beating them, coming in drunk and high out of his mind ... and one other strange thing I noticed." He paused, frowning.

"Yes?"

"Well, it's strange, ever since he moved in, the rats in the walls have been coming out and dying like crazy. His room was full of them this morning. It almost seemed like he was poisoning them somehow. Of course, I'm happy to get rid of the pests, no complaints there, but it's very strange, you'll agree."

Marty and Hastings exchanged looks. "Practice makes perfect, I guess," Marty said grimly. "A little warm-up for the main event." They stood up. "Well, thank you, Manuel, Fernando." They shook hands.

"I guess that's that," Marty said with resignation as they got back into the car.

"What do you mean?" Hastings said curtly.

"He's gone! What can we do? Hire some sort of private detective or contract killer, like in a fucking film? Look, Si, I'm going to need a long convalescence after this. Guy's gone, and running after some assassin in South America whose name is probably a fake isn't going to solve anything! I'm sure we can put ourselves back together, given time."

Hastings couldn't believe his ears. "Guy was like a brother to us — to me, if not to you. I know that this bastard killed him, and I'm never going to rest until Guy gets justice. And what if the killer isn't satisfied with just knocking off one of us?"

"So what the hell are you going to do?" Marty looked exasperated and exhausted. His knuckles were white on the wheel.

"I'm going to Colombia. We just got a big royalty check. I can't just mope around here. If I can find Nuñez, I'm going to."

Marty just stared at him. "What are you talking about? Do you know what your chances of finding him are in his own fucking country?"

Hastings lit a Silk Cut. "Well, nothing we've ever done has been considered sensible, has it? I'm going to take my holiday in Colombia!"

SIX

"Attention, passengers! We will soon be making our approach to Bolívar International Aerodrome. Please refrain from smoking or injecting until the warning signs are turned off. Also, please ensure that you bring all of your carry-on luggage with you upon exiting the aircraft, and do not leave behind your sample of No-Catch Cocaine, compliments of the Colombian Cartels! Enjoy your stay in lovely Bogotá, and thank you for flying Air Cartel!"

Hastings gazed out the window at the lush rainforest sweeping underneath the plane as it gradually descended toward one of the most remarkable cities on the globe, let alone South America. The whole continent had been kept in a state of near-anarchy since the arrival of the first Europeans, with revolutions and insurrections too numerous to count. The coastal Republic of New Portugal, founded on and still practicing slavery, was still by far the strongest, if not the richest state on the continent, with a large, well equipped army and a population of half a billion. Most of the people of that country lived in a state of dire poverty, and the nation was regarded with opprobrium by most of the world.

The former Spanish colony of Colombia ranked only slightly higher in the eyes of the world's idealistic democrats. A pseudo-military oligarchy ruled the country with an iron fist, but it was widely acknowledged that the Colombian Cartels, the only genuine large-scale corporation in the country, was the real power behind the state. The company was formed by a committee of rich coca growers when drugs were legalized. Being the wealthiest men in the country, they had quickly consolidated their power. Their most audacious act had been the hiring (for a rumored billion-mark fee) of a German engineering firm to build a transparent, self-supporting dome made of space-age polymers over the city of Bogotá. The cost for the maintenance of this outlandish project on a yearly basis must be astronomical, but so was the wealth of the men who built it. Vehicle operation was restricted to certain hours under the dome, and fresh air was pumped in by massive generators. The air was laced with a weak concentration of cocaine, a feature designed to keep the population pacified and happy. Apparently it was effective, since there had never been any sign of social unrest in the capital since the dome's unveiling. The rest of the country, and the continent, had been in constant turmoil since the European colonizers abruptly ended their rule. The cocaine-laced atmosphere also attracted tourists from around the globe in search of a worry-free holiday. Most of the arable cleared land in the nation was devoted to growing the coca plant, and a considerable porton of the population was under its influence at any given time.

The argument with Marty the day before had gone on for a couple of hours. He had accused Hastings of total feyness, as he put it, being willing to throw his life, or at least his career, away in a foreign land in search of pointless vengeance. Hastings had in turn told Marty that he was cowardly and disloyal. They had not parted on good terms, leaving the possibility of any continued musical partnership or any friendship at all in serious jeopardy, but Hastings had booked a standby flight to Bogotá the next morning. He had been much entertained during the flight, despite his despondence, by the presence of a pretty young diplomat from the Democratic Federation of Greater Costa Rica in the seat beside him; she had filled him in on some of the basic points of Colombian society and customs and had given him some direction for his enquiries, as well as a good view of part of her upper thigh.

When the plane had touched down and taxied, two soldiers came on board and opened every item of cabin luggage. This took about an hour. Hastings' seatmate explained that the Colombian authorities seemed inexplicably concerned about what foreign visitors might be bringing into the country.

Stepping off the plane, he was hit by a wave of humid heat, forcing him to remove his finest Mod leather coat. A far cry from the unhealthy, smog-laden air of New York in the fall. A bus took them through the terminal and the entrance of that wonder of the world, the great dome of Bogotá. The only way it could be detected was by the glint of the late-afternoon rays on its transparent surface. As he shaded his eyes from the glare, he shook his head in astonishment at the thought of billions, even trillions of dollars wasted on this ultimate civic extravagance, built for no reason but pomp, while the bulk of the people lived at starvation levels all over the continent.

His bags were inspected again inside the airport, but he finally managed to check his luggage (one small suitcase and a knapsack) and phone one of the cheaper hotels his new friend had recommended, called the Villa del Palmar. Having safely booked a room, he sat down at the airport bar to consider his still mainly unformed plan of action. He had decided that even before he checked into his room, he would visit the British Embassy to try to find a sympathetic ear. It was a slim chance, but if the Empire's authorities were willing to assist, he would gladly avoid the unpleasant task of scouring the criminal underground of an unfamiliar and possibly dangerous city. If Her Majesty's servants were unwilling to assist, Plan B would have to be trying to hire some local help. And Hastings didn't speak or understand a word of Spanish beyond *gracias*.

He finished his drink and hailed a taxi, an ancient Chevrolet Model A convertible from the thirties, and managed to convey his destination to the grinning driver. The streets of Bogotá were a madhouse of activity, even more so than the Latin neighborhood in New York. No one wore gas masks to protect from pollution, and instead of the fixed, sedated stares he was commonly used to seeing, most of the people seemed be filled with a manic, cheerful energy. Hastings began to feel something of the same elation as he breathed in the surprisingly sweet air; it felt like a mild cocaine high, which, he suddenly realized, it was. The atmosphere also seemed to be temperature-controlled in some way. It was not as hot here as it was at the airport. A new sense of enjoyment took hold of him. Every street seemed to be a marketplace, where peasant farmers loudly peddled their coffee, bananas, and other tropical goods. As the cab left the crowded poor areas on the outskirts of the city, the markets disappeared, to be replaced by prim-looking shops, although the crowds remained. He noticed what seemed to be a chain of identical shops placed every few blocks, with the sign *Farmacia Recreativa*. He took this to be the Cartels' official outlet, and they certainly seemed to be the busiest shops in the city.

The streets in the area he was passing through were wide, clean avenues of gray stone lined with square low-rise buildings. It could have been the respectable business district of any provincial town in Virginia.

At last, the cab entered a shaded backstreet of older-looking, well-kept houses, many of which had flags hung over the doors, denoting international embassies. Hastings saw those of Costa Rica, France, Germany, and the Tatar Republic before the cab pulled up on front of a lavish European-style brick home flying the good old Union Jack. He gave the driver what he hoped was a good tip and was rewarded with an ecstatic parting grin. He strolled up the palm tree-lined walk and rang the doorbell, which played the opening strains of "Land of Hope and Glory." The door was opened by a tall, very thin old man wearing a suit resembling worn-out butler's garb. The man said something unfriendly in badly accented Spanish, looking Hastings up and down and making him feel quite self-conscious in his flares and lime-green T-shirt.

"Hello."

The man said nothing but continued to examine him disdainfully.

"I'm English. I wonder if you could let me in to speak with the consul?"

"English, eh?" The butler's wheezing voice sounded as disapproving as he looked, but he opened the door wide enough for Hastings to squeeze through. "Lost your passport? On some kind of New Age voyage of discovery, having tribal hallucinations with the natives, are we? We see your sort from time to time. You think you can flaunt Her Majesty's laws and the rules of polite society and decency whenever you can, with your drugs and pop music, but you're happy to throw yourself on the mercy of her servants when you're in need." The rant seemed to take a lot out of him, for he leaned on the railing of the staircase, wheezing a little.

Hastings felt himself flushing. He was hot, tired, and his bags weighed heavily on his arms. "Listen, chum, I'm on very important business here. I'm going to see the consul, whether you like the sight of me or not!"

The old man moved to block Hastings' path and was about to elicit another angry retort when a loud voice boomed from deep within the building. "I say, Boyle, what's the fuss about out there? Can't get a wink of sleep in here!" This was followed by a guffaw. A small, very fat balding man wearing a brown suit with a plum-colored waistcoat and a golden fob-watch emerged into the hallway. "Well, what have we here? A lost traveller? From old Blighty, are we?"

"Virginia, sir, but your ... man here doesn't seem to want to let me in."

"Hmmm ... well, he's got a job of work to do, you know. An important function, what what! Regardless, you don't seem very threatening, albeit a bit scruffy, and I haven't had a visitor all day! That will be all, Boyle."

The old man slouched off, disappointed, grumbling under his breath, into a small room near the door.

The consul lowered his voice. "A fine secretary, but a bit of a soggy blanket, what what! I'm Sir Andrew Laurence Fairweather-

Smyth, of the Shropshire Fairweathers, at your service! Come in, come in!"

He led Hastings into a spacious office that contained several overstuffed leather chairs and sofas and a gigantic oak desk. The beige-papered walls were lined with trophies and photographs, most of which showed a much thinner, youthful consul playing polo or cricket. "Ah-ha, you've noticed my trophies and awards, dear boy! No polo in these parts, alas, although we sometimes manage to cobble together a cricket match." He squeezed his rotund frame into the chair behind his desk. "I was stationed in Kashmir before this posting, staring down the Tatars, and I must say it doesn't feel like much of a promotion. One becomes rather lonely with scaly old Boyle as the only decent English company for miles around! Ha! So, what can I do for you, young man?"

Hastings explained his troubles at length. He didn't conceal his purpose for being in the country, mainly because he couldn't for the life of him think of a more likely story to explain what a British pop star could be looking for alone in South America. When he finished, Fairweather-Smyth knitted his brows.

"A homicide, you say! An investigation the police won't assist with, eh? Taking it all on yourself for honor and friendship's sake, mmmm? It's all a bit too *Boy's Own Paper*, don't you think? I'm sure you could have found some Virginian authority to take your story seriously?"

"I could not," Hastings said flatly.

"Well, well, you know your own business best. Long time since I was last in those parts — and only on holiday at that. I prefer the heights of the Pamir, with a good horse under me and a division of fierce Gurkhas at my command, though those days are long over for me. I'm afraid, Mr. Hastings, that, though I greatly sympathize with your heroic, um, initiative, my hands are rather tied on this matter. This simply isn't my jurisdiction. As you may know, relations between Colombia and the Empire are more than a little strained at the moment, due the Guyana Question, and we can't afford any negative interactions that, shall we say, could adversely affect negotiations. You may have to avoid the Colombian authorities altogether if you want any direct answers to your questions."

"So you can't help me?"

"Now, now, you haven't let me finish, my boy." Fairweather-Smyth leaned back in his overstuffed chair, which looked dangerously like it was going to fall over backward, and lit up a peculiar-smelling brown cigarillo. "I'm an old-fashioned chap, but a reasonable one. I don't pretend to understand the likes of you, with your strange clothes and funny ladies' hairstyles and newfangled ideas about anarchy and all, but I do understand that every generation's different. The result of a limited democracy! Got bairns of my own back home, and God knows what they're up to as we speak. Worse than you, I imagine. And I do definitely appreciate a man of action and pluck."

The consul, Hastings thought, looked like anything but a man of action. But he certainly liked the sound of his own voice.

The man leaned forward with a conspiratorial look, and the front legs of his chair landed with a thud. "I can put you in touch with a good local man. He's sometimes ... in Her Majesty's employ, if you know what I mean."

"You mean he's a spy?"

"Not quite. His specialty is finding things and people, and that sounds exactly like what you need at the moment. He's been useful to me on a couple of occasions." The consul leaned forward even farther, arching a brow. "But mark my words, my boy, if you cause too much of a stir and bring any unwanted attention to the Crown in these parts, I'll either disavow you entirely or have you in Colombian prison on trumped-up charges within a day. Am I understood?"

Hastings decided it would be wise to avoid a visible reaction to the sweaty little man's threat, lest he should actually be capable of carrying it out. He nodded.

"Good!" The consul opened a desk drawer, took out a business card, and passed it to him. "He seems a bit of a shady character but is a really decent sort overall, and his Queen's English is excellent. I don't suggest calling ahead; his secretary will pretend to have no idea whom you are talking about. His front is as a respectable businessman, an exporter of tropical fruit and coconut-flavored beverages. He is also, from what I've heard, an excellent defenseman in a football match."

"Thank you, sir," Hastings said, standing up. "This is a start, anyway."

"Good luck, and if you get any solid evidence, concrete stuff, mind, I might be help you at that point. Now, won't you stay for a gin and tonic? I don't get the chance to talk sport and home much in these god-forsaken parts. Do you swing a bat?"

"Haven't for a while. I'd really better crack on, but thanks for the offer." Hastings beat a hasty retreat to the door. The effort of being polite to the plump servant of Empire was starting to wear him out.

*

It was now 5:00 p.m., but the subequatorial sun seemed to beat down even harder as Hastings shouldered his way through the crowds. The temperature inside the dome, though supposedly controlled, seemed to have risen considerably. Upon checking into the hotel, which was priced a little beyond his means, he had found that the investigator's office was fortuitously only a few streets away, so, after enjoying some of his complimentary airline cocaine, he set out into the streets once more. He had also managed to locate some of the strangely alluring cigarillos that the consul had been smoking, noting with amusement that they too seemed to be laced with cocaine. The whole country seemed to be made of it. Even more amusing was the fact that a stodgy old pillar of Empire could be seen smoking them openly with such relish. It was like the stereotype of the opium-eating Indian army officer succumbing to the exotic lures of the conquered culture.

Hastings enjoyed the sights and sounds of the streets, lost in his impressions, until he suddenly came upon the street he was looking for, the El Camino Real. At Number 56, in a shabby two-story building, he saw a sign that said *Miguel Gonzalez: Bebibas Gaseosas*. Ascending a steep staircase, he found himself in a dusty, wood-floored office, lit blindingly by the setting sun. Great clouds of dust circled in the beams. A stout, middle-aged lady in a green dress with her hair in a tidy bun was tapping away on an ancient typewriter. The tapping echoed off the walls. Another office was presumably behind a glass-windowed door near the desk. She looked up as the creaking floorboards announced his entrance.

"*¿Necesito usted ayuda?*" she said.

"Umm, Señor Gonzalez, *por favor*."

"You have no appointment?" she asked, switching to heavily accented English.

"No, but I've just come from the British Embassy. Sir Fairweather-Smyth sent me. My name's Simon Hastings." He tried to inject a sense of importance into the words, as though sent on an important mission.

"Hmm, well, I never hear of any Mr. Fairwatersmith, but I see if Mr. Gonzalez will see you." She disappeared into the office, returning a few seconds later. "Okay, go in." She resumed her work, ignoring him.

Inside the inner office, a radio was playing a version of "Vegetables" by The Beach Bums, sung by a Spanish-language choir over unobtrusively soft jazz instrumentation. Gonzalez sat engulfed in sunbeams and dust motes behind a large but battered desk. He looked to be in his thirties, with shiny, longish brown hair and a light green zoot suit. He looked, in fact, disturbingly like the man that Hastings had come to Colombia to confront, albeit better put together. He didn't get up when Hastings entered but looked penetratingly at him for a few seconds. His eyes were an intense blue that looked out of place on his olive-hued face. When he spoke it was in perfect, barely accented English.

"Welcome, Mr. Hastings. Yes, I am mildly familiar with your name. Not all of my people are ignorant of cultural events of the north. Though my tastes tend toward softer music, as you can hear." The easy listening rendition of the song was mercifully coming to an end, to be replaced by Don Leitch's latest light-folk hit, "Cosmic Wheels." Gonzalez stood up abruptly and shook Hastings' hand.

"Well then, if you know who I am, you will probably have heard of the very recent death of my friend, Guy Calvert," Hastings said guardedly.

"There was something on the news last night about a dead pop star in Virginia, a famous one." Gonzalez extended a case of brown Colombian cigarettes. Hoping that they were cocaine-free, Hastings accepted one and lit up. It was indeed free of such additives. "But we don't get much substance in our foreign news here, Mr. Hastings, just the very bare facts. Tell my why this news has brought you all this way, and then to me."

After Hastings had finished his story, Gonzalez smiled ruefully. "A very tall order you wish to set me. As you can see, dark-haired men in baggy suits aren't exactly uncommon here. And the name he used in New York was no doubt false." He paused. "Nonetheless, I will take on this case, for the sake of your loyalty to your friend and for a good-sized fee payable upon satisfactory completion. I admire any man who devotes his time to trying to free people from the chains of such governments as we now have in this oppressive world." His blue eyes glowed passionately from under dark brows.

Hastings was somewhat taken aback by this outburst. "Everyone I've seen here seems fairly happy."

"You haven't visited the barrios, my friend, where the majority of the population lives. The whole country is under the thumb of the cartels, and the few wealthy people all work for them," Gonzalez growled. "The image of freedom presented to foreign tourists is false. If any man manages to escape from this cocaine-induced trance that they keep us in and dares to speak his mind, he very likely won't see another morning." He walked over to a cabinet in the corner and unlocked it. Inside were several oxygen tanks. "Many times each day I have to try to clear my head in order to retain my freedom. You people up in the Virginias, you think that drugs are wonderful, that these companies provide their products generously for the benefit of humankind. They are parasites whose growth can't be stopped. They govern this world, those makers of drugs, along with other corporations, not our so-called elected governments. They keep your people in thrall just as easily as they govern these grinning half-corpses, my countrymen. People are much more pliable when they are stoned by the TV or by 'recreational pharmaceuticals.'" He stopped suddenly and sat down.

"Look, friend, I'm well aware of the problems of the modern world. I don't like it any more than you do, but you'll have to excuse my ignorance of a country I've never visited. Now, are you going to help me or not?" said Hastings.

He didn't much like being lectured; it had always been the only source of friction between himself and Guy, aside from Guy's predilection for homemade fixes. And Gonzalez's speech had caused an unexpected bubble of guilt to rise to the surface; was his whole generation of rebels merely a stooge for international capitalists? He quickly repressed the thought.

Gonzalez had sat down with his head in his hands after his outburst, recovering his equilibrium. He raised his head and smiled slowly. "I'm sorry, *amigo*. The strain of trying to keep a clear head in a city where my government puts drugs into the air to keep me from thinking for myself wears me out. It's a wonder that we are not all insane here. Of course I'll help you, for a price to be determined. It will be affordable, I assure you."

"Why don't you move away?"

"It's not that easy. I work sometimes for the government, and that's why I'm allowed to stay in business. The good money is accompanied by certain disadvantages, one of which is that I know too much about the inner workings of our society, and if I tried to leave, I would probably be jailed ... or killed. I chose the wrong line of work. But enough of this. I doubt that the government, or the Cartels for that matter, will object to you trying to track down a criminal who may or may not be working on his own but is either a pharmaceutical smuggler or a man who concocts his own chemicals — a madman. Such activities are, of course, the worst crimes that that can be committed in our country, since they take profits directly out of the coffers of the Cartels. I would avoid dealing with our authorities, though, if I were you. As high as my price is, theirs would be higher and potentially much less ... pleasant. I will make inquiries. You go to your hotel and wait for my call. When I have some information, I will contact you."

"You're sure that this man isn't working for the Cartels?"

"If he was, you would never have seen him. The Cartels have a hundred years of homicidal experience behind them, and they don't countenance mistakes from their operatives. He is likely not working alone, but my supposition, for the time being, is that he's not in the employ of the corporate masters of Colombia. And besides, I know the Cartels' product list very well, and those that our quarry was selling don't sound familiar at all."

"Where will you start?"

"Not many Colombians visit Virginia for any length of time. This man will have had to give his real name to reenter the country. I have friends in customs at the airport who may remember him. Naturally, he may have contacts there as well, or he would never have gotten out in the first place. Nonetheless, I may have some success if he was not too careful." He extended his hand once more and ushered Hastings to the door. The secretary didn't even look up as they passed her.

Out in the light again, Hastings found that the street life, which had seemed so gay and lively earlier in the day, now seemed unnaturally vibrant, as though the people were animated puppets possessed by a malignant will. Their smiles looked ghastly in the red glare of the setting sun. A profound depression fell on him. When he reached his hotel, he decided to skip dinner and went straight to his room. He was glad that he had brought his portable tape player. Lying on the sheets of the queen-sized bed, which reeked of ingrained smoke, he fixed the reels in place, put his headphones on, and set his pack of Silk Cuts beside him. The sound of the new Delia Derbyshire album, his latest favorite, soothed his ears with layers of buzzing synthesizer. He fell asleep during the second piece.

The phone rang shortly after 11:00 p.m.

From *The Modern City: An Urban Theorist's Travelogue*
by Prof. S.R.J. Kilbey

Surely the greatest affront to good taste in the world today is Bogotá, Colombia, the largest city in this rapidly developing country. Like all such countries, Colombia contains two solitudes, which rarely meet: a small, extremely wealthy ruling class and the great mass of peasants who serve them and starve for them. The middle class, mainly made up of tradesmen, is growing but small.

It is truly disgusting that in a country where the majority of people live in abject poverty, the city's government, at the bidding of the all-powerful Cartels, which dominate the political and economic life of the nation, has spent an undisclosed sum that may venture into the trillions erecting the famous dome, the so-called newest Wonder of the World. All readers should be familiar with the appearance of this dome; we have seen it on countless television programs and tourist brochures. This dome serves no apparent purpose but to appear grand and imposing, and it certainly is an engineering marvel (for which Germans were responsible). It is also expensive to maintain, since the temperature inside would be unbearable on sunny days without some regulation (it is, nonetheless, kept at a tropical temperature much of the time, possibly to keep the populace in an enervated state). The dome houses much of the government, embassies, and the business district, as well as wealthy and middle-class neighborhoods. Barrios cling to the outside of the dome like limpets on a rock, hence most tourists wisely choose to stay within the dome's welcoming interior, stimulated by the trace amounts of cocaine in the atmosphere.

The money pit of a spectacle, combined with the absolute indifference of the city's government to living conditions outside the dome, earns Bogotá my lowest rating. Only through a healthy infusion of proper democracy will this city ever be restored to the provincial beauty that it once possessed.

SEVEN

"I've been lucky, Mr. Hastings," Gonzalez said, sitting at ease on a chair in Hastings' room. "My contact has access to some pretty complete records at Bolívar Airport. Because of security features embedded within, it is nearly impossible to fake a Colombian passport, so our friend, whose real name is Ramón Rosas, has had to come and go under his own name, which I'm sure does not please him. But he wouldn't have expected to be followed here, or even to be suspected of this murder in any way by someone so far away. He would have little cause for fear. I have looked him up, and I have a good idea of where he can be found."

"Very well," Hastings replied. "You do work fast."

"Of course. I am the best, and I've spent my whole life learning the darkest secrets of this city. Do you know how to fire a gun?"

"Of course not!" Hastings was shocked. "I am, in case you haven't noticed, what people like to call a hippie. I don't believe in the things."

Gonzalez threw back his head and laughed loud. "And what, my dear Mr. Hastings, did you expect to do when you came here? Did you think that when discovered Rosas would happily offer to hand himself over to the authorities? We need to bring this man in ourselves if we want the police to do anything. It's the Colombian way." He held out a shiny black pistol. "Careful, it's loaded."

As he regarded this symbol of everything The Spheres stood against, Hastings began to feel that this trip had been a rash idea after all. But he had come all this way to bring the killer of his best friend to justice, and this was no time for faintheartedness. He wrapped his shaking fingers around the barrel, wincing in disgust. Gonzalez watched him with amusement.

"Well, it seems you have gained some resolve. We'd better go. I will tell you about the illustrious career of our friend Rosas on the way. We're going to a very interesting part of town, where a handgun is a necessary part of one's wardrobe. My car is outside."

The night was jet-black and cloudless as they walked out of the lobby. Most of the streetlights appeared to be inactive, and only a few cars and no pedestrians were out on the roads. The air was perfectly still under the windless dome. Hastings noticed with astonishment that there were several strange lights, like hovering UFOs, placed at even intervals in the blackness. Then he realized that these were the night beacons, designed to warn airplanes away from the dome. Gonzalez's car, a beat-up old Holden from New Wales, was parked at the curb.

"I have another car, a much nicer German model, but we don't want to draw attention," he said, holding the passenger door open. "You are going to see the real Bogotá, the bars of the barrio, which the criminal elements tend to frequent." The engine started with a cough.

"You already know exactly where to find him?" Hastings asked skeptically as the car sputtered onto a main street.

"Please give me some credit, Mr. Hastings!" Gonzalez puffed cheerfully on a cigarette and offered him some oxygen from a small cylinder. "We've got to have our wits about us. Well, Rosas was indeed already in my files, which made the job quite easy. I even have a photograph, in case you've forgotten what he looks like. A very dangerous man, perhaps even a wanted man, with some dangerous friends. He was extremely lucky to make it past the officials at the airport. He used to work, many years ago, for the Cartels, in their security department, which means that he has much blood on his hands. He was fired, reputedly for some clumsy overenthusiasm — massacring a whole village, I believe — and somehow managed to evade his own executioners or was for some reason allowed to escape. Since then, he's made his living peddling homemade concoctions and serving as a part-time contract killer for small-time criminals. Not a skilled killer, but a ruthless one. He also has contacts in the slave trade. I don't know where he holes up, but judging by his extrovert behavior in New York, I would say that there are three or four bars where he's likely to spend his time."

"Won't someone recognize you?"

"That's a risk we'll have to take. However, there are almost as many investigators and informants as there are criminals in Bogotá, and I always take precautions. But, Mr. Hastings—"

"Yes?"

"I would recommend that you not speak while I make the inquiries. British subjects, and foreigners in general, are not highly regarded here."

The landscape had gradually begun to change during the drive. The streets around the hotel and business district had been deserted but clean, with few open establishments. Now, every second storefront seemed to be a bar of some kind, and the buildings were gradually becoming more run-down. There were many more people walking the streets, which were littered with refuse. Obviously, the wealthier neighborhoods were better served by the city, just as they were in any city in the world.

The car approached what looked like a border crossing post.

"What's that?"

"We are about to go outside the dome. The barrio has grown up outside the city limits, and there are too many people living in it for the government to be able to wipe it cleanly from the map." Gonzalez chuckled. "Their location outside our beloved plastic home may explain why the inhabitants of the barrio, despite their poverty, seem to be lot more sharp-witted than my dome-dwelling neighbors. As a respectable citizen with a good business front, I am allowed to enter and exit the dome as I please, a luxury not afforded to the poorer citizens. I suggest again that you don't speak. If we aren't allowed out, we may never find our man."

The car drew up to the booth, and a blue-uniformed guard

approached. He looked in, his gaze lingering disapprovingly on Hastings, who was starting to wish he'd brought different clothes and got a "straight" haircut. Gonzalez spoke in Spanish, and the guard grunted. He looked over Gonzalez's papers for a few moments then gestured threateningly at Hastings. Gonzalez hurriedly added something else, which must have worked. The guard let out a gruff guffaw, smacked Gonzalez hard on the shoulder, winked exaggeratedly at Hastings, and waved the car through. Gonzalez sighed with relief.

"What did you say?"

"I told him you are a visiting client, a soft-drink importer from New Orleans, and that I am taking you to the barrio to pick up some whores. These fellows appreciate that sort of thing."

The neighborhood they were now in was one of the strangest places Hastings had ever seen. It was a shantytown. All of the one-story buildings were either constructed out of corrugated sheet metal or rough wooden planks. There were neon signs on many of the buildings, and large groups of ragged but lively-looking people, mostly men, stood clustered around the entrances. Many were either staggering about or holding each other up. Here and there a scantily clad woman teetered around on high heels from group to group, soliciting business. Even larger piles of garbage filled the gutters. Just as in Spanish Stockholm, there were street musicians playing on many of the corners.

Gonzalez parked. "Welcome to the barrio. Better leave the car here. They don't see many vehicles around here."

The air was palpably thicker when they got out of the car, the remnant of the day's equatorial humidity. After passing a few shadowy side streets, presumably the residential areas of the barrio, they came upon a metal edifice larger than any they had come across, a sheet metal palace. It had a massive neon sign flickering above the door shaped like a nude woman, with the words *La Virginiana* emblazoned across her breasts.

"A likely criminal hangout!" Hastings said.

"Exactly. There are more dangerous felons here tonight than there are in the government jails." Gonzalez grinned maliciously. "So try to look as evil as possible, my dear hippie."

A bouncer who looked about eight feet tall glared down at them as they went by. Inside, the bar was unbelievably crowded and noisy. There was no live entertainment, but the sounds of the jukebox and of the shouting and laughing and breaking glass created an almost unbearable cacophony. The air reeked of beer, tequila, and stale sweat. The male patrons seemed to be divided by two fashion styles. About half of them wore zoot suits in pastel shades, some with fedoras and all with dark hair slicked back rakishly. The other half wore leather or denim vests that revealed enormous hairy arms and violent-looking tattoos. Some of these men were shaved bald.

"Even here, there is something of a social divide," Gonzalez remarked over the racket as Hastings nervously glanced around him. "The men in the vests are mostly gang members. We'll try not to talk to or even look at them. The suits are criminals of a more sophisticated stripe, white-collar crooks. Keep an eye out for our man Rosas."

They began to push their way delicately through the crowd. Most of the men paid no attention to them, but some shoved back aggressively. Hastings was careful not to look into their faces as he hurried quickly past. After a few difficult turns around the room, Hastings touched Gonzalez on the arm and shook his head. Gonzalez gestured toward the door.

Back out in the night air, Hastings breathed in deeply. "Lovely place. We may as well look for a needle in a bloody haystack." The phrase sounded oddly familiar. Hadn't someone he knew used it recently?

Gonzalez patted him reassuringly on the back. "We've only started, dear fellow. Stiff upper lip, isn't that what you British say? My first day on the case, and you're ready to quit! If we don't find him in the places I've chosen for tonight, I'll do more research tomorrow. I am the best, after all."

"You're right." Hastings smiled as he accepted another cigarette. "Sorry. It's been a long—" He froze, staring across the street.

"What?"

"Quick, get your photo out. I think it's him!"

Gonzalez swung around, feeling inside his jacket. There was a group of three men in suits standing outside another, smaller bar, engaged in animated conversation. All three appeared to be fall-down drunk. Rosas was holding the floor, waving his arms as he told some anecdote, at which the others laughed raucously. There was no doubt as to his identity — the longish, greasy hair, the diminutive stature. These things had all been tattooed on the back of Hastings' skull the night he stood on the stage at Elysian Fields and watched Rosas smile in satisfaction as Guy's life ebbed away.

Gonzalez looked discreetly from the photograph to the man on the other side of the street for a few moments, frowning. "That's him, all right. This is lucky, almost too lucky. I'm not sure I'm comfortable with such quick results. We'll just wait and see what his next move is."

They moved away into the shadows. Now that he had found the murderer, Hastings' mind was in turmoil. Part of him, a part that he had always ignored and suppressed, was filled with anger and hatred. He felt an itch in his left hand, the side of the pocket that contained the gun. But what would killing Rosas accomplish? Guy would never sing on this Earth again, no matter what. With Gonzalez's connections, and hopefully some evidence if things were handled properly, perhaps Rosas could be brought to trial, if not necessarily for the crimes he committed in Virginia. And if Gonzalez were telling the truth about his society, Rosas would probably pay the ultimate price. But not before Hastings had the chance to ask him some pointed questions about his activities.

They didn't have to wait long. After about ten minutes, Rosas rolled up his right sleeve and jabbed a small syringe into his arm with evident relish, then waved farewell to his two friends and headed off down the street. The two pursuers let him get a block ahead of them and followed. After a few more minutes, they were away from the main strip, and the street became much quieter. There were very few pedestrians about as they slowly followed the staggering man. He was kicking up clouds of dust from the road as he lumbered.

Just as Rosas turned down a side street and Hastings was about to speed up to keep him in sight, he heard Gonzalez yell from behind him, "Look out! Run!" He heard what sounded like a muffled shot and turned to see Gonzalez go sprawling, his gun half out of his pocket. He stared despairingly up at Hastings, an unspoken apology burning in his dying eyes. Three men dressed in black were running toward them, dark blurs in the night. Hastings turned to run, but before he could take more than a couple of steps, he felt a blow to the back of his head. Blinding light and excruciating pain filled his head, and he felt himself falling as well.

Perhaps he would be following Guy sooner than expected, he thought before darkness came.

EIGHT

Hastings jolted back to consciousness. There was a splitting pain in the back of his head. He could feel a breeze or a draft on his left side, and it was surprisingly cold; the air felt thinner. Wasn't he in Colombia? He tried to open his eyes but was unable to for a few seconds. When he did, he found himself sitting upright in a damp, dark space. There was water trickling down stone walls. He could see what looked like a cold flagstone floor beneath him. When he tried to move, he found that he was tied to a chair.

"Mr. Simon Hastings." A figure stepped from the shadows. "I trust you are feeling better." The figure was that of a tall man with graying, close-cropped hair, wearing a modest but obviously expensive business suit. He had elegant, aquiline features and mild-looking brown eyes, but his thick brows added a hint of brutality. He too had a Spanish accent, but, like Gonzalez, he spoke fluently in an educated tone.

"Where am I? What have you done with my friend?" Hastings could barely speak, the pain in his head was so intense.

The man smiled. "I can answer both of those questions, but I don't think you will like the answers." He came closer and unceremoniously stuck a cigarette in Hastings' mouth; he spat it out defiantly. His captor shrugged and sat in a chair to the right, crossing his legs.

"Since this is my country, it is my right to be the one asking the questions, but there will be plenty of time for that, time which you will not enjoy. Your friend is dead. He was known to us. This brings me to your second question. You are in Medellín, at the headquarters of the Colombian Cartels. I am Ricardo Alvarez, Director of Security. I am also Minister for the Environment in the Government of Colombia. I am holding you on suspicion of illegal pharmaceutical trafficking."

Hastings' head was swimming. Another man dead, this one on his account. "I'm not a drug dealer... I have a perfectly good reason for being in your country," he managed to stammer. Anger and resentment, as well as the pain, were clouding his brain. "And if I'm suspected of this, why am I not in police custody?"

Alvarez gave a short, barking laugh, which was incongruous with his sophisticated exterior. "As your friends Gonzalez and Rosas may have warned you, there is a very fine line between the duties of the authorities and company security—"

"Rosas?"

"Yes, and do not play stupid with me. Your activities in the country were monitored from the moment you stepped off your flight. Do you think the presence of a known radical and hellraiser in our country would go unnoticed?"

Despite his discomfort, Hastings couldn't help but feel flattered by this description of himself. Alvarez smiled again. "Though my daughter, who attends private school in Upper Canada, enjoys your music very much, and I do not forbid her to listen to it. A stage, you know." Hastings opened his mouth to speak, but Alvarez waved him to silence. "You were followed to the British consulate, where you presumably notified your countrymen of your status as a tourist for cover. You then contacted, a little to our surprise, Miguel Gonzalez, with whom I am very familiar, a man known to harbor some very dangerous views indeed. He had been of some use to me in the past, but I'd had my eye on him for some time for stepping outside acceptable boundaries.

"But the reason for your presence here was still a mystery to us until you arrived for your meeting with your third partner, Rosas. We have been watching him for a while also, having heard of certain very undesirable activities of his that affected our profits. Activities that made us very angry. He is a slippery one and has managed to avoid leaving evidence so far.

"Yes, we do officially require evidence before arresting someone; we try to stick to that most of the time. Fortuitously, you were followed right to him, and our agents decided it would be opportune to remove the threat. Perhaps regrettable in some ways. The only reason you are still alive is that you are a foreigner, and we need to preserve our good foreign relations. If someone knows you went missing here, that would not be good. Still, I have not quite decided what to you do with you yet. We know Rosas recently visited you in New York. International illegal dealing is a very big crime."

"Rosas?" Hastings croaked.

"He escaped yet again, unfortunately, by slipping down an alley while we apprehended you. But he won't evade us for long. Now, what shall I do with you?" Alvarez crossed his legs, leaned back, and took a long pull on his cigarette.

Hastings finally pulled himself together. He must try to reason with the man. "Listen, Mr. Alvarez, you've got this all wrong, and a good man has died because of your error."

Alvarez shrugged casually. "Many good men have died at my command. More good ones than evil, most likely. That's the nature of my work. But if I am incorrect, please do fill me in. I have plenty of time."

Alvarez's attitude toward the killing of Gonzalez, and the story his people had concocted, sent Hastings into a rage. He could no longer control himself; he had heard plenty about these multinational executives and the way they played fast and loose with the law, seemingly living in their own world where they could get away with whatever they pleased. "I'll fill you in all right, you sick bastard," he almost roared, straining at his bonds. "Rosas is responsible for the murders of two men in New York, ironically a couple of your best customers. I came here to track him down. And you let him get away!"

He cursed and raved in this fashion for a few minutes, while Alvarez looked on stonily, then finally calmed down and related the facts. He was getting tired of explaining himself.

When he had finished, Alvarez got up and paced the room for a few long seconds then stopped and stared hard at Hastings. "Calvert is dead, eh? My daughter will be heartbroken. Now that you mention it, I did hear that some British pop star had died. I will confirm this story. I will also have a chat with my friend Fairweather-Smyth, who, if you are telling the truth, was overly cautious in sending you to that amateur Gonzalez. I would have been perfectly happy to assist you. We could have helped each other! The consul should have told you that avoiding the long arm of the Cartels is impossible in Colombia. I will be back, and if you are lying, diplomacy be damned, you won't live another day!"

He roughly untied Hastings' arms and offered him another cigarette, which was grudgingly accepted. Then he left. Hastings heard the lock turn in the heavy metal door.

He looked around him. He was in what was once likely a storage room; the walls, ceiling, and floor were concrete, not stone, which, he noticed with a shiver, was stained a dark red in many places. Water dripped from several cracks in the walls and ceiling. The two wooden chairs were the only furniture and a naked bulb the only light. No doubt this room was designed to break the will of the captive.

It was at least a couple of hours before Alvarez returned; hunger pangs were clawing at Hastings' stomach. He was slumped on the floor, heedless of the dirt. He had passed out for a while, but his head still pounded. He raised himself slowly to his feet, noticing that Alvarez had changed into some sort of fancy black evening dress. "What's the time?"

"Six p.m., Mr. Hastings. You were out for about sixteen hours, you know, and completely oblivious to your helicopter journey to our lovely highland corporate headquarters. Our men are good at their jobs." Hastings noticed that he had not shut the door behind him, but a heavy-set man in a black uniform with a large gun stood outside. "The facts would appear to confirm your story. I owe you, ahem, an apology for our hastiness. You have come on a brave and foolish mission, sir. Well, follow me, and we can continue this discussion in more comfort."

Hastings painfully followed him out of the door, up a flight of stairs, and into the pink marble-floored lobby of some large building. There seemed to be no one around. The guard accompanied them. The entered a large elevator. The guard would not return Hastings' gaze, standing at attention with his gun across his chest, his face impassive.

They disembarked at the fortieth floor, went down a long white hallway, and into an office. The guard remained outside. The office was by far the most opulent Hastings had seen. There were priceless-looking antiques in display cases around the room and several paintings that looked like the work of the renowned and recently deceased Photographic Realist painter Federico Picasso, the value of which must have been in the millions of pounds. There was a massive desk, a few well-appointed chairs, and a luxurious crimson shag carpet. A large window with open curtains opened on a beautiful valley panorama of rolling hills and thick, emerald jungle stretching into the distance, where he could see the outskirts of a large city. The sun was beginning to set, filling the room with blood-red ambiance.

"Please forgive our rough treatment, Mr. Hastings. Welcome to Medellín. We may have had our information mixed up, but we thought we had to act quickly. Unfortunately, I am forced to admit, our actions deprived us of our real quarry in the end. This does not happen very often." In the red glow, Alvarez looked positively satanic. "Some port?" He poured two glasses of rich burgundy liquid from a crystal decanter and seated himself behind his desk with a sigh.

And you killed a man who had helped you in the past, thought Hastings but kept that thought to himself. The man who sat facing him obviously possessed no conscience. "Well, you can make it up to me by helping me track down this arsehole again," he bluntly said instead.

"That would be my pleasure, but there has been an unfortunate complication."

"Which is?"

Alvarez now wore an impishly coy look, which Hastings found annoying. "Rosas, as I said, ran away into an alley. We have had the police tear apart every shack in that neighborhood, during the course of which they made several coincidental arrests based on what they found, which made them very happy. In one filthy place they were directed to they questioned a woman of ill repute, who, under the influence of, ah, some mild interrogation, admitted to being the current paramour of the elusive Rosas, who had run out of the house in great haste minutes before my men arrived. Other tenants of the neighborhood were able to confirm that Rosas lives there. The woman produced this list from his lodgings, which, as you can see, has your name on it. Curious, hmmm? We originally thought it was a contact list, but now its meaning seems more sinister, would you not agree?" He handed Hastings a sheet of paper with a list, in two parts, scrawled in a messy hand.

Hunter Burlington
Guy Calvert
Simon Hastings
Martin Sharpe-Thornton

Maurice Wyatt
Daevid Mallorn
Rick Farren
Ed Barrett

Hastings was very familiar with all the names. He looked up quizzically. "This must be a hit list!"

Alvarez continued smiling in his inscrutable way. "So it would seem, so it would seem. A strange pastime, assassinating minor pop stars! It appears you are a marked man."

"That was why he looked so upset when I wouldn't buy any of his drugs."

"Indeed. These other men, you know them?"

"Yes, they're outspoken rock musicians. They all share the beliefs and to some extent the sounds of my band. We've gigged with all of them. Obviously, this man is supposed to or wants to kill us all. Why?"

Alvarez put a finger to his mouth. "I know Rosas' history very well. He is not the type to take an interest either in cultural or political affairs. Our supposition must be that he is working for someone else, and not necessarily someone in this country. I know all of the rich madmen and madwomen of Colombia intimately (some might say that I am one of them!), and I don't know of anyone who would want to knock off northern pop stars, even for sport. We are an insular people. Rosas spent a great deal of time out of the country last year, but we do not know where. We assumed he was working in the slave trade somewhere. As long as he stayed away, we were well satisfied. It was stupid of him to come back. Let me tell you what I think." He was silent for a few moments.

"Yes?" Hastings' head was still aching, and he was feeling rather faint. He sipped some of the port to steady himself.

"Rosas, during his travels, has met with someone who has contracted him to do these killings, presumably for a large fee. He is not the sort to turn down large financial gain — who is? — and having worked briefly as a member of my security force, albeit not one of the most skilled, killing is not an activity to which he would give a second thought." Hastings felt a chill run up his spine and shifted uncomfortably in his chair. "It would be easy enough to follow one of you home and shoot or stab you, but the mastermind of this plan has been clever and has decided to boldly pin the killings, should they be discovered, on the Cartels. It is intended to be the perfect crime — committed by our former employee, with what is purported to be our products. This incenses me, especially since it involves betrayal by a once-trusted member of our team. A very careful, seemingly foolproof plan. Despite the potential danger to him here, Rosas has been instructed to go to ground. He is taking a break to return home to enjoy some of his earnings, to renew some of his business contacts, and if anyone suspects anything, to make it look like he is returning to report to his bosses — myself, in other words."

"Why did you fire him?"

Alvarez shrugged. "I had orders to downsize. Others had more seniority and far more skill, so I unfortunately had to let him go. He may have turned into something given a longer trial. We offered him a very generous severance package, including an extension of his dental benefits for a year."

"And you don't sell a drug called Cortezuma #1?"

Alvarez looked offended. "Give us more credit than that. The Cartels are very concerned about the political correctness of our product names, and this insult to a great Spanish hero and a conquered king by combining their names would be very unpopular!"

Hastings gazed out the window. It all fit together. If Alvarez was right, a great deal of preparation had gone into these murders, and there would be more to follow if Rosas were not caught or the targets weren't at least warned of the danger. He might already be running out of time; Rosas may even have left already, and England would likely be his next stop. The Cartels' security obviously wasn't as proficient as Alvarez liked to think. There was only one thing to be done, and one person to do it.

"Mr. Hastings." Alvarez had stood up and was pacing slowly and precisely, like a caged lion. "I think that you had better return to your home country, to London, if that is where your friends live. I cannot assist you in tracking down Rosas in Britain. It would mean a great deal of trouble, and not only with your friend Fairweather-Smyth, if Colombian operatives were to be found working in England. MI5 is a rather bumbling group but nonetheless not one I care to alarm at the moment. We are currently involved in a silly little border dispute with one of your colonies to the east of here, and my hands will be tied until that is resolved and our countries are allies once again."

"Understood," Hastings said, longing to be out of the company of this most disturbing man. "Well, if you could kindly return me to Bogotá, as quickly as possible, I can be on the next flight to London. I assume considering that all of the rest of the people on the list are there, I'd best go and warn them about the danger."

Alvarez held up a hand. "Not so fast, Mr. Hastings. I am as interested — for my own reasons — in ending the activities of our little assassin as you are. You will be taken directly to the airport for an overnight flight, and we will endeavor to find out what your hotel has done with your baggage. I have one request, with which I cannot, naturally, force you to comply." His eyes glinted evilly, as though he was enjoying the idea of "forcing."

"And that is?"

"I would like you to carry a gun. We have developed a new prototype weapon, a sonic gun. We also have needle guns that inject poisons, which might seem appropriate in this case, but we are also eager to move to the forefront of sonic attack weaponry development. It has only been ... tested ... a few times here, but it is effective. This will be an excellent chance to give it a field test. The European authorities know nothing of it and should not be able to detect the presence of its use in a corpse."

Hastings swallowed in disbelief. Was he living in some kind of a thriller novel? "How does it work?" he almost whispered.

"It is simple. It works on the blood vessels in the brain, causing massive cranial bleeding when a certain unhearable sonic wave is delivered directly at the target's head. The finer details do not concern you. There is only one drawback: you must be quite close to your target, because the range is very short. We are working on a better prototype, which will eliminate this annoyance, but if you use it, you will never be arrested for any crime. It will look like the deceased has had a brain aneurysm. The weapon will not be seized by the customs officials in Britain, because it is designed to look like a small, travel-size rechargeable electric hair dryer."

"As you said, you can't force me to carry this."

Alvarez's huge brows clouded, and he leaned menacingly over Hastings. "That is correct, my peace-loving friend. But consider for a moment the forces with which you are dealing. Someone is determined to kill off your silly little movement, as insignificant as it seems to most of us, and you are on their list. Do you think that Rosas is anything but a tool? If he disappears or is captured, do you think they will not send someone else to kill you? You may never rest again, and no one in your government will ever believe you because, thanks to the closed-mindedness of the New York police, you have no evidence of foul play in the death of Guy Calvert. You need to protect yourself ... and you can do me a favor in the process. If you should meet Rosas, and I'm very sure you will, it would warm my heart to know that this traitorous worm has been dispatched by a weapon I helped design."

Despite the overwhelming miasma of evil oozing out of the man, Hastings knew he was right. Someone wanted Hastings dead, and all of his social activist musician friends too. He was the only one with knowledge of the situation, so he was the only one who could prevent further tragedy.

"All right," he said wearily. "I'll take your gun."

"I knew you would, Mr. Hastings. You see, you and I are not so different as you think. We will both kill for the right reasons. Now, let's head to the cantina ... all this plotting makes a man ravenous."

From *The Modern City: An Urban Theorist's Travelogue*
by Prof. S.R.J. Kilbey

Old Mother Londinia is one of the world's oldest and largest cities, celebrated in countless stories, ballads, and legends, the hub of the English-speaking world and the globe's oldest empire. But this proudest of cities also provides us with prime examples of the most disturbing trend in urban development: suburbanization. The last twenty years have seen an incredible expansion in the breadth of the city's metropolitan boundaries, well into Kent, Hampshire, Sussex, etc. The massive influx of immigrants from the four corners of Empire, as well as from the depressed postindustrial North, has created a demand for cheap, quickly built housing. This demand has been met, but with no regard for aesthetics or quality of environment. The suburbs are filled with domiciles identical down to the last nail, and oppressive glass office towers and industrial parks filled with faceless factories. The seats of government have naturally followed the glitter of money to these soulless areas of sprawl and so-called "progress."

This has left the inner city, home to the shrines of England's history, the Tower of London, the former Houses of Parliament, the Edward Hall, and Disraeli's Synagogue, inhabited mainly by a mixture of impoverished senior citizens too frightened to leave, unwashed bohemians, criminals, and adventurers, although there are still neighborhoods, like Mayfair, where some middle-class and respectably wealthy families reside within impenetrable fortresses. The east end of the city is almost entirely abandoned and left to the rats. This shocking state of disrepair in the heart of the world's greatest metropolis is a repulsive blot that we can no longer ignore; it is time to restore London to her state of former glory and to recognize the wonderful history contained within her innermost boundaries, rather than chase forevermore a vision of progress and new money bereft of foresight, beauty, and dignity.

NINE

The area outside Arrivals Gate 7 at Lord Palmerston International Airport was a hive of activity, and Hastings' eyes searched in vain for a sign of his brother in the excited crowd. He wasn't surprised that Henry hadn't shown up; in fact, he had expected it. For a businessman, Henry was neither punctual nor dependable in any way and was a difficult fellow to like in most regards.

Hastings' younger brother had supposedly been dispatched in his brand new car to bring him to their father's house in Watford after meeting his flight, which had arrived late at 4:00 p.m. Hastings, despite sleeping through most of the flight, was exhausted. Henry lived in Beckenham in a palatial flat but was at least good enough to visit their ailing father every four months or so. Their mother, a chain-smoker, had died of lung cancer five years before, and their father had never really recovered. He now smoked about five packets of various brands of unfiltered cigarettes a day, as well as a pipe, cigars, and snuff. It was Henry's theory that Raymond Hastings was trying to hasten his return to his wife's side, being too much of a coward to take his own life. Simon didn't think that was funny; he thought their dad was just lonely and needed some attention. Tobacco was substituted for the need of friends and acquaintances.

Simon had decided that his return to England would be a good opportunity to lie low and visit his father, for whom, though he had been much closer with their mother, he still felt some lingering fondness. He would also save money on accommodations, given that his own flat in London was likely too dangerous to visit, although Alvarez had insisted he take some funds to assist in his search for Rosas, for whom he really seemed to have it in. Hastings felt as though he had been turned into a paid assassin himself — a very unsettling turn of events. He had gone from being a musician in a band that advocated for all the best causes, from disarmament to environmental preservation to the more abstract concepts of brotherhood and universal love (and sometimes free love), and now he was carrying around a bizarre spy-gun looking to dispatch an assassin.

Giving up on trying to find Henry in the crowd, he picked up his suitcase and bag and shouldered his way down an escalator to the southbound platform of the Chelmsford-Palmerston station on the Suburban Line. There was little time to lose. He would have to make it surreptitiously downtown by that evening if he were to effectively warn his friends. Many lived in neighborhoods lacking telephone service, but they could generally be found at Middle Earth, the UFO Club, or the Mountain Grill, and would be easy enough to find, given a few days. He hoped that his father wouldn't want to talk too much and that Henry wouldn't show up at the house to antagonize him.

With difficulty, he managed to force his way onto the platform to await the next train for the long journey across the city to Watford. The crowd was hysterically thick and covered the entire platform, surging toward the oncoming train as though its members were about to throw themselves, lemming-like, in front of the first coach.

The Underground traveled aboveground this far out into the suburbs, so, although he didn't get a seat, Hastings could at least gaze out the window at the rows of houses instead of into the eyes of ashen rush-hour commuters, facing the frantic, competitive end to another day of office drudgery.

The Underground system had been expanded in recent years to cover all the suburban areas of the city, supplementing the train lines, which as anyone who has lived in or visited London knows is a very good thing; the city was in grave danger of choking on its own fumes, as was happening in Tokyo and Peking and would in

New York as well if the authorities were not careful. The nationalist threats to the dominance of the British Empire were extinguished in the early 1960s, and an overwhelming wave of immigration by British subjects from the colonies and also refugees from the almost-vaporized areas of the brief East European Nuclear War had expanded the city borders to make it by far the largest metropolis on Earth.

It now stretched from Oxford to Southend, Cambridge to the Channel. The counties of Kent, Sussex, Essex, Hampshire, Wiltshire, Buckinghamshire, and Bedfordshire no longer really existed, having been declared boroughs of Greater London only the year before. The offices of national and mayoral governments had been relocated to a gigantic complex in Luton, and the old central boroughs had been left to rot into a network of bohemian and criminal enclaves that attracted radicals of every stripe from around the globe. Hastings himself had lived in Notting Hill for a few years before the band started off. It was at Guy's insistence that The Spheres had moved across the Atlantic to test the uncharted waters of Virginia, where, he reasoned, "They're badly in need of some enlightenment in that benighted colony."

Most of Hastings' friends, including the men on Rosas' hit list, still lived in the neighborhoods of Kensington, Camden Town, and especially Ladbroke Grove. Maurice Wyatt, Daevid Mallorn, Rick Farren, and Ed Barrett were amongst the leading rock musicians in Britain, but none had succeeded as fabulously and commercially as The Spheres had in Virginia, where there was less competition. Each had, however, made his mark on pop culture and had led the fight against government control and censorship of music and morals, a fight that they finally seemed to be winning. Some of their records were even played on the BBC. Maurice Wyatt was the leader of The Wylde Flowers, a jazz-rock group known for its mind-blowing extended instrumentals. Daevid Mallorn, originally from New Wales in the South Pacific, had also played with that band but had since formed his own group with New Walesian and

French expats, The Flying Teapots, known for their anarchistic views and humorous lyrics. Ed Barrett was the former leader of The Peuce Frank, the original underground band, and Rick Farren was a dangerous political radical as well as a musician, known for his daring acts of vandalism outside the gates of Buckingham Palace and other sacred places of the nation (such as wrapping his feces in the flag and setting them on fire, then throwing them over the gate). The Royal Family had since moved permanently to the safer glens of Scotland. Hastings would have to track down all of these fellows before it was too late and one of them was found dead.

For now, however, he would have to deal with his family. The tube train was nearing Watford Station 1, and he managed to force his way off with a great deal of difficulty. As he exited the station, dragging his suitcase tiredly behind him, he was surprised to see the ancient family Mini waiting outside. The plume of smoke drifting out of the driver's side told him his father was at the wheel.

A rare smile cracked Raymond Hastings' papery, deeply lined face as his son squeezed through the Mini's passenger door. A small, broad, man with thinning gray hair, thick glasses, and a plain, unremarkable face, he was no more noticeable to passersby during his morning walk to the newsagent than an old log by the side of the road.

"Hullo, me son."

"Hullo, Dad. How'd you know I'd be here?"

His dad chucked. "I knew, when that other good-for-nothing son of mine didn't ring me back today, that you'd be making your own way. I'm none too pleased with him."

"How's the leg?" Raymond had found it painful to drive for some time due to a leg injury he sustained while working at the steel screw, nut, and grommet factory where he had spent most of his adult life, before the injury had happily ended his working days. Unfortunately, his wife had died not far into his early retirement. Raymond's rusty driving skills were now showcased as the Mini veered dangerously from lane to lane. His son soon began to fear for his life.

Raymond lit a fresh cigarette from the butt of his last, grinding out the old one in the car's overflowing ashtray. The car reeked so badly of stale smoke that even a habitual smoker like Simon felt sick to his stomach.

"So, son, Colombia? What was that all about?"

"Needed a quick holiday, Dad, after that tragedy. Didn't want to face the press." He could safely have told his dad the truth, but it didn't seem necessary or particularly believable.

"Strange choice for a holiday, eh? And only a couple of days! But then you were always the strange one. Sorry about yer pal, son. He was a good young man at heart, just lived a bit too hard. Let that be a lesson to you, if my own clean living ain't enough." His face cracked open in another smile. He was a meek sort of man who rarely offered any kind of advice or remonstration and had spent his own life working for unkind, uncaring masters, so the younger Hastings appreciated the attempt at counsel.

"You're right, Dad. I'm going to take it easy for a while, then figure out what to do with myself, now that the band is done." He actually had no firm conception of what his next move should be, but he was determined not to hash this out with his father.

"That's good, son. You've had your fun, but a man's got to do hard work at some point in his life. It's good to see you." His father offered him a filterless Regal.

A fine drizzle began pattering on the roof of the car; one thing never changed about England: the sun never, ever bloody seemed to come out. Raymond pulled the car into the drive of the small suburban bungalow where Simon Hastings had spent his formative years and where he had first jammed with the juvenile Guy Calvert and Marty Sharpe-Thornton in the basement as school kids. Similar houses stretched out around it in a maze of identical streets where few ever walked but cars sputtered endlessly by. Few trees had been planted, but tiny, limp shrubs had proliferated, sown over time by indifferent gardeners, clinging to life in tiny front gardens. The network of streets was left bare, like a skeleton under the relentless pall.

Another wave of incredibly thick, tobacco-laden air hit Hastings in the face as he entered the dusty front hallway. It was almost like trying to move underwater. Night was beginning to descend, thankfully concealing the ugliness of the neighborhood for a while, so Hastings switched on the hall light.

"Make yourself at home," his father said with another dry chuckle, followed by a brief coughing fit. "You know your way around. Want a cuppa?"

"Sure, thanks." Hastings collapsed onto the sofa in the bay window, lungs aching, pulling a half-full Player's packet from under him as he did. "So, how are *you*, Dad?"

"Not too bad, son." His father's voice floated, muffled, from the kitchen. "Nothing much happens around here, you know."

Little in the front room had changed in the years since Hastings last visited, except that many more layers of dust had accumulated on top of the photographs, bland washed-out prints of rural scenes, and vases. There were also a couple of dozen tobacco packets littered around the room, on the floor, and on the furniture, as well as cigars, cigarillos, roll-your-own pouches, and pipe tobacco.

The photographs were all quite old, of his father and mother in happier, newlywed days, or when the boys were young. Nothing since. Raymond lived entirely in his past. One thing that Hastings always admired about his seemingly commonplace family was the strong bond that had existed between his parents. This was not something Hastings had observed in any other relationship he had known or seen, and it was a romantic ideal that he would otherwise have dismissed. Even Henry hadn't been such a bad kid when he was younger, before his four years at the famous London School for the Exploitation of Economic Opportunity (LSEEO).

The death of Linda Hastings, the glue who bonded them

together, had shattered Raymond's life and scattered the family unit. He awoke to find that the world was actually a very cold, hard, unforgiving place; maybe he had never noticed that. When she had died (ironically, the oncologists hinted they thought her cancer was unrelated to smoking), he had barely spoken for two years but had started his own insane smoking habit.

It was at this time that Simon had started visiting less frequently, unable to stand the dreariness of the permanently dim bungalow; his own rock-star life was so much more colorful.

At least Dad was now talking again.

"Here we are," Raymond said, returning to the room with a tray. "Nice cup of English tea for you. Can't get it like that over in the colony." He set the tray down on a table. It nearly fell off because there was a pack of cigarillos underneath. Hastings reached out to remove it. Seeing the packet in his hand, his father said, "Thanks, don't mind if I do," and took one out. It was one of those awful port-scented ones that Hastings really detested; the smell made him feel like vomiting. "So, do you still see that girl you told me about?"

"Teresa? Yes. She's been out of the country for a while, but she might be back in New York now. I'll give her a ring in a bit, I think." Teresa was a free spirit. She had no income except that which came from a large inheritance; though born in New York, she had come from a rich, old-money European trading family reputed to have strong underworld connections. This didn't bother her friends in the musical underground, since she spent most of it on promoting radical causes and gave a couple hundred quid to panhandlers every now and then; she sometimes even took these unfortunates into her flat. She had been disowned by her family, but not before she had come of age and run away with her money.

Teresa was a follower of the Communist ideology of the nineteenth century German philosopher Engels, who had also been the scion of a rich family but had thrown it all away in the name of the brotherhood of man, finally to be martyred in the

Polish Uprising of 1877. Her latest expedition to the Andes, which she had coyly called a "mountain-climbing adventure," really had the purpose of helping rebuild villages recently destroyed by the flooding created by the construction of the Pinochet Dam, which had caused so much international outrage earlier that year before being forgotten by the wealthier world. Most tragedies in "developing" countries tended to be after their twenty-second spot on the nightly news.

Teresa had engaged in some memorable fights over the past few months with Ned Loogeant, who was no match for her advanced intellect and trained boxing skills. Smiling at the memory of those happy times, Hastings suddenly found himself missing her intensely. He snapped his attention back to his father, who also had a faraway look in his eyes, which added a certain dignity to his wizened face, despite the smoldering cigarillo dangling forgotten from his lower lip. Raymond peered at him owlishly and adjusted his spectacles.

"Look, Dad, I've got a few loose ends to tie up in town, so I was wondering if I—"

The front door suddenly crashed open, and Henry Hastings came striding in. "Si! How are you, you dirty old hippie!" He walked over to Hastings and wrung his hand vigorously but without sincerity. From the neck up, Henry essentially looked like a short-haired version of Simon, though he wore a permanent expression of smug confidence. From the shoulders down, he was the image of the stylish City businessman, always in a hand-painted silk tie and waistcoat with Arabian leather shoes. His smart new forest-green Krupp-Benz was no doubt parked outside. He flung off his trench coat and sat down on a dusty chair. "Hullo, Dad! Keeping well?"

Raymond looked angry for possibly the first time in many years. "Where the hell were you today? You're brother's visiting for the first time in ages, and you couldn't even be trusted to meet him at the airport!" Both Hastings brothers stared at their father in surprise. Raymond's face was flushed a deep red; Simon wondered if the years of intense smoking had enlarged Dad's heart.

"Ah, well, had a sudden meeting come up and couldn't avoid it, could I? Didn't even have time to phone." Henry had a funny habit of clipping off the front of his sentences, maybe be because he felt his time was at such a premium. He added a question, Cockney-style, to the end of many sentences, even though his accent was actually quite neutral. He shrugged nonchalantly. "Know how it is, Si, don't you? Not cross with me?"

"Of course not," Simon murmured, wanting to avoid a confrontation. But their father was in one of his rare animated moods and would have none of it. His voice trembled as he stood up and jabbed a yellow finger in Henry's direction.

"I tell you, you little shit, sometimes I wonder if someone slipped the wrong baby into your incubator. I worked all my life at that horrible job just to provide a decent standard for my family, and what have you done? Went off and became some kind of prancing financial industry dandy who won't even do a favor for his family—"

"*I* became a dandy? I'm the success, aren't I? Just take a look at this twee little—"

"That's enough!" Simon stood up. "We're not going to dig up any old issues here. We've been over our differences before, both in politics and fashion—" he turned to Henry "—and there's nothing to be accomplished by fighting."

Their father sat down. "Your mother would be ashamed of you, Henry. You're a discredit to our family."

The two sons froze in shock. This was the first time their dad had mentioned their mother, to the best of their knowledge, since the last dirt had been shoveled onto her casket. He was shaking visibly and sweating.

Now Henry completely lost his cool. "Just what the hell do you mean by that, you desiccated old corpse? Do you think she'd be proud of you smoking your life away in here, staring out the window all day?"

Simon sensed this was the boiling-over point of a long-standing conflict he didn't want to be involved in, so he slipped off to his father's rarely used study to try ringing Teresa. It was just after noon in New York, almost the time that she would be getting up if she had just arrived back in town after a long flight. The line rang five or six times, but he finally heard her voice on the other end.

"Yeah?"

"Terry, it's me, Simon."

"Simey! Where the hell are ya! I've been back for almost two days, and no one knows where you are! What's going on? What happened to Guy? Did someone really murder him? Are you in New—"

"All right, all right! Listen, I don't have much time. I do miss you, and I'd love to fill you in on all this, but I've got to deal with some life-and-death situations. First, Guy was murdered, and I know it. That idiot Marty still has his doubts, I'm sure, but I don't."

"Billy doesn't. He's been trying to get the cops to investigate, but nothing's happened yet. The Hammer had him buried right away. What the hell's going on over there? You at a soccer game?"

He had to raise his voice over the yelling from the front room. "Nothing. I've been to Colombia, but at my dad's in Watford now. How soon can you get here? I could use some help. More people could get hurt, and it all depends on me."

"Colombia! What the ... oh, all right. I can be there tomorrow. Can't you tell me anything else?" She sounded worried, which was out of character.

"Not really. Just get here as soon as you can. Here's my father's address. I'll be waiting."

After he had given her the address, he said, "I've got to go now."

"Okay. Bye, Simon. And Simon..."

"Yes?"

"I miss you too," she said hurriedly, and the line went dead. But he felt a lot better. He heard a loud bang from the front hallway. Raymond was sitting with his head in his hands, breathing heavily as the Krupp-Benz screeched emphatically away. Hastings walked over and laid a hand on his shoulder.

"Don't worry about it, Dad. Henry's a twit, but he may still turn out someday."

His father raised his head with an attempt at a smile. This almost made his glasses fall off. He looked drained by his uncharacteristic outburst. "I just wish things had turned out differently," he said softly. Tears were gathering in his eyes. Hastings felt a surge of pity for his father and wished he could stay to comfort him, but there was no time.

"Listen, Dad, I have to go out now — it's really urgent. Life-and-death stuff. When I get back tonight, we need to talk about this tobacco habit of yours, and some other stuff."

Raymond looked like he wanted to protest, but he had no energy left. He simply nodded. Hastings took the car keys and a forgotten pack of Dunhills from the coffee table, and with a last concerned look back, he left.

TEN

As the Mini puttered on the M7 past row upon row of faceless suburban homes toward the old boroughs and larger, newer cars flashed by, Hastings drew up his plan of action. He would stop off first at Middle Earth to see if any of his friends were on the evening's bill. Most of them would be easy to find, but Ed Barrett often went missing for weeks, off on some dangerous acid trip in a flophouse. His friends had become quite concerned of late. Hastings only intended to stay a few nights, keeping an eye out for Rosas; he didn't even know if the man was in the country, and if he managed to warn his friends about buying the man's products and what he looked like, he would consider his work done — and then it would be time for a real break. What else could he do? Then maybe he and Teresa could go away from a while to some place where he could rest up and consider his next musical options.

He was now passing through a district of factories with billowing smokestacks. Finding the gray industrial landscape depressing, he switched on the car's ancient radio, and after a burst of static, the voice of Ron Peele, the BBC's star DJ, emerged: "That was the latest off Steve Took, 'Seventh Sign.' Now, here's a song by martyred British rocker Guy Calvert, who died just four days ago; a loss that many, including myself, will be mourning for a very long time." One of The Spheres' lesser-known album tracks, "Barren Planet" (Hastings had actually written the lyrics, but most people assumed that Guy had written everything), a song about ecological destruction, came on:

> *The sands have run down the glass,*
> *The long day fades into sunset,*

The wind blew all they had built away,
When they decided not to pay their debts.

They never found their way home,
The barren planet mourns alone.

Listening to the song, with its intricate lead lines and hypnotically droning rhythm section, awakened the need to play again. He had been so busy, and in so much distress and danger, that he hadn't noticed for the first time in several years days had passed since he last picked up a guitar. He wondered what the rest of the boys were up to and whether he would ever return to Virginia. As he reached the end of the M7 and exited onto the North End Expressway, the song reached its delicate bridge:

They'll never return,
They threw it away.
They watched it burn,
And danced in the flames.
And laughed in their pain.

He shook his head; really rather depressing, that one. Actually, they all were. What a gloomy bunch of sods. He needed to write some cheerier material, if only for his own sake. He had always intended to, but he just seemed cursed with a natural melancholy. Every time he tried to write a happy tune, it came out sounding hollow and insincere.

After another twenty minutes in heavy traffic, he arrived in Covent Garden and parked at Long Acre and Mercer. It was seven thirty, and the sound checks at Middle Earth would just be ending. Getting out of the car, he felt the strangely shaped little gun digging into his side, and the sense of absurdity and unreality that was plaguing him intensified.

Taking a deep breath, he noticed an unpleasant, acrid smell.

It smelled a lot like New York. Perhaps London was finally going to the environmental dogs too. The city certainly did not keep up the downtown boroughs as it once did; only the sites and neighborhoods of tourist value, like the Tower and the Palace, were cleaned regularly and guarded heavily. Visitors had to make appointments just to enter the British Museum, although not many had wanted to since the majority of the exhibits from the decaying old edifice had been moved years ago to the new National Museum in Oxford. Tourists really didn't come to London any more, turned off by the unkempt streets, blackened buildings, the lack of a theater district — and the possibility of getting mugged at any time. As in the barrio, the streets were full of people, mostly hippies and bohemians of all races and genders, strolling or hanging out on the corners, smoking joints. He began to feel right at home.

There was a high turnover amongst shopkeepers in the inner city. He noted with interest which shops and cafes were still open, which had shut down, and which were new additions. He resisted the urge to pop into old Mr. Chong's Fish and Chips for a quick bite of haddock. He even met a couple of old acquaintances (everyone was impressed to see him) and received still more condolences about Guy. He also found out that the bill at Middle Earth featured both The Wylde Flowers and The Peuce Frank, a great stroke of luck. Hastings felt his spirits lift again. He'd be able to corner Maurice Wyatt and possibly find out where Ed Barrett was currently hiding out. Perhaps he could even make an entertaining night of it.

As he approached the cellar-based club, he began to wonder why the hell the band ever left London in the first place. New York, even the inner city, had never really appealed to him; there was too much of a visible clash between wealth and poverty; the rich jostled shamelessly with the poor, ignoring the outstretched hands of beggars, going to luncheon meetings in their expensive suits. In downtown London, just about everyone fit society's current definition of poverty, but few cared about that and people were generally willing to help out; the life of the community was enough to sustain anyone, if you were into that sort of lifestyle.

On his way into the club, he stopped at a chemist to pick up some pharma. Feeling a new distaste for the products of the Colombian Cartels, he decided on some synthesized opium produced by United Chinese Chemical, although for all he knew they could be bastards, just like the Cartels — or even Rosas' employers. Was there such a thing as a decent corporation? There certainly weren't any decent record companies; they would try to screw you over in a second if you weren't careful.

Illegal drugs sold by street dealers were much, much cheaper and stronger, but considering that he was on someone's hit list, it would have been suicidal to take that risk. He wondered whether he would have to live the rest of his life with that fear.

The door staff at the club knew him very well from the countless gigs he had played there back in the day, so he was able to avoid the cover charge. The room was packed with revelers, and he had trouble forcing his way through the cheerfully stoned crowd toward the backstage area. The stage was unguarded; unlike New York, London clubs had never hired bouncers to control audiences and had been rewarded thus far with little trouble.

Middle Earth was not a large club but was definitely one of the major centers of the London counterculture. Like-minded people of all ages came there by night, even from the suburbs, to experience a kind of communal freedom that everyday prosaic life denied them, a life of long working days, business attire, financial pressures, television and sundry electronic distractions, and the ubiquitous easy listening music piped into every office, restaurant, and shopping mall that slowly wore down a person's soul.

Backstage in the grungy dressing room area, Hastings found The Wylde Flowers getting ready for their set. Maurice Wyatt, a shortish, thick-set fellow with blonde hair, a big beard, and an impish smile, was getting out his drumsticks. Wyatt, after embracing him, said in his high-pitched, gravelly voice, "We're playing an early set, Si, so we'll chat afterwards, okay?"

Hastings was about to protest and ask Wyatt to delay for a couple of minutes, but the diminutive drummer had already disappeared, so he returned to the audience to catch the set. He nervously scanned the audience but saw no one that looked remotely like Rosas.

The Wylde Flowers were not a particularly charismatic group of performers, but their distinctive sound more than made up for their static presence. Their tunes were mostly instrumental, improvised, and at least ten minutes long. This is still a trend in modern music, and it can be traced directly back to the beginnings of The Wylde Flowers and The Spheres. Probably due to the length of their pieces, which bored most casual listeners to tears, they had achieved only modest success but had acquired a die-hard following across what remained of Europe. They had no guitar player, just bass, drums, and an incredibly fuzzy, impossibly loud organ. Guest musicians appeared from time to time, often showing up well into a piece to honk on reeds and winds.

The band's musicianship was incredible, and the audience showed its appreciation by gyrating along with Wyatt's frenetic drumming. There seemed to be no end to their infectious musical energy. Hastings found himself watching the audience with longing and sadness. There was no greater feeling than that of melding with a crowd of ecstatic listeners, sharing in an experience for which the musician was only the medium by which a mysterious force took hold. It almost justified one's existence on Earth, even though Hastings was reluctant to give this power a name. Then he was jerked out of his overwrought reverie by his name being called out on the PA.

"Simon Hastings, please approach the stage. We have a guitar for you to play! Simon Hastings!" Mitchell Ratledge, the organist, was saying in his lazy, melodious baritone.

Wyatt, grinning widely, caught sight of him and brandished a shiny chromium Mustang at the front of the stage.

"There he is! Mr. Simon Hastings, ladies and gentleman, of The Spheres! We didn't expect him to be here tonight, or even in the bloody country at all, but we're honored by his return. We'd like to take this opportunity to play a new piece titled 'The Music of The Spheres,' in memory of our late friend and yours, Guy Calvert. We're sure that the spirit of the band will go on. Simon's going to jam along, aren't you, mate?"

There could be no doubt of that. Hastings was relieved to feel the same old swell of power through his body as he strapped on the guitar with a smile and a nod to Ratledge. He barely noticed that the audience was giving him an extended ovation, he was so wrapped up in the anticipation of playing again. He plugged into the Vox amplifier that the roadie had lugged onto the stage and adjusted the volume.

Ratledge led the tune, which, he noticed with surprise, had been adapted from the melody line of "Barren Planet," but played faster, jazzier, and with a few sevenths thrown in. He followed the band's chords for a few minutes while Ratledge soloed. When he got the nod, he felt so good that he went immediately, without any buildup, into a blistering, fast lead high on the fretboard that pained his fingers. He ignored the discomfort; it was as though he was forcing all of his anguish into this one performance. His days of contented semistardom were behind him. The fight for the things he believed in, which had often seemed abstract and symbolic, was now far too real in the light of the knowledge that someone with money and malice to burn had carefully planned to have him killed, presumably for the sole ideological reason that he was a left-wing musician who advocated for socialism and freedom of expression. They had failed so far, but Hastings had no idea how to fight back; he had only his music and the comradeship of the people before him now.

His lengthy solo reached a blazing finale, and he snapped out of his trance, letting go of the guitar's neck and wincing. He looked at his hand. The fingertips were cut and bleeding slightly from the pressure he had been applying. It was all he could do to scratch out the complementary chords to finish the piece. When it was over, the audience gave him an even longer ovation, almost hysterically. He felt almost crushed by this outpouring of affection and left the stage with tears in his eyes as the band crashed into its final number of the evening.

Backstage, he slumped down in the nearest chair and lit up one of his father's Dunhills, an action he regretted immediately; the cigarettes must have been months old at best, and the tobacco was stale and brittle. The members of The Peuce Frank were going through their own pregig pharmaceutical rituals. They were justly reputed to be the scene's biggest acid-heads and spent a lot more time in their LSD-induced fantasies than they did in the concrete world.

"Killer playing, man," Bill Filmour, the Frank's lead guitarist said thickly, approaching. "You're still the best, Si."

"Get away." Hastings laughed. "I don't have half your technique."

Filmour frowned a little. "Technique doesn't mean much. You've got some feel the rest of us are lacking. Guy had it too. You gonna be here for a while?"

"Yeah, I'm going to stay for all the sets."

"Well, here." Filmour held out a bit of yellowy paper. "We've just been given the most outrageous acid. Far better than that weak shit they sell in the shops. Roger's cousin makes it in his basement with a kid's chemistry set. I don't even remember being here last weekend — I think I was literally out in space somewhere. You look like you could use an escape yourself."

"Thanks, mate."

Filmour nodded in his amiably vague way, flipped his long, straight hair out of his face, and went to do his final tune-up. The Wylde Flowers were taking their time finishing their last tune, so Hastings placed the paper under his tongue. It was true; he could use an escape. The acid shouldn't take full effect before he had a chance to talk rationally to Wyatt about the danger that faced them all.

The piece finally ended, and The Wylde Flowers lurched offstage, looking as weary as Hastings had felt after only one song.

"That was beautiful, Simon," Wyatt said. "I've heard you play well before, but never like that! You'll be happy to know that we got it all on tape. We'll release an EP!"

Hastings rallied his energy. "That's great, Mo. You're a great band. I'm glad I found you here tonight — but there's something I have tell you, and it's not too pleasant."

He started to tell his story for what felt like the umpteenth time, but as he did, he began to feel very peculiar; the acid was kicking in quicker than predicted. Wyatt's face had turned a strange shade of blue, which slowly became more intense, and his blonde stubble was shining a blinding neon yellow. Out of the corners of his eyes, Hastings could swear that he saw several bright orange lizards gazing intently at him from under a table before flicking out of view just as he turned his head. As people moved in the background, their lines became badly blurred, and he thought he heard crows cawing raucously somewhere in the distance.

"Are you all right, Si?" Wyatt's blue face twisted with concern. "Did those maniacs slip you something homemade? Some of their bloody cleaning chemicals?" He reached out to steady Hastings, who was feeling more and more unstable by the second. "Sit down for a while."

"I'm ... okay. It is some powerful stuff, though."

"So ... I get the gist. Some sort of capitalist assassin. What should we do?"

"All I can tell you ... is that you should keep an eye out ... and tell everyone you know ... for this man. He didn't exactly ... blend in in New York, so I doubt he will here. Maybe we can catch him out. And ... if you see any of the other fellows from the list ... Ed Barrett ... help me warn them."

"You *have* had a hard time lately, haven't you, old son?" Wyatt rested a sympathetic hand on Hastings' shoulder. It felt like a ton of bricks.

"I'm afraid so ... Mo." He was now forcing the words out; he could no longer feel his tongue moving as he spoke. The orange lizards had ceased hiding; one was perched on Wyatt's shoulder, staring impudently at Hastings with glittering diamond eyes. *Why lizards?* The very light in the room had taken on a strange, seductive red hue, and all sensation was gradually leaving his body. He staggered.

"Si? Jesus, man, sit down!"

The first beats of The Peuce Frank's set crashed into his addled brain like a train wreck, cutting short the cawing crows that were actually their intro tape. In the uncontrolled state of his cortex, the volume was intensified until it felt like his whole skull was reverberating. Had someone got a hold of his sonic gun and used it on him?

He felt himself falling but couldn't stop. As Wyatt hurriedly reached out to catch him, Hastings fell heavily to the floor.

He got me somehow, he thought groggily. *Stupid. Wasn't thinking. Thank God it's over.*

ELEVEN

Though he waited for a state of merciful unconsciousness to envelop him and save him from his agony, Hastings' mind refused to pass out, and through the nightmare hallucinations that followed, he slowly realized that what was really happening was not poisoning but instead the worst acid trip of his life, perhaps of anyone's. He had no idea where he was, and he felt and saw nothing real as he was taken by The Wylde Flowers to their house, a rambling Queen Anne at the top of Clarendon Road.

For hours, he was tormented by visions worse and more vivid than any nightmare he had ever experienced. Against a deserted urban background, the animated corpses of Guy and Gonzalez, both vomiting unbelievable amounts of bright crimson blood, attempted to strangle him as they accused him in chilling zombie whispers of causing their deaths. Rosas and Alvarez appeared, linked happily arm in arm, dressed in devil's costumes complete with pitchforks and horns. For some reason, The Hammer was with them, carrying an oversized beer stein that must have held a gallon of stout. The Hammer gestured rudely at him then poured the beer over his own head, urinated on a wall, and disappeared in a puff of black smoke. Multicolored lizards constantly gnawed on his limbs until there was nothing left but curiously bloodless stumps, which waved around pathetically. His beloved Gibson made an appearance, but every time he reached out with his stumps, sobbing, to gather it in, it danced away, laughing, on two black-stockinged legs. His father also briefly took a bow, ten smelly French cigarettes dangling from his mouth and a smokestack protruding from the top of his head, which belched black fumes. At last, after a seeming eternity of this torture, he finally passed out into a dreamless sleep.

When he finally woke, he found himself in a dim room. It was dark, but as he lifted his head, he could see that the walls were painted navy blue. There were no decorations on the walls, but several small tables held lava lamps of various colors. The beams mixed in a rainbow on the walls. He was lying on one of two large, soft sofas that took up much of the space. He was thankful to find a large glass of water on the floor and drank the whole thing in a gulp. He felt horrible, but he wasn't dead.

It was the second time in three days that he had thought himself a dead man and the second time he had been rendered unconscious. *I can't take much more of this*, he reflected ruefully. Then he remembered Teresa, who had been speeding across the Atlantic to comfort him, and wondered about the time.

A soft knock sounded at the door, and Mo Wyatt's head peered cautiously around the crack. "Si? You awake?"

"Yup," he croaked.

"Jesus, mate, we were scared stiff!" Wyatt said, advancing and rubbing sleep out of his eyes.

"What time is it?"

"Four a.m. You were tripping for about five hours there before you fell asleep. I've been catching a few winks meself for a while, but I thought I'd come and see if you were still alive! Filmour feels really bad about it; he said he shouldn't have given you such strong stuff, considering the stress you've been under. Especially when I told him the whole story."

"I thought I'd been poisoned."

"Small wonder, Si. I thought so too for a while! But don't worry, we'll all be careful, and if this bastard's around, we'll take care of him. Our bit of London doesn't take kindly to capitalist infiltrators and thugs. Funny." He leaned back on the other couch.

"What?"

"This almost provides a bit of contrast, doesn't it?"

"How so?" Hastings' head was hurting too much for abstract conversation.

"The message must be getting out, if someone's willing to resort to these tactics. Turns out we're a serious threat after all. Now we'll have to prove we're up to the test."

*

Hastings' head continued to pound all the way back to his father's place in the weak late morning light on the M7. He had slept for another six hours, but the rest and water had done him little good. He would have stayed downtown for the day to try to track down some of his other friends, but he had called his father first. Teresa had been true to her word and had left on a flight that arrived in London early that morning. She had called him from the airport, waking Raymond and frightening him half to death, to tell him that she had arrived and that she would be at the house shortly by taxi. His father had said that she had sounded very worried when she found out Simon hadn't arrived home yet, news that wouldn't have fazed her at all just a couple of weeks before. But then a bad trip (he'd had a few) wouldn't have seemed to him like a near-death experience, either.

He remembered the gun that Alvarez had given him and checked his pockets. It was still there, an innocent-looking device you might find in a teenager's bedroom. It was even pink. As he wrapped his hand around its sleek plastic handle, he reflected on the fact that, no matter how loathsome firearms might be in principle, the greatest pacifist in the world would still derive an almost childlike comfort from possession of one in his time of uncertainty. Of course, it was hard to take comfort from a weapon, however lethal, that looked like a miniature hair dryer. Well, Rosas would be in for the coiffing of his life if he should get up to any of his dirty tricks in London.

After another monotonous drive under an ominous sky, he finally reached the Watford exit and turned onto his father's street. As he pulled into the drive, the little car's engine sputtering pathetically, he could see Teresa's face peering out the front window. A light rain had started. The neighbor's child, whom Hastings had never seen, was throwing a ball against the garage door, making a sound that reverberated throughout the deathly silent suburb. The child looked up him with oddly penetrating, coldly luminous eyes that sent a chill through Hastings' body; then he extended one tiny finger in Hastings' direction in the international symbol of insolence. The boy was wearing the neon contact lenses that were in vogue with kids. They made him look like an invader from a planet of evil dwarfs. *So old for their age in some ways*, he thought, *devoid of innocence. Damn the makers of those lenses!*

Then he shook himself, returned the gesture with both hands and a grin, and turned the door handle, cursing for the millionth time his inescapably morbid thoughts.

Teresa threw her powerful arms around him as he entered. She was dressed in an ankle-length Peruvian dress, a shawl, and a wide-brimmed straw hat covering her long, dark-red hair. Teresa had an open face, large eyes, arched Italian eyebrows, and, unusual for the times, she never wore a trace of makeup.

"How are you, you bastard!" she roared with typical exuberance in her rich, low-toned voice.

"Well ... not so good, actually, Ter. Had a bit of a bad trip last night. Hi, Dad." He slumped down in a chair as his father slouched into the room. He was smoking a briar pipe and had an old felt hat on, perhaps his idea of dressing up to receive guests. He looked like a wizened version of Dickens' classic detective, Hercules Watson.

Teresa sat down beside Simon and put a hand on his knee. "Now, you've got to tell me what the hell's going on, Simon."

Raymond looked troubled. "And where were you last night, boy? I hope you weren't into those drugs again — remember what happened to your friend? I've been worried sick. I haven't heard from your brother since our row, either, although I suppose that's a mixed blessing."

Hastings held up a hand. "One at a time, please. First, Dad, I'm here now, and I'm all right, and so's the car — that's all you need to know. Second, you probably won't hear from my good brother until he needs something from you. Last, Teresa, I'm going to need a nice big cuppa before I can tell you everything that's gone on in the last week. I'm exhausted and sick, and as unfair as this might seem, I'm tired of telling this story too. I'll probably have to tell it a few more times in the next little while."

"Well, sorrrrryy…" Teresa reached out and roughly mussed his hair. "But seriously, sorry, matey. You English and your tea. The old cure-all. If that's what you need, go ahead."

After several cuppas, Hastings finally felt well enough to tell her his version of events. For some reason, the telling didn't seem like such a trial this time.

"Shit," Teresa said. "I knew the Establishment would declare war on us sometime. Didn't I tell you that a bunch of times? Still, I never thought they'd be so clandestine about it."

"We don't know who's behind this, remember. It's just a theory."

"But a good one. Haven't you been paying attention to what's been going on in New York lately?"

Hastings shook his head. "I stopped reading the paper. It just makes me angry."

"The gangs of hooligans? The ones, probably paid, that go downtown and attack what they call 'hippies' and 'freaks'?"

Like the ones that attacked the cab that fateful night. "Yeah? So, I've seen them. What's the connection?"

Teresa scowled. "You really are out of it, aren't you? Haven't you watched TV or read the papers at all? Haven't you heard how capitalist right-wing politicians and their media mouthpieces are deliberately fomenting violence and prejudice by pitting common workers against their natural allies in the urban counterculture?"

"Right, yes, workers, capitalists…" he mumbled into his chest. Although he'd given more than his share of such speeches, he sometimes tired of endlessly hearing them from Teresa.

"For Chrissake, Simon, it's gotten worse since I left on my trip, only a month ago. Just a couple of days ago, Baba Frank got beat up on the subway by some of those punks with the designer masks."

Hastings had to stifle a guilty smile at the thought of the stoic way in which Baba Frank would likely respond to getting rolled by hooligans.

"There's been some violence in central London, too," Raymond offered meekly, relighting his pipe. He had shuffled back in to catch the tail end of the conversation. "Glad I live out here. The hippies and the soccer yobs have had a few battles. It's the same lads from bad families who beat up on the Asians and coloreds."

Teresa's brows grew thunderous at his use of the word "coloreds." "Sorry, I meant visible minorities," Raymond added hastily. "Should know to mind my p's and q's better by this point, after living with Sunny Jim here all these years." Teresa walked over, lifted up the detective hat, and planted a forgiving kiss right in the middle of his forehead. He blushed. "But why all this so suddenly?"

"It's elementary, my dear Mr. Hastings. There's a new counter-movement against the reforms that have been passed in the last few years. Certain politicians want to return to the age when workers and especially women couldn't vote, when members of the producing classes couldn't change jobs to better themselves but could be fired without warning. They had to listen to royal-certified music and watch approved dramas on the damn TV, while big businessmen and the government colluded to keep themselves in luxury. All the while draining the resources of our colonies and treating immigrants like slaves. Why, they even tried to brainwash us when we were kids! You must remember."

Raymond rubbed his forehead. "I certainly do, dear." He looked profoundly miserable and a little guilty, perhaps remembering how happy he personally had been in those times, which were dark for so many others. "But don't blame me — I was a Labour man all my life, although they never got anywhere in the polls."

"I'd never blame you for anything, Mr. H.," Teresa said, bathing him in one of her radiant smiles. "You're too sweet." Raymond blinked back. She was certainly doing a good job of cheering him up. "But you really shouldn't smoke so much. You're setting a bad example for Simie."

"Ahem, well," Raymond said, butting out his latest. "I'll just go put another kettle on, shall I?" He shuffled quickly out of the room, almost losing one of his slippers.

Teresa turned her smile on Simon, who had hurriedly put out his own cigarette. "So, Simon, what's next?"

From *Battle for the Pluriverse, Vol. 2*
by Mort Moorhen (New Worlds Publishing, 1970)

As the mutants attack, their ruined features, hideously scarred from a thousand ritual tortures, now fortunately hidden under heavy steel masks, Jerry Carpathia can't help regretting letting the Steel Daffodil convince him to get involved in such a messy situation in this backward corner of the Seventh Pluriverse. There she is, a few paces away, chewing on an unlit cigar as she shoots up an attacker in his mainline with her serum gun, until he falls writhing in delicious agony and is carried off by rippling, sentient pavement. Antimatter flares are going off everywhere, and Carpathia finds himself on the defensive from no fewer than three buzz-cut-wearing, scab-scalped mutants bearing primitive "machine guns." He dispatches them quickly with a swathe of lime-green serum, and they die screaming their thanks. A dicey business indeed, but he has to keep in mind that the only reason for their attack is to gain release from the agony of the state of eternal boredom and small but painful punishments in which their masters keep them. How can he but pity those who endure such a plight?

"Having fun yet?" the Steel Daffodil yells, her golden hair and cleavage glowing in the unholy radiance. He tranquilizes another opponent into blissful oblivion but feels a tug on his coat as he does so. He turns around, and as always, there's no one there. That pesky conscience again, elusive but ever-present, turning his days into a tragedy of ethical proportions.

TWELVE

Teresa, always brimming with energy, was unwilling to let Hastings take another nap to remove the giant black bags from under his eyes, the last outward manifestations of the previous night's ordeal. She made Raymond rush them to the Underground, grumbling that all their stinky old city needed was another polluting gas-burner on the M7. Raymond didn't utter a single word on the way to the station, just gripped the steering wheel ever tighter and looked absolutely desperate for a smoke. When he dropped them off, he roared away, tires squealing.

"What's his problem?"

Hastings grinned. "Addiction. Not everyone's as perfect as you claim to be, my dear."

"I know. It's a curse." She took his arm and walked close to him as they descended the escalator to the platform. They received plenty of stares, not many of them friendly. Watford, an extremely conservative suburb, did not possess anything like a bohemian community. One group of loutish teenage boys dressed in Watford football jerseys who got off at Harrow made a point of delivering a few insults in their direction, something about the "hippie poof" and his "tart," but one vicious glare from Teresa abruptly shut them up.

During the long ride, she filled him in on the latest news from New York. There had been no further developments in the case of Guy's death. The mayor, who had hinted at a possible pending investigation the day after the incident, had been relieved of his duties in the fallout from a sex scandal involving several city politicians, a movie star or two, three clergymen, and the star player for the New York Tobacconists rounders team. The police had issued an official statement that the final verdict in the case was one of accidental death by misadventure from the intake of toxic chemicals, probably imported illegally from Colombia. The Colombian Cartels, Virginia Office, had also issued a statement, reassuring the public that despite widespread rumors that chemicals from their country were to blame, Colombian Cartels products were guaranteed to be nontoxic and safe when used appropriately. There had been little public opposition to either statement, except perhaps in the downtown core, where someone had organized a tiny, pathetic march.

Marty had apparently disappeared the day after Hastings left and was said to have told someone he was going back to England to live with his mum in Coventry. Billy Prestwick, after a couple of days of making vitriolic attacks on the police in the press, had also made the sudden announcement just hours before Teresa's departure for London that he would be moving to Portland in the Central North Autonomous Territory, where his sister resided, as far away from the corruption of New York as possible. The Hammer had joined the Muttonchop Killers.

Hastings was amazed. "All this in only a matter of days?"

Teresa sadly shook her head and leaned on his shoulder. "Yup. It's almost as though without Guy's leadership, the rest of you just immediately fell apart."

He was more than a little annoyed at this. "What do you mean? I haven't fallen apart."

"Sorry, I guess not. Although you have to admit running off to Colombia was ... impulsive."

"Perhaps. But at least I had a purpose. And what's this about The Hammer? Did the Muttonchops kick out Bludgeon Nightstick to make room?"

"No. They claim they're going to pioneer a two-drummer sound. As if they're not obnoxious enough already."

He laughed. "You can say that again. Well, good riddance to that alcoholic bastard."

They were silent after that, and after transferring to the Central Line at Paddington, they reached the fragrant, welcoming confines of Ladbroke Grove without further incident.

"I always love coming to London," Teresa said gaily as a few strands of sunlight unexpectedly imbued the street with an idyllic glow. "We should stay here, at least for a while."

Hastings shot her a quick glance. She always had a way of echoing his thoughts. Was it love? It did seem strange, since he had spent so much of his time in a community where the word "love" was bandied about in an endless mantra by stoned hippies, and there seemed to be so much brotherly love to go around that anyone should feel such a selfish, possessive variant, but there it was for the first time in his life.

Once again, he was welcomed by several old acquaintances as they walked arm in arm down the street. He decided to risk lighting up a smoke, despite the chance of ruining Teresa's gay mood and bringing her ire down upon him; the weather was so beautiful, it seemed ridiculous not to indulge on such a fine day. There was a slight autumnal nip in the air, the kind that makes a person feel just that little bit more alive. Teresa was so wrapped up in the sights and sounds of the busy neighborhood that she didn't even seem to notice.

After a few minutes, they reached the Mountain Grill on Hastings' favorite street, Portobello Road, where Daevid Mallorn could often be found at this time of day enjoying a tea, some macrobiotic delicacies, and holding forth on his beloved Eastern philosophy and the politics of absurdist resistance. Mallorn was basically a more genial, expressive version of Baba Frank of the Asparagus Stalks and had been good friends with Hastings for many years. He had spent his youth traveling the world, and he had picked up a number of unconventional ideas and culinary tastes.

Sure enough, they found Mallorn seated comfortably at the prized window table of the café, conversing in between mouthfuls with Steve Brock, London's preeminent street busker. Both were rail-thin, with unkempt blond hair parted in the middle, but Mallorn had the pointier nose and a narrow goatee jutting off his chin. Also present was Mort Moorhen, the noted new wave science fiction writer. Mallorn and Brock greeted their friends with excitement, and the always well-mannered but quiet and intense Moorhen nodded gravely from behind his bushy beard.

"Have you come for oolong tea and couscous, friends?" Mallorn said, bringing over two extra chairs. His slightly lined face shone with a pixyish energy as he jabbed his fork into some kind of raw potato and radish dish. He and Brock could have been brothers, with their similar features and taste in colorful, mad-looking clothing.

"Well, we might have a bite while we're here, Daeve," Hastings said, "but we're actually here for rather a more pressing reason. Some bad news, in case you haven't heard yet, and a warning. I know the world sometimes passes you by around here."

Moorhen's ears pricked up at this. He had a taste for a dark tale (and still does, as anyone who's read his latest, *The Grey Passage to the Vacant Beyond*, will agree).

"Well, do tell, then," Mallorn said, wiping some fragments of parsley from his tiny blond goatee, the eyes in his gaunt face gleaming with interest and charm.

Hastings, surprised that his friends hadn't heard the news yet, sighed, drew in a breath, then thought better of it. "Teresa, you know the whole story. I'm tired of the telling. Could you please fill the chaps in?"

While she enthusiastically launched into the story of her heroic Simon's half-week in Hell, he went to order a coffee, which he carried to the doorway to soak up some of the day's fading rays.

"You shouldn't drink that stuff, it'll kill you," Mallorn called out, interrupting the tale.

Hastings ignored him. A light, refreshingly cool breeze was wafting in to complement the carefree atmosphere. This street always had a few pleasing sights to display. Few people in the area owned vehicles, so, aside from a few parked delivery vans, pedestrians walked unrestricted and freely on the road. Today, a Caribbean man with dreads so heavy that his face was totally hidden under his drooping ebony fronds was covering the pavement with chalk pictures in bright pastels, mainly of idealized country scenes and exotic animals. He was very good. The sparse rays added a surrealistic glow to the man's work. Hastings wished he could step right into one of these otherworldly illustrations and forget the problems of life in our troubled dimension, where visions of beauty and potential always seem to come up sadly short of realization.

Groups strolled the pavements, laughing and talking, the older, more conservative inhabitants who had never left the neighborhood mixing easily and without tension with young, colorfully dressed bohemians, many of whom carried instrument cases slung over their shoulders. It often seemed like everyone under forty in Ladbroke Grove and Notting Hill was in a band, but there was no sense of competition, and all styles of music were welcome, from all of the traditional musics of the world to ska and reggae, to psychedelic rock and roll. It was an oasis of culture in a country where the life had been sucked away for years from the arts. Afterward, the neighborhood was to become a bit more gentrified, which was a great source of disappointment for people like Hastings and his friends, but to this day there is still a special atmosphere in this small corner of London.

"Simon! C'mon back in," Teresa called. He turned back to the café, finding the party much more subdued than it had been when they arrived.

"This is terrible..." Brock, who had a couple of tears running down his own prominent nose, was interrupted by the muffled sound of an explosion not far in the distance. It was accompanied by a dull roar that Hastings couldn't place.

Mallorn shook his head sadly, wiping away his own tears, and sighed. "Not again."

"Fucking bastards!" Brock exclaimed, jumping up and striding over to the doorway, along with several other patrons, who were also muttering and cursing. His lanky limbs were quivering with suppressed violence. Hastings and Teresa joined them, curious. Moorhen remained at the table with Mallorn, his face inscrutable under its layer of fur as he sipped his tea.

"It's those goddamned thugs again," Brock said. "They come in from the suburbs in gangs — usually football hooligans boozed up after the games, and they try to do damage to the neighborhood. They police won't stop them." He spat forcefully out onto the pavement. "They do more than break windows and shit like that. They even beat up a poor old gran the other week, just minding her own business. There's more of them every time."

"Half of them come from Tory party meetings, not football matches," growled another man with bushy black sideburns. "That bastard Powell whips 'em up into a frenzy at special meetings." Due to a gerrymandered electoral system in which the boroughs of central London were joined into huge super-boroughs with the suburbs, the MP for that part of London had always been a Tory, despite receiving votes from almost none of Ladbroke Grove or North Kensington's inhabitants.

"Well, they won't have the chance to do any more damage today!" Brock roared. "I'll kick all their bleedin' heads in first!" An angry mutter of approval and agreement went up from the predominantly male crowd that had assembled outside, and Hastings felt his own repressed rage and frustration responding. *Let them come*, he thought. *It may not solve things, but I may get a little symbolic revenge for Guy by knocking a few teeth out today.*

"Simon ... be careful, please. You're no fighter," he heard Teresa say from behind him, but it barely registered. He could feel his body shaking slightly in primal anticipation. He felt nauseous and lightheaded with the fear that always accompanies impending violence.

The sounds of smashing glass and sharp explosions were joined by the uncontrolled roar of a large group of approaching men. The sounds came nearer for about a minute. Then, suddenly, a crowd came bursting around the corner of Westbourne Park Road. There must have been a hundred men of different age groups, Hastings estimated, at least half of them wearing sinister red gas masks. So that rubbish had finally arrived in Britain from Virginia — or did it originate here? It was only a matter of time before the new populist political situation and migration policies boiled over into open conflict.

The mob was escorted by several cars, which drove behind, wildly sounding their horns. The hooligans were smashing windows as they came and throwing what looked like homemade bombs made of bottles. Plumes of smoke billowed in the distance, indicating they had already started several fires. Men and women, mostly elderly and many people of color, stumbled choking out of the fires, while younger people frantically tried to put the fire out with blankets and tea towels.

"Bloody hell!" Brock said. "There's never been this many before." Nevertheless, he turned to the multicultural crowd surrounding him, which now almost matched the group of hooligans in size. "Well, it's time we fought back, isn't it?"

His followers bellowed.

As one, the crowd of longhairs, East Indians, and Rastas marched toward the mob. The closer they got, the more frenetic the vandalism of the hooligans became. The weak rays of sunlight that had imparted a sense of peace to the street were now buried beneath a flotilla of thick, gray clouds that hovered menacingly over the impending battle. Hastings could now hear the vandals jeering: "'Ey, 'ere come the hippie boys for a stompin'!"

"'Ere come the immigrant-lovin' hippies! Oh, 'oim so froitened! Where's me mum?"

"We're gonna kill the lot of them commies and take their women! Bloody welfare cases."

There were now only a few meters separating the groups. The Ladbroke Grove defenders grimly ignored these jibes. They had armed themselves with whatever they could find in the alleys, broken bits of pipe, wood, glass. They marched under Brock's direction in a surprisingly united line. Hastings walked directly behind Brock, unarmed, his fists clenched tightly in a bizarre mixture of terror and anticipation. He could feel the veins in his neck and forehead pumping.

Then the hooligans charged with a deafening holler. The lines quickly dissolved into a flurry of hand-to-hand combat. Hastings felt himself confronted by a massive, gorilla-like bald man. He carried a cricket bat in his right hand.

"All right, lovey. It's lights-out!" the monster hissed, then jumped ferociously at Hastings, who leapt desperately into his enemy's body to grapple with his arm before he could bring the bat to bear. It was his only hope to avoid being knocked senseless. He was borne down by the weight of his opponent but managed to roll away, realizing that the man had lost his bat in the fall. Hastings nimbly scrambled to where it lay, jumped up, and swung it wildly with a yell. When he looked down, the gargantuan man lay prostrate, blood oozing from a large, serious-looking gash on his temple. The bat was splintered. Hastings felt sick and guilty, but he had no time to reflect on what he had done as another hooligan, this time a small, blonde, ratty-looking type with a crew cut and dressed in a bomber jacket, had finished knocking down the other speaker from the café and was brandishing a knife at Hastings with an evil grin.

The time Hastings took the offensive, leaping forward and aiming a blow with the bat's remains at the man's knife hand. His aim was true, and the man dropped the knife with a curse, holding his forearm. Without a second thought, Hastings brought the bat down with full force on the crew cut. The man went down without a sound and lay on his back, twitching grotesquely. The bat was almost down to the handle.

This time, no one immediately confronted him, so he took the opportunity to look around him. The air was filled with smoke from the homemade bombs, and one of the cars was on fire. Steve Brock was taking harsh knocks by the second, but they seemed to have little effect on him in his berserker state. He swung his wiry arms like windmills, bowling over any hooligan who wandered into his path. Then Hastings saw with a shock that Teresa had joined the fray on the other side of the crowd and was applying a choke hold to a man twice her size. Hastings vaguely remembered her saying she'd taken some rare form of Chinese martial arts training during her teens. It was impressive to behold.

She wasted no time but went on the attack against an even bigger man, downing him with what looked like a classic karate chop. Aside from those two, the locals, who were not much used to fighting, were getting the worst of the battle and taking a serious beating. He had no more time to admire Teresa's combat skills, because he was set upon by a third opponent, a skinhead with brawny tattooed arms wearing a gas mask and bearing yet another cricket bat. Just as Hastings ducked to avoid the first swing, the sound of rapidly approaching sirens drifted into the smoke. Everyone stopped dead in an awkward moment of silence.

"All right, boys, we've had our fun," yelled one of the invaders, the only one wearing a smart suit. "Let's clear off, on the double." The mob swiftly dispersed, leaving their unconscious and wounded on the pavement. The locals stood around in shock and confusion.

Four police cars pulled up, screeching their brakes, their headlights switched on against the unusual murk caused by the fires. Momentarily distracted, Hastings shielded his eyes and stopped paying attention. Hearing a rustle behind him, he turned around too late to see his previous opponent's fist coming at his head.

Oh, no ... not again. A crunching sound, a blinding light, and then he fell.

THIRTEEN

Again, Hastings didn't pass out entirely but instead lay in a daze for several minutes, oblivious to everything that was going on around him except the intense pain, experiencing hallucinations of himself committing horrible murders in a waist-deep pool of blood. He did feel a pair of strong arms lift his head, which was placed into someone's lap. When his mind cleared a little, he saw Teresa's concerned face peering down at him.

"Oh, brave little Simie! Are you all right?"

He struggled to sit upright, feeling nauseous. A fine drizzle brushed his face. The police and most of the wounded were gone; so were the hooligans and most of their smoke. The usual token visit to break up the fight, then the bobbies had gone their way. The wrecked car was giving off an acrid stench. Most of the local heroes had scattered at the arrival of the police. Brock, Mallorn, and Moorhen, the latter two of which had watched the fight from the safety of the Mountain Grill, stood beside Teresa. Brock was covered in scratches and cuts but looked very pleased with himself.

"Got knocked on my bloody head again ... where'd the fuzz go?"

Brock shook his head angrily, his eyes still blazing. "They just dispersed the crowd, laughed a bit at us, and took off. People can come and try to set fire to our fucking neighborhood, and they won't do a thing!"

"Simie here took down a couple of men, didn't you?" Teresa looked a little proud as she helped him to his feet. One of the sleeves of her dress was torn, and her face was smudged with dirt. "My little fighter."

"That's about a third of your tally," Moorhen observed dryly.

Hastings said nothing; the memory of the animalistic pleasure he had felt in taking his enemies down was still disturbing him deeply, but he checked his pocket for his special gun, which he had forgotten about again. It was still there, awaiting its one moment of dreadful glory. He was glad that he had not remembered it in the heat of battle, or a man might now lie dead by his hand.

"And what about Her Ladyship here!" Mallorn exclaimed, shaking water out of his hair. "Like the Goddess of War, striding into battle to aid the puny male in his hopeless hour, knocking her enemies about like nine-pins—"

"That's enough, please. If you've never seen a woman taking care of business, you clearly don't get out much." If there were any stirring speeches to be made, Teresa preferred to be the one making them.

"Moorhen here was taking notes through the whole thing, the cold fish! Coming soon to a bookstall near you, *The Battle for Ladbroke Grove!*"

Moorhen smiled slightly and didn't seem embarrassed at all at this mention of his nonparticipation.

Mallorn's face had reddened a little. "I was there with you in spirit, my dear. You know I'm a pacifist, and besides, you chaps seemed to have the situation well in hand."

"I'm supposed to be a pacifist too," Hastings mumbled. He could not understand why he should feel so guilty about protecting the place he loved deeply from despicable invaders bent on destruction, but he did.

"What was that, Simie?" Teresa took his arm.

"I said don't start bickering. And stop calling me Simie."

*

It was early in the evening. A few telephone calls and visits to those lacking telephones had led to an impromptu conference in Daevid Mallorn's one-bedroom flat. Teresa and Steve Brock had taken turns making the calls while Mallorn had brought Hastings to his "doctor," which might not have been the best idea. Mallorn's doctor had never taken classes at any kind of medical school and practiced "holistic" medicine without a license. She prescribed herbs, which she also sold in her shop, for almost any malady a patient could arrive with. Mallorn said that he and "everyone in the know" swore by her services, even when they resulted in a case of the runs.

The doctor, a corpulent figure with a mass of tangled gray hair who had smoked a large, ornate hookah throughout the examination, concluded that not only was he suffering from a concussion, but the water element had also become unbalanced with the fire element in his cortex, a condition that could lead to serious spiritual duress if left unchecked. For this she had prescribed a herbal supplement to be taken orally. She claimed it was grown in a secret valley in the Hindu Kush and would restore the sacred balance; she also provided a very pungent herbal poultice to be held to his head for two hours. She refused payment.

Hastings now sat dazedly in a corner of Mallorn's crowded flat, holding the poultice to the bump on his head with one hand and his nose with the other. The oral concoction had numbed every part of his body but his head, which still hurt quite badly. And he was pretty sure he could feel the runs starting already. He was puffing on a large joint to try to kill the throbbing and the smell.

A pall of smoke hung at the ceiling, produced by the marijuana, hashish, cigarettes, and cheroots of the assembled company. Mort Moorhen was there, scribbling furiously in a notebook, along with Maurice Wyatt, Bill Filmour, and Roger Lakehead of The Peuce Frank, and Brock and his bandmate from The Sonic Assassins, Stick Turner. Teresa, Mallorn, and his "partner in auras" (girlfriend) Shakti Yoni, rounded out the group. The whereabouts of Rick Farren and Ed Barrett were the only item on the agenda.

Barrett, well known as a genius but something of a loose cannon, had never been quite the same since leaving The Peuce Frank the year before. He had started buying a new, dangerous substance called "crack" off the streets, which had driven him completely mad for a short time, and though his friends had managed to wean him off the stuff, he had never been coherent enough since then to resume working. After a brief attempt at a solo career, he had abandoned a half-finished album and disappeared into the deep underground network of basement flophouses, where people stoned out of their minds on homemade mixtures lived out the remnants of their miserable lives. Even the most rabid aesthete like Guy had (generally) known better than to fall prey to the endless quest for new, unlicensed sensations and forsake mainstream pharma for the dangerous products of the cellars of the city. If Guy had lived, there would have been a good chance that, should his music career ever have stumbled, he would have ended up in a chemical den somewhere, dreaming away his last years. Barrett had already made that choice.

"Well, obviously in the case of Ed, we have no bloody idea where he is, but we do know the sort of place we're likely to find him," Mo Wyatt said. "We'll just have to search. I wonder why whoever's doing these killings considers poor Ed important enough to bump off. I mean, he'll die soon enough on his own."

"True," Bill Filmour said. "But it's possible they still consider him important as a symbol. He's still remembered by our fans."

"Or maybe they haven't followed the scene in a while," bearded Stick Turner pointed out dryly, absently playing with his saxophone reed, which he had brought in hopes that the meeting might turn into a jam session.

"Regardless," Teresa put in impatiently, "his name was on the list that Simon saw. We have a responsibility to find him. He can at least still be saved from himself."

"Fine. Some of us will be charged with searching for Ed." Mallorn had taken on the responsibility of chairperson, a right he felt should be his since they had convened in his flat, interrupting his and Shakti's evening ablutions and the ritualistic drinking of their jasmine tea. "We'll try every rubbishy hole we know of tonight, tomorrow, and every day thereafter until we track him down. Obviously the Frank boys should be involved in all this, since he's their mate. I'll come along. Maybe if we find him we can get him to Ms. Moonstone for a good cleaning out, eh Simon?"

Hastings had discarded the smelly poultice Ms. Moonstone had given him and was quietly sipping an ale, a much more pleasant anesthetic. "I'll come too. I rescued Guy from flophouses a couple more times than I care to remember."

Wyatt smiled. "I remember those days. All right, what about Rick Farren? Where the hell's he?"

Steve Brock piped up, coughing out a cloud as he did so. Teresa made a face and went to stand by the window. "Rick's still in hiding from the fuzz; they want him for blowing up that statue of the queen and her doggies a couple of months ago, remember?"

Mallorn frowned. "Yes, we've had a few disagreements over his methods. But he's still a friend. Well, those of who aren't involved in looking for Ed will have to try to track down Rick. Hopefully this mysterious Latin assassin won't have a better idea of these chaps' whereabouts than we do."

"All right, so me, Stick, Mo, and presumably old Moorhen here, if it's up to it, will search for Farren. Mort?"

Moorhen started, dropping his notebook. "Yes, absolutely. Whatever it takes."

They decided that Farren would likely have taken refuge amongst his fellow anarchists. Sometimes he hid out in a dried-out sewer pipe under a road in Wandsworth (where he swore he'd once seen an alligator or some kind of small dinosaur). He discovered the pipe when on the lam from the police for blowing up an (empty) bank. He could have got life on one of the Hulks on the Thames for that.

(These details, by the way, are being divulged in this narrative only because I have chosen a pseudonym to mask the identity of this intrepid urban guerrilla and his band; he is a long-time acquaintance of mine but has wisely chosen discontinue these activities. The authorities won't get a word out of this scribe!)

"Someone call Rod Blair," Hastings suggested. "He's good pals with Farren, isn't he?"

"Good idea," said Steve with a nod.

This is where your narrator must again place himself briefly into this story. I was indeed contacted shortly after the incident described here, by Stick Turner. I am still offended to this day by the fact that he did not tell me the reason why he was seeking Rick Farren or invite me to this council. As it happened, I had no idea where he was, not having seen him in months myself. Apparently, it was decided that they could not risk my journalistic zeal overcoming my tact, and that if I were to leak these events in the press, it would warn the assassin of pursuit, thereby forcing his hand and making the investigators responsible for a death. Imagine! That point is, I must admit, somewhat lost on me. I am a great believer in the power of the public to do good if properly aroused and feel, moreover, that more trust should have been put in my discretion; but I digress.

"Okay, guys, that's it." Teresa strode commandingly into the center of the room, surveying the assembly with a look of disgust, like a general inspecting a badly turned out regiment. "Butt out your cancer sticks, and let's get going. And don't spend any time sampling the delights of these flophouses yourselves, or I'll personally kick your asses. This is serious."

After a few minutes of mild protests and milling about, three groups split apart, one to try the old Seaman's Rest in the Docklands, where several local anarchists were known to tipple and hold forth on their theories over important pints of Raspberry Wheat ale from Upper Canada, the other groups to start touring dens in the Central and East London areas, not exactly a savory task.

Hastings had decided that his group had best start their investigation at one particularly notorious house of ill repute in Fulham, an illegal basement drug den known to its customers as Benny's. It had enjoyed a relatively illustrious history for an establishment of its kind. The cellar of the house had been an infamous opium den in the eighteenth century, featured in the social novels of Sir Walter McPhee and immortalized by Boswell in his history of the city. Not much had changed since. It was one of the places where Hastings had searched for Guy when he disappeared for two weeks after a badly received gig. The proprietor, Benny, a shaven-headed, one-eyed Cockney who apparently didn't indulge in the products himself, cooked up most of the chemicals consumed there in a private room and never divulged his recipes to anyone.

His wife, a buxom, raven-haired Irishwoman, served as the devil's waitress, walking around to the filthy cots and doling out the "medicines," as they called them. Their prices were considered quite reasonable. When one of the "patients" died, they were removed by night by members of the Brennan Boys crime family, and whence the corpses were taken, no one knew. The existence of the place was well known to the police, who, it was rumored, were well paid by the Brennans to stay clear.

Mallorn wrinkled his nose as he, Hastings, and Teresa entered the slimy, dark alleyway ("Old Mainline Lane," the graffiti called it) customers had to pass through to gain entrance to the basement. The evening air was noticeably chillier; it was a colder than normal fall for the south of England. Hastings shivered in his thick denim jacket.

"I deeply regret having to come to such a place. It reeks of sin," Mallorn said.

Hastings laughed hollowly. "Sin? I never thought you were so old-fashioned, Daeve. One man's sin is another man's paradise, I've heard." He descended the two stairs to the chipped green door, almost slipping on the well-worn surfaces, and delivered three quiet knocks and one loud one on a heavy brass knocker shaped like a boar's head.

"Where'd you learn that?" Teresa said suspiciously.

Hastings rolled his eyes. "I told you, I had to come here to save Guy's life. It was Marty, by the way, who taught me the knock. I'd be surprised if they haven't changed it by now."

The door squealed open a couple of inches, and a fat, frowning face with an eye-patch peered out. "Wod'ya want?"

"Hello, Mr. ... Benny," Hastings said politely. "You may remember me, Simon Hastings. A friend of Marty Sharpe's. He used to come here sometimes."

"Wrong knock. Knock's changed. Go away." The door started to close.

"Listen, Benny, stop." The door stayed open an inch. "I've got an important message for a friend, a customer of yours. It's a life-and-death situation. Is there an Ed Barrett here?"

"No Barrett. No Sharpe. Fuck off." The door started to close again.

"How much?" Teresa's brazen Virginian voice boomed out behind Hastings, making him jump.

"Eh?" The voice behind the door sounded muffled but intrigued.

"How much do you want for us to come in?"

There was silence for a few seconds as Benny considered his price. "Fifty quid."

Teresa reached into her pocket, pulled out a large roll of bills, and stripped three off. Mallorn's left eyebrow shot up. "For emergencies," she said with a cheeky grin. Hastings didn't know whether to be admiring or appalled. She squeezed the banknotes through the crack.

There was a crackle, then the door opened wide, revealing Benny in all his corpulent glory. He wore a stained white undershirt, which was too short. His hairy, rotund belly fell out over his beltline. He scratched the stubble on his head and regarded them with beady eyes, blinking in the permanent half-light of the alley. "In," he growled.

They heard the door slam behind them, and they were

enveloped in the rank odors of sweat, urine, feces, and burning chemicals.

Mallorn's face creased in disgust. "Let's get this over with."

Hastings nodded, lit up a smoke to try to kill the smells, and began to inspect the denizens of the cots. There were about fifteen wooden cots, with thin, dingy, stained mattresses on them, but no pillows or blankets. The room was lit by two naked bulbs dangling from the low ceiling. The floor was bare flagstones, on which the odd well-fed rat could be seen scurrying about its business. There was water leaking out of a large pipe on one wall, forming a filthy pool where two rats were happily bathing like a couple at the seaside. A horrible odor wafted from the door to a lavatory that had likely not been cleaned in months, even years. Roughly half of the cots were filled with huddled forms, all motionless. All appeared to be male. The atmosphere of despair was almost palpable, clinging like an aura to these lost souls who had chosen a slow, sordid suicide over a quick and clean one.

Benny had disappeared back into a private office, but the proprietress came puffing up to them. She was as large as her husband, with long, greasy hair, wearing a blouse unbuttoned to reveal cleavage that resembled a shady Alpine valley nestled between two massive, rounded peaks. The effect was, however, completely unerotic. She grinned at them, incongruous in her occupation and location, showing two rows of broken or missing teeth.

"Well then, me dearies, what can we do for you? Three beds and three spoonfuls of Benny's best?" She brandished three needles in one hand. At least those were new and still in their packaging. Her warm voice sounded like that of the proverbial Irish country milkmaid and contrasted sharply with her sordid surroundings. Hastings found himself wondering about her history, how she fell in with Benny and came to run one of London's filthiest drug houses.

"No, thank you, madam." Mallorn inclined a little in a small bow. Hastings and Teresa exchanged looks of amusement. "We're here to find a friend; we deeply regret the imposition, but we would not be here if we could avoid it. We know how much emphasis you place on discretion. Do mind if we look around for a few minutes?"

The Irishwoman beamed. "Oh, aren't we a well-spoken little man, then?" She patted Mallorn's cheek. He flinched slightly. "Of course you can, duckies. Just don't disturb the customers. They're likely to 'freak out,' as you young 'uns say, if you bother them too much."

They thanked her and began a circuit of the room. Hastings shuddered as he looked into each of the desolate faces they passed. Their eyes were glassy, staring at nothing. None of them appeared to see him, or if they did, they were indifferent. They were a mixture. Some were stereotypical hippie druggies, but there was one man with recently clipped, now messy hair, dressed in parts of a once-immaculate business suit. The suit was covered in dried vomit, and he was drooling. An open briefcase lay beside him, and torn papers were strewn all over the bed. Hastings turned quickly away, feeling his gorge rise.

"Legalizing and regulating drugs was one of the few intelligent things this government's ever done," he remarked to Teresa. "Who knows how many people it's saved from places like this?"

"I'm not sure," she murmured. "They're here because they still can't get what they want from the legal products."

The next man, who had long, matted hair and a bushy beard and sported biker colors on his dirty leather, started, sat up, and stared with wide eyes at Hastings, mumbling something incoherent. As his whisper started to climb rapidly to a scream, Hastings was forced to beat another hasty retreat. Although he was disappointed at not finding Ed Barrett here, he approached the last cot with some relief. He did not, however, relish the prospect of spending the night in one nightmarish den after another, looking for a man no one had seen in weeks. Mallorn, who evidently had no stomach for the task at hand, had gone to stand by the door and was shifting uncomfortably from one foot to the other. Teresa followed Hastings as he walked over to the cot, in a corner underneath the only window, which was so grimy that it let in almost no light. He leaned down then recoiled with such force that he fell back into Teresa and almost knocked her over.

"What the hell, Simon?"

"My god, Teresa, it's Marty!"

FOURTEEN

It was indeed Martin Sharpe-Thornton lying almost dead to the world on the cot. He had certainly fallen into a sad state in a very short time. His clothes were soiled, and his long, curly hair, which no one had ever seen even slightly out place or unclean, was oily and tangled. A pile of used needles lay beside him. His mouth hung open, and a thread of spittle was dripping out.

"Jesus!" Hastings exclaimed. He couldn't believe it. Marty had not gone back to Coventry to stay with his mum. He had come directly to London and headed straight for the nearest flophouse. How could Marty, always in control, have broken into pieces so quickly? He looked at Teresa and Mallorn, who had cautiously wandered over when he had heard the commotion. "We've got to get him out of here."

Hastings reached out and lightly shook Marty's shoulder. His eyes opened, and he looked directly into Hastings' face. Then he let out a piercing yell and started thrashing about. "Go away, go away! I thought I got rid of you! Go back to hell with the rest of them! Go away!" He closed his eyes and passed out again, sweat running down his face.

"He thinks you're a nightmare," Mallorn said.

"Thanks for pointing out the obvious."

"'Ere, wot's this?" a voice said angrily from behind them. "Disturbin' me fuckin' customers, eh? What did I tell ya? Clear off!" Benny shook his finger at them.

Teresa advanced on him, the tendons in her neck standing out like cables. "Listen, you fat piece of shit! You go and mind your filthy business before I rip a few layers of blubber off you. We're leaving, all right, and we're taking this man with us. You got a problem with that?"

Benny, for all his bluster, seemed to be a bit of a coward when confronted by equal aggression. He shrank away, holding his palms outward. "Awlright, dearie, no need for that sorta language. Just take yer friend and get out, there's a good girl." He leered and winked at her in a ghastly fashion.

Teresa regarded him with total derision. She seemed to tower above him. "You're a fucking vulture, Benny. You should stop taking advantage of people with problems and do something worthwhile with your life."

Benny's face turned a deep shade of purple. "Don't you preach at me, little lady. I'm runnin' a business 'ere, plain and simple." He gestured toward the door. "Now get out, and don't come anywhere near 'ere again, or I can have somethin' very nasty done to you."

Hastings and Mallorn lifted Marty's rigid form with great difficulty and carried him out the door, which slammed behind them with extra emphasis.

"Well, we won't be able to go back there any time soon," Hastings puffed.

"You do have a way with people, Teresa," Mallorn added.

"Why would we want to?" Teresa spat. "That was one of the more depressing experiences of my life, and I've seen a lot of crap."

"We haven't found Ed yet, have we? Just this poor sod," Hastings grunted. Marty was heavier than his skinny frame would have suggested.

"Now, who wants the task of getting Marty somewhere safe so he can come down?" Mallorn asked.

"I suppose you would prefer that honor," Teresa said, casting her penetrating eye on Mallorn's sheepish face. "You didn't seem to have the balls for this business."

"That's enough," Hastings said. "Daeve, you take Marty to your place and try to clean him up, and go easy with the weird healing herbs, will you?"

"Sure, sure." Mallorn looked hurt. "But your head does feel

better now, doesn't it?"

Hastings was surprised to notice that the pain had indeed lessened considerably. "Why, I guess it does," he said, smiling a little.

"You shouldn't put these things down," Mallorn said, "until you've given them a really good go. I'll get Marty cleaned up, don't you worry. Come back to my place tonight. I'll try to make up a bed for you two. And be careful. Even our pit bull here couldn't defeat some of the people who run these places in hand-to-hand combat."

She rolled her eyes. "Okay, Daeve, let's get you a taxi."

*

After they had bundled Mallorn and the still unconscious Marty into a taxi (several had deliberately passed them by, presumably deterred by the sight of three long-hairs supporting what looked to be a corpse), Hastings and Teresa renewed their search of the city's houses of sin.

First, they visited MacPhaill's Magick Emporium near Leicester Square. It sold ornaments and decorations but had a back room that was even dirtier and housed even more lost souls on any given night than Benny's. There they observed the more passive ecstasies of opium eaters who lay on boards covered with rags in a dimly lit room filled with the eerie sounds of bubbling hookahs and the soft laughter of dreamers lost in their private fantasies, visions so beautiful they made a return to reality far more intolerable and undesirable. They were quickly sent packing by MacPhaill's courteous but firm helpers, but not before they had ascertained that Ed was not among his clientele that night.

They visited the notorious Miss Maddeford's in Camden Town, an old-fashioned brothel that had once catered to Members of Parliament and sundry knights, lords, and barons of the realm but had fallen on harder times. It now also sold concoctions brewed by the matron on her kitchen stove to supplement business lost to the decline in the downtown upscale sex trade. These home brews had caused several deaths over the years, but since a large portion of the male members of the London constabulary (and some female) had spent a great deal of time in the welcoming bowels of the brothel, Miss Maddeford was largely left alone. She owned several houses around town and spent her weekends in a sumptuous mansion in Richmond, where her parties, still attended by many members of the empire's richest and most famous families, were legendary. Though helpful, she was unable to remember coming across Ed or Rick Farren within the previous few months, although they had both visited within the year.

They reluctantly stopped in at Dr. Mick's House of Morphine, a den in a house near the University College Hospital. The proprietor was a crazed surgeon who had worked at the hospital for twenty years and had been helping himself to stimulants, antipsychotic medications, ether, opiates, and morphine for almost as long. This place was only frequented by the most hardcore boredom-driven thrill-seekers, since the doctor's mixtures of these medications had caused countless fatalities over the years. When a customer expired, the doctor would take them discreetly with the help of associates across the road to the rear entrance of the emergency ward into the morgue, leaving a toe tag on the corpse that read *Illegal Drug Addict: Accidental Death.* Nothing had ever been suspected, since the hospital admitted many such cases each night, and many died in the emergency room. The doctor numbered many of his most distinguished colleagues amongst his best customers, so any potential scandal was hushed up.

In each of these establishments, Hastings had inquired about Ed, but no one had seen him for weeks. In each place, Teresa had picked a fight with the proprietor, accusing them of taking advantage of the mentally ill. One of the girls at the brothel had taken a swing at her, but Teresa had subdued her and pacified her by telling her that she had no moral quarrel with the legal aspects of prostitution in the house, only with Madame Maddeford's dangerous cocktails.

This had led to an argument on the way to the next place, wherein Hastings had told her keep her bloody mouth shut, or they'd get nowhere, and what made prostitution more ethical than selling drugs anyway? Teresa had retorted by telling him that he was chauvinist swine, that selling your body of your own choice was one thing, but selling deadly mixtures of chemicals was another matter entirely.

Now they were no longer on speaking terms as they got out of their own taxi outside of Daevid Mallorn's flat, which was over the top of an extremely foul-smelling fish market. The pavement reeked of rotting prawns and crabs twenty-four hours a day. It was one o'clock in the morning, and they were both dead-tired. Hastings now had his splitting headache back and reminded himself that he had better go and see a legitimate GP as soon as possible. Two nasty knocks on the head in a week must not be good for a chap.

Still not speaking, they dragged themselves up the steep, creaky stairs, finding Marty lying on the sofa, knocked out. A wet bandage had been stuck to his head. The sickly-sweet smell from it filled the room, competing with the odors of stale smoke, incense, and the fishy smell from the street. Heedless, they threw themselves down on the cushions Mallorn had placed on the floor for their bed and lay on their sides, facing away from each other. Hastings passed out immediately.

*

The were awakened only a few hours later by Shakti Yoni, who inadvertently stepped on Teresa's arm on her way to the kitchen.

"Owww!"

"Sorry, dear," flaxen-haired Shakti said in her luxuriously low-toned, soothing voice, leaning down and patting Teresa on the head. "You go back to sleep." That, however, proved impossible as their hosts began to loudly bang pots, pans, and plates in the kitchen. Even Marty started to stir, moaning and gurgling horribly.

"For Christ's sake," Hastings growled and glared at his watch, which said five thirty, but eventually he rose and went to take a shower. At least there was running water, and Mallorn had put out some clean-looking towels. It was still quite dark outside, but the first birds could be heard energetically chirping.

When he emerged dressed in an Indian tunic that Mallorn had laid out for him, he went to the kitchen and found a bizarre spread set out on the tabletop. There were at least ten bowls filled with unidentifiable fruits and grains. Teresa, dressed in a crimson sari, and Marty were seated at the table. Marty looked terrible. There were huge bags under his eyes, which were so bloodshot, the whites looked solid red. He had also changed into some of Mallorn's Indian garb, which was nothing like what he would normally wear.

"Simon," he croaked flatly, staring down at the table.

"Well, well, well," Hastings said, glancing from Marty to the "food" on the table. He could not for the life of him figure out what most of it was. "Fancy meeting you at Benny's, eh?"

Hearing the hostility in Hastings' voice, Mallorn tried to smooth over the situation. "We've prepared some real delicacies for you to put some spring back in your step this morning, Simon. The bowl here's what the citizens of the South Pacific Jersey Island chain eat for breakfast every morning. It's a fruit called pikkupo, and it's as tasty as can be."

Hastings gingerly placed a segment of the soggy yellow fruit in his mouth and swallowed. It was horrible.

"And here's some organic oatmeal with dried beets, a delicacy from the steppes, quinoa with bean sprouts, and some black tea with clarified butter. Help yourself." Mallorn beamed and planted a kiss on Shakti's head.

Hastings cast a baleful eye at Marty. "Well, well," he said again.

"Glad we found you before you enjoyed too many more cocktails. What about your mum?"

Marty curled his lips into a ghastly smirk. "Yes, well, that was my original intention. Instead, I got off the plane like a robot and headed straight to good ol' Benny's. Hadn't been there in years. Lost my luggage, too."

"How long had you been there?"

"Only a day and a half, actually. But as you can see, I'd been going at it pretty heavy. I suppose I was more down than I thought."

"I'll say!" Teresa cut in. "You could have killed yourself."

"Maybe that was the point," Mallorn said calmly. "But don't worry, Marty, you're back with friends now."

"Well, I was grateful this morning to wake up and see your ugly mug over me instead of Benny's. Thanks, chaps — and ladies," he added with a smile in Teresa's direction, then popped some beets into his mouth.

"You'd better get cleaned up, sunshine, because we have work to do," she said. "The man who killed Guy is probably in town, and Simon found evidence in Colombia that both of you were on his mysterious hit list."

"Really?" Marty went a shade paler still, almost dead white. "I suppose I've had a couple of close scrapes, then. I knew I'd come close to death. Maybe it was the shock that sent me over the edge."

Hastings reached over and clapped him on the shoulder. "Looks like you'll be joining my detective work after all. And it won't be easy finding this slippery character. Now," he said, turning to Mallorn, "how's about some eggs and toast, eh — and coffee!"

"I'm afraid we don't consume such poisons," Mallorn said mildly but firmly. "These things are hellish for your digestion. But I've got some organic spelt bread. Would you like that?"

Hastings laughed. "Don't worry about it. We'll find a bite on the way. We have work to do!"

From *The Young Person's Guide to the Music Business*
by Archie Richardson (Your Best You! Press, 1970)

No business offers the enterprising young man or woman more exciting career opportunities than the world of pop music. You don't have to be an extroverted rock star to reap the benefits of involvement in this exploding global industry. There's money to be made and prestige to be won through careers in music production and engineering, artist development and relations, marketing and promotion, concert bookings, and stage management — something for everyone!

Hob-nob with the greatest musicians in the world today while contributing to their success! Learn how to manipulate the public's taste and exploit opportunities within the cultural marketplace! Be a part of the wildest, most happening party scenes in the world today! And I mean WILD!

The music industry has doubled its sales of LPs, eight-tracks, and cassettes within the last three years. In my role as Promotion Director for Columbus Records, the world's leading record manufacturer and distributor, I have helped to break the careers of the Kidney Stones, the Sugar Pops, the Georgia Sludge Monster, Judee Sill, and Grovel, to name but five of the diverse million-selling acts I have guided to the top of the international charts. This book and my experience can be your guide to sure success in a world of glamor and luxury. Read on and learn!

FIFTEEN

It was evening when they finally gave up the search. They had spent the last thirteen hours visiting not only drug dens, but almost every bar, club, and café in the area, with no success. A few people reported Barrett sightings within the last couple of weeks, but no one knew his present whereabouts. The Peuce Frank boys, who had also been combing the underworld as far east as Limehouse, had experienced the same results. Mallorn had been given the task of phoning around to all of their friends on the music scene, as well as Ed's mum and sister. As Hastings, Marty, and Teresa trooped wearily through the door of the apartment, he shook his head and sadly took a bite of his unflavored soy yoghurt.

"No news, I'm afraid. Shakti even went as far as going to the police, who of course sent her packing, even though she changed into her navy business suit, which we only use in absolute emergencies. And Steve called; it's the same situation with Rick Farren. It's like they've both disappeared off the face of the Earth."

Hastings' face was grim as he slumped down on a kitchen chair. "Let's hope that's not too close to the truth."

"Now, Simon, I don't want to upset you, but after another day of this, we may have to, well, devote a little less of our time to this. Aside from meditating hopefully in anticipation of their safe return, naturally."

"What the hell do you mean?" Hastings glowered at him.

"What he means, Simon, and I happen to agree," Teresa said gently, "is that, although we're not saying we think you're obsessed or anything like that, and we do understand your need to avenge Guy's death and prevent new ones, we do have to try to get back to normal soon. Marty's here now, and as he said to you at lunch, he'll be ready to start playing again soon. Your record company is probably wondering what to do with you. We'll keep an eye out for the missing guys and this assassin character you've talked about, but it's time to think about the future. Ed will turn up eventually; he always does. If we can't find him, it's doubtful the killer will be able to."

Marty nodded. "Simon, I cared as much about Guy as you did, and I'm just as pissed off as you that there's some hitman out there waiting to poison us, or worse. But since there's no justice system for us to call upon here, our hands are pretty much tied. We'll just have to be watchful."

Hastings considered these comments for a minute then nodded slowly. "Maybe you're right. We won't give up the search, but it's time I thought a bit about myself. And maybe if the police won't help us — and we know they won't — it's time we enlisted the help of the greater community."

"What, you mean like putting up posters?" Marty looked skeptical.

"Well, there aren't really a lot of chaps in London who would fit the appearance of Ramón Rosas, are there? There's no way the authorities will ever take us seriously, so it can't really hurt things. We don't have to specify exactly why we're looking for him or mention him by name."

That is what they did, although your narrator is ashamed to admit that he never noticed anything of the like about town. In my defense, I did leave that week for a short stay at the family estate near Aberdeen. And aside from the one phone call described earlier, no one ever really enlisted my aid in this case. I heard rumors in the succeeding year, but I never really did have any idea of these events until Hastings finally filled me in. More's the pity.

The posters contained no details about why Rosas was wanted, only that he was a criminal who had seriously hurt members of the community. The citizens of the West End looked after their own, being used to indifferent treatment by law enforcement agencies, and would respond if the man was seen. Aside from keeping an eye out themselves, there was little else Hastings, Marty, and their friends could do. They briefly discussed hiring an investigator, but Hastings left that in Mallorn's hands; he had lost his taste for cloak-and-dagger sleuthing since his Colombian misadventure.

He was in a position where he needed to make a decision for the sake of his own mental health, and though his burning desire for revenge and his wish to protect his people had not abated, he could see there was little else to do. He agreed reluctantly that the next day he and Marty would visit the corporate offices of Aureola Records to find out if they still had a recording contract. Some source of income was needed; since his early teens, there had been no occupation other than musician he had ever visualized making him happy.

Hastings was certain of two things: he had not seen the last of Ramón Rosas, and the mystery of who ordered the killings would someday be solved.

*

The next day, as promised, Hastings accompanied Marty by rail to the Bromley offices of Aureola Records (a holding of Empress Tobacco Ltd., which itself is a division of The Magister Corporation Plc.), the world's second largest record company, as judged by annual sales figures. Bromley, once a peaceful semirural suburb, is now the southern business center of London. The relationship between the new wave of rock and roll bands and the traditional record companies was a strained one at best but had become one from which it was hard to break free. Hastings was not the only musician to recognize the hypocrisy of activists out to change the world passively watching their music and views marketed as product by corporations whose profit-mongering was the very opposite of everything they stood for. The issue had been nagging in the back of his mind for some time, as it had been for all the members of The Spheres (the Hammer probably excepted). The topic had rarely come to the forefront of any conversation; they had been too busy working, recording, and basking in their newfound celebrity to become too discontented with their handlers at this point in their career.

The Spheres had believed they needed the money the big company provided in order to obtain the necessary exposure to start an international career and to assist in subversively spreading their message, the old "infiltrate from within" theory that has always failed throughout history. But now that their records were selling in large quantities, Hastings had come to realize that all they really were was a cash cow for the company, while receiving a minute percentage of the profits as a royalty in return. In short, they were being robbed. The entertainment industry had attached itself like a leech to the ever-changing counterculture and showed no sign of letting go. The musicians continued to innovate, and the industry reaped the rewards. Daevid Mallorn had recently taken the daring step of cutting The Flying Teapots' ties with Virginia-based Columbus Records, signing a contract instead with London independent Groovy Melon Productions, which was run by an old Jamaican fellow from his basement and was mainly known for calypso recordings. Mallorn claimed (although he was known to lie simply to amuse himself) that his band's popularity and financial security had actually improved since the change. Now that The Spheres were likely done as a band, it was high time for the two surviving members to consider a similar step.

Hastings broached the topic gingerly as they sat enjoying some watery tea in styrofoam cups and soggy crumpets in a brightly lit, sterile Bromley teashop, gaining strength for their impending visit. Marty still looked something like an embalmed corpse but said he felt decent. The shop was full of businessmen in pinstripes.

"Well, Simon," Marty said thoughtfully through a mouthful of crumpet (he had only just recovered his appetite), "it's not like the paradox of our relationship with these shifty bastards hadn't occurred to me before. And you're probably right. If we're going to form a new band, and you want to make a break from Aureola, I think now's the time. But I do think that we should see what they might offer us. I haven't had a chat with anyone from the company in quite a while."

Hastings frowned. "Yes, Marty, but Guy was their star, and as far as they're likely concerned, he was the sole reason for our success. If anything, I'm afraid they'll cut our advances and royalties, and I'm not prepared to accept that kind of insult after all the profit we've made for them in the last couple of years."

"True, true." Marty grinned and shoved the last piece of breakfast into his mouth. "This was a disgusting meal. Well, we might as well find out, eh?"

They finished their tea in silence then went back out into Bromley High Street, where a chilly breeze was blowing and the sun was finally peeking out. It was a short walk to the high-rise office building that housed Aureola. On their way through the characterless suburban business district, they passed several fast food chain restaurants and two massive supermarkets on opposite sides, wedged between the skyscrapers.

"Nice atmosphere."

"You can say that again," Marty said, neatly tripping up a middle-aged, well-dressed businessman with his umbrella.

They could hear him yelling back at them for a few seconds, but presumably intimidated by their "antisocial" exterior, he did not follow. Marty chuckled. "Welcome to the future, old boy," he said softly, with a surprising trace of sadness, maybe regret that his own anger had briefly gotten the best of him.

The old security guard at the desk recognized them and gave them a friendly nod as they clomped across the heavy pink marble floor, their footsteps echoing hollowly in the bland emptiness. Hastings pressed the button for the ninety-ninth floor.

"Here goes then," he said grimly. The stepped out onto a lush carpet in front of a reception desk in a large room lit by tall windows. The full eastern morning sun was streaming in blindingly. The company's workspace was modern and open-concept. The offices, with the exception of those belonging to the executives, were made of head-high cubicle dividers. The receptionist, whose blonde hair was pulled back tightly into a bun, regarded them coldly over the top of her spectacles.

"Yes?" she said in a voice like glass shards.

"We're here to see Franklin Ferris. Tell him Simon and Marty from The Spheres are here to see him."

The secretary's demeanor abruptly became obsequious. "Well, our Virginian stars! This is an honor. You'll have to forgive me; I'm new here. Please, help yourself to some tea and have a seat." She picked up the phone to dial Franklin Ferris.

"Pretty bird, huh?" Marty whispered as he sat in one of the plush chairs. Hastings rolled his eyes and remained standing.

A minute or so later, an eccentric figure came bounding up to them, dressed in a pair of purple flares, a tweed blazer, and an impossibly wide tie. He had short, very messy hair and a pair of huge sideburns. His face was covered in an unnaturally wide, beaming grin underneath a pair of bulging eyes. Franklin Ferris was head of A&R for Aureola and probably the most influential music industry personality in the whole kingdom. He had signed up The Spheres after going mad over one of their shows at the UFO. A mostly decent sort, he had once confided in Hastings while extremely high that he often felt uncomfortable as a go-between dealing both with the underpaid talent and his padded employers. He had later vehemently denied saying any such thing. He was good friends with Billy Prestwick, a former Aureola employee himself, and possessed a similarly effusive personality.

"Simon! Marty! How the fuck are you!" he fairly screamed. Heads bobbed up over cubicle dividers for a few moments before disappearing again. "Wow! You both look like shit! But," he sobered suddenly, "that's understandable, considering what you've been through. I cried for hours, I tell you, when I heard about Guy. But come in, lads, come in! Thanks, Trixie," he said with a wink at the secretary and led them toward the back of the room. Ferris was considered important enough to have his own office beside those of the president and vice-president of marketing. Both of those doors were shut.

"Come in! Come in!" Ferris bellowed. "Try to find somewhere to sit, I dare you!" There were a desk and several chairs in the room, but all were covered in papers, LP sleeves, fast food bags, and pieces of swag. Posters adorned all of the wall space, including a huge one of The Spheres' album cover for *Astronomy*: a photograph of the Crab Nebula. An expensive mini-computer (just introduced to the market) took up the whole desktop, part of the floor, and a whole shelving unit along one wall. Hastings settled himself down on top of a Wimpy's bag. "I'm run off my feet, like everyone else here. The latest thing is to try to figure out whether we'll get into this new 'compact disk' thing out of Asia, or just stick with good 'ol tapes, LPs, and eight-tracks." Ferris plumped himself down in his chair. "So, lads, I guess you want to know what's going on here, with your contract and all, mmm? And I'd like to know what happened to old Billy."

"The thought had crossed our minds. As for Billy, he's disappeared to somewhere in the western Virginias. So's Electron Z."

Marty pulled out his smokes and lit up. "You see, Franklin, we've decided to continue on with a clean slate, maybe not as The Spheres, but we'd like to know what interest the company may have in a new project involving myself and Simon."

"Hmm, interesting, lads. You see, with Guy's death, sales of Spheres albums have jumped about three hundred percent in a few days."

"Nothing sells like death," Marty said. It was a truly disgusting thought, getting rich off the corpse of their friend.

"Indeed, indeed," Ferris said, looking momentarily down at his desk. "Terrible, but true. Good for your bank accounts, anyway. Now that I now where you're at, I'll see that your latest checks are expedited. Anyway, my professional opinion, no offense, is that

The Spheres are dead as a band. Because of this terrible tragedy, the name is identified by the public almost solely with Guy. But I do think that the two of you on your own would be a successful act. We'd be interested in that, especially as you two wrote all the music, didn't you?"

"Most of it," Hastings said. "But what about the contract?"

Ferris stared blankly back. "What about it?"

"Well," Hastings said, trying to speak gently, "the old contract is presumably null, now that the band is broken up. We'd like to renegotiate."

"Renegotiate? Why? Isn't the old contract good enough?"

Hastings shook his head. "Frankly, no. The royalty rate is insulting. We won't want a higher advance, but we we'll want a higher percentage of sales."

Ferris's eyes started to pop out even farther than normal. The morning sun made their bloodshot surfaces shine like diamonds, and his face had become deeply flushed within seconds. "I don't understand. You're already tied with the Beach Bums for the highest royalty rate we give out!"

Marty leaned forward and spoke persuasively. "Come on, Franklin, you know as well as we do that our royalty only amounts to a few pence per band member for each unit sold."

"But that's standard procedure!"

"Well, standard procedure is morally incorrect. I'm sorry."

"What are you trying to do to me?" Ferris cradled his head in his hands. "You know I'll never convince the bosses to give you a higher royalty. Maybe if the band was still together, but this is completely unreasonable. You'll ruin me!"

Marty and Simon looked at each other and rolled their eyes at his histrionics. "I'm sorry, Franklin, but if you can't arrange what we want, we're going to leave your company. I doubt they'll even miss us."

"Wha—for who—after everything I've done for you..." Ferris had pulled a three-quarters-drained bottle of whiskey from a desk drawer. He took a long, gurgling pull, finishing the bottle. "Where will you go? We're it, you know. The biggest and the best... Well, that's that. You're free then, you bastards. I told you, they'd never let me offer you more than you're getting now. Get out of here."

Sorrowfully, they rose to leave. Marty was already out the door and Hastings half out when Ferris suddenly rose.

"Oh, fuck it!" he shouted. "This is terrible. I can't do this anymore."

They stopped.

"Come back in, please. Sit. Sit. If I had any more spirits in here, I'd offer you a drink. Now, you say that Billy's disappeared."

"As far as we're concerned. That's right. He cracked up."

"So he's not your manager anymore?"

"Looks like."

"Well, how would you like a new one?"

"You mean— "

"That's right." Ferris beamed widely, and his teeth were lit up like bulbs by the sun. "I've made a decision, rather more quickly than I like to do things, but there, you've forced my hand. I've had it with these bastards. I'm quitting on the condition that you make me your manager."

Hastings couldn't believe his ears. "You'd give up your plum position to manage a new band, one that doesn't even exist yet?"

"It's not as cushy as you think, what with Sir Philip next door breathing down my neck all the time. I think I'll be able to make a go of it if I can find a couple more clients. There comes a time in a man's life when he has to choose a side. I've never been satisfied with the way things are done here. I will, however, need twenty percent commission on any bookings or contracts I get you, and a budget."

"Done!" They stood up and solemnly shook his hand.

"That's that, then! Smashing. I'll get your checks on the way out. Just give me a minute to write my resignation letter. I hope I won't have cause to regret this."

"I sincerely hope so as well," Hastings said.

SIXTEEN

Hastings and Marty got down to work after that meeting. Their first item of business was to decide what sort of band they would like to form. They agreed that neither of them was willing to totally abandon the free-form, improvisatory style they had been developing at the time of Guy's death. In fact, they both declared themselves ready to take matters a step further and, like The Wylde Flowers, abandon traditional songwriting forms altogether if need be. The restrictions imposed by keeping songs under five minutes in length limited, they felt, both their pleasure in playing them and an audience's potential benefit from listening. Money would not be a problem for a while; they were expecting more very healthy royalty checks from the post-death sales of *Musick of The Spheres* and *Astronomy*, their two releases. They were content to let Aureola pursue and pay Electron Z and the Hammer. Guy's royalties were to be paid to his family in Bushey.

They rented a house that day in Notting Hill, on Pembroke Crescent; the bottom floor to live in and the top floor for rehearsals and to have a place for their homeless friends to crash in. Steve Took moved in the first week, sleeping happily on the floor, and he showed no sign of leaving in the ensuing days. Over the course of the next two weeks, they managed to put out enough feelers on the scene to set up auditions with four drummers. A tall, scruffy red-haired young Scottish fella barely out of his teens named Basil Baker came immediately to the forefront. Although his style was the most unorthodox of the lot, and he sometimes seemed to lose control altogether (he occasionally even lost the beat), his frenetic enthusiasm was infectious and powered their jams to new heights. He only seemed to possess one set of clothes, a fact that Marty and

Simon deemed to be none of their business.

The problem of keyboards was solved when Teresa announced that she had taken advanced piano lessons for several years as a young girl and had always nurtured a secret desire to play in a band. She had always been envious of Hastings and the fact that he had an outlet for his artistic expression. Though shocked to find out something so important that he hadn't had an inkling of before, Hastings readily gave her an audition on a borrowed organ and was astounded by her abilities. Fortunately, Marty agreed wholeheartedly with her addition.

They immediately went out and spent some of their royalties on a full setup of organ, synthesizers, and Mellotron. A new band was born. Whether an internal romantic relationship might someday interfere with their rapport as bandmates remained to be seen. Teresa could be stubborn, to say the least, and Hastings was also used to having his way.

Naming the group was another issue. Since Guy and Hastings had come up with The Spheres, Marty felt it was his turn, but Hastings was also strong-willed about such issues, and they argued about it long into one night, almost losing their tempers until finally coming to a consensus. They liked the cosmic connotation of a name like The Spheres but racked their brains unsuccessfully for over an hour until Daevid Mallorn, who had come over to jam, suggested they name themselves after their own second album.

"Why the hell didn't I think of that?" Hastings grumbled as he fell asleep in an old armchair they had found in front of a house on Ladbroke Road. Most of the furniture had been acquired that way.

"Don't worry about it," Mallorn said. "We can't all be clever."

The next day, they held a meeting with Franklin Ferris to decide how Astronomy would present themselves to the scene. Rumors had already been circulating about the new band, and many people were looking forward to their debut. A full-page story had already appeared in the *NMT*, and Ron Peel's show on the BBC wanted to set up a radio session. A week of solid jamming had led to a fine new set of seven numbers. Hastings had written the lyrics, but for the sake of democracy, the vocals were divided between himself, Marty, and Teresa. They all seemed to possess adequate voices, although none could provide the incandescent charisma that Guy had brought to The Spheres. The sound of the new group was harder-edged than that of the old band, mostly due to the drumming style of Basil Baker, who never seemed to let up.

Hastings' lyrics were no longer idealistic, wistful, and tinged with fantasy; his experiences in the past month had shattered any illusions that a peaceful hippie revolution was underway or could ever really be successful. Most of the world was still dead-set against them, and a widespread movement was not forthcoming, especially since the supposedly mind-freeing drug culture had been controlled and subsumed by big business. They would forever be preaching to the converted or controlled and packaged as product by corporations.

A contract was signed with the proprietor of Groovy Melon Records, Ezekiel "Shorty" Mackintosh, for a forty percent royalty on gross revenues. His distribution was not the best, but even if they sold a quarter of the albums and singles they were used to selling, they would still make more money than they had with Aureola. An album would be due in no more than two months' time.

Ferris started a postering campaign for the band's first gig, to be at the UFO on Tottenham Court Road. The posters competed for space on Central London's streetlamp poles with Mallorn's "wanted" poster asking for information about Ramón Rosas. Mallorn had taken on a private investigator, but in typical fashion, he had actually hired a psychic medium who was apparently wandering the streets of the city, arms outstretched, trying to detect Rosas' aura as he walked. Several people had spotted this bizarre figure on the Embankment by Blackfriars Bridge, seemingly involved in deep conversation with the Thames and making rude gestures at the infrequent passing trains. Hastings did not expect any results from that area, but his lust for revenge, once recently all-consuming, was fading fast in the glow of his excitement about the new band. He did, however, as a precaution, keep his weapon, the deadly hair dryer, on him at all times. In the back of his mind, he knew whoever had wanted him dead would not give up so easily after just one attempt.

A month and a week after that fateful night in New York, Marty Sharpe-Thornton and Simon Hastings had set themselves back up again in their hometown and were ready to continue their career, a little more world-weary but still in fighting shape. Ferris proved to be just as energetic a manager as Billy Prestwick had been, perhaps even more so. The whole scene was buzzing about the gigs that Astronomy had planned, a series of three shows over three weeks that would culminate in the Groovy Melon launch party at the UFO, where The Flying Teapots and Astronomy would concurrently release their new LPs. The third act for the bill would be The Fairport Convention, a new band that had stunned the scene with their daring fusion of traditional folk music and rock and roll. It would be an exciting time.

*

The night before the band's first gig at UFO, the band members invited some of their friends over to the house for a party they considered a wake finally to send Guy's spirit off to wherever its final destination might be (into the body of a dolphin or ancient sea turtle, Mallorn said) in a way that he would have approved of: with gaiety and conversation. Somehow, your noble scribe seems to have been excluded from this occasion, but I digress once more.

It was a chilly night. Cold rain and wet snow were lashing through the streets, borne on a stiff north wind, but inside the house it was warm and mellow. Teresa had turned off all the electric lights, which only worked sporadically anyway, and had lit several oil lamps and candles.

There were fifty or sixty people crowded into the small two-bedroom house (Basil Baker had been sleeping on a sofa in the rehearsal room; Hastings/Teresa and Marty took the bedrooms) for the party. Some were talking and passing around joints, and some were jamming in small groups with acoustic guitars. Franklin Ferris was holding court about the music business with a rapt circle around him. Mallorn was entertaining in the main parlor, dominating the conversation as always.

"Simon, your view of humanity is far too bleak. I've no quarrel with negative philosophies, but you have your own life to consider. We don't want you to develop an ulcer. You're full of hate, understandably, but you were getting there long before Guy died."

"He's got a point, Simie." Teresa sat with her arm draped across Hastings' shoulders.

He scowled. "You're one to talk. And don't call me Simie. It's hard not to feel bleak about bloody humanity. I don't believe in false optimism. Look at the scum that leads our society. When they're not starting wars and turning a blind eye to our Empire's economic exploitation of poor countries, they're abusing their own people and the natural world. People go around with empty dreams that they can't even describe to themselves. They think that having a certain amount of money and prestige, things that are only important to our species of arrogant, hairless monkey and to absolutely nothing bloody else, will lead them to some kind of nirvana. But it's all for nothing. It's frustrating to think of the potential that we have, which will never be realized. It makes me ashamed to be human."

Teresa sighed.

Mallorn pointed a bony appendage at him. "But that's just it, Simon. It *is* all for nothing. Or a great big mysterious something. That can be a source of comfort to you, in a strange way. When all's said and done, every act, for good or ill, done by men and women, is forgotten and gone. The universe is too great to pay attention to the pitiful deeds of one small species of limited ability and imagination, inhabiting one miniature speck of dust. That is my source of optimism. We're part of something too great even to comprehend. Our minds, even the most powerful ones, can't even begin to conceive of the greater reality that surrounds us. We just have to try, well, to be the best we can."

Teresa sighed louder. They ignored her.

"That's little comfort when you have to deal with small-minded idiots every day and see what they do to the planet and to each other. This state of mind you recommend is impossible to maintain — I strongly doubt you're anywhere near it yourself."

Teresa just stalked off.

"Damn straight," Marty muttered. "Humanity is a cancer that consumes itself and everything around it. Nothing cute about that." He was carefully unwrapping a single-serving needleful of Kässel's popular nonaddictive heroin substitute.

"Look," Mallorn said with a look of priestly benevolence, "I admit that I get annoyed too — well, more than annoyed. But you have to try to gain some perspective is all I'm saying. I've been fortunate to have been born with a brain with advanced cognitive abilities. As have all of you. Or most of you. I may not be the most brilliant chap on the planet, but I've got a good nut. I perceive more than the average person, I suppose, either that or the average person isn't capable of proper comprehension due to the circumstances of their lives and education. We just need to try to find a way to draw them out, to find the best in them. They're not any different to us in their souls. These dreams that they think will be satisfied by money, power, romantic love, and sex, they're just symptoms of a greater need. We're fortunate that we're closer to the answer than they are, but it's always helpful to remember that we're not really that much closer to understanding ourselves."

Teresa had slipped back with drink in hand. "Well, it doesn't make violence and suffering any easier to watch, does it? What are we supposed to do about these things? Try to send out good vibes through the tops of our heads? Half the fucking planet lives in poverty to serve this empire's need for luxury, and the situation shows no sign of improving. People's ignorance is not an excuse! This mystical shit's all very well for party talk, but people with a conscience have to do something to improve the lives they see around them, no matter what it takes."

"Amen, sister," Steve Brock chimed in. His gangly frame was stretched out full-length on the floor in the middle of their circle. His cuts and scratches had mostly healed, but he had a recently acquired black eye from taking on a seven-foot skinhead he had seen kicking a cat.

Mallorn now looked mildly upset. "I'm not promoting indifference to suffering. You're deliberately misunderstanding me. I'm just saying that approaching things with a clear mind will keep you happier, more fit to help, and better prepare you. Our music must not just be an expression of anger and bitterness but instead must inspire people to better themselves. I think we can all agree on that."

Teresa ignored him and launched into her favorite topic. "Now, Engels said that what the proletariat needs is leaders who—"

The company was mercifully saved from yet another Engelist rant by the sound of the front door banging open. It continued to clatter in the wind as a ragged figure stepped in and stood dripping puddles on the floor while it blinked its eyes in the light. It was a tall man with a round face and long, stringy hair, wearing a shredded motorcycle jacket and tight blue jeans. They stared at him in shock.

"Bloody hell, it's Rick Farren!" Mo Wyatt exclaimed, nearly dropping a hunk of Stilton on Brock's head. Brock sat up abruptly.

"Well, fuck me! We've been looking all over for you, mate!"

Farren wearily closed the door behind him, stripped off his jacket, and collapsed on the floor beside Brock. "I heard there was a party here tonight. You know I never miss one, boys." He was renowned for his swagger.

"Where the hell have you been, you bastard? We looked all over the fucking city for you," Brock said, clapping Farren on the back.

"Speaking of revolutionaries, eh?" Mallorn said to Teresa with a wink.

Farren paused a moment to be introduced to her and to rakishly kiss her hand, then got up and struck a dramatic pose. "Ah, what an ordeal I've been through, my friends. On the run from the agents of our fascist government. Shot at, tear-gassed, you name it! I've barely escaped with my life. I haven't picked up a guitar in months."

"That's what happens when you choose violent methods to express your dissatisfaction," Mallorn said.

"Shut up, Daevid, you old windbag," Farren growled, not without affection. "By the way, Moorhen, are you taking this down?"

Sure enough, Mort Moorhen was sitting quietly in a corner, scribbling down the conversation with a can of bitter positioned in front of him.

"It'll be a good idea for a story. Just don't use me real name. Well, it was like this. I'd just finished a fun little job where I blew up that statue of the ruddy queen and pony in Green Park, and I thought I'd gotten away scot-free. I went down to my hide-out in the sewer to cool it for a few days, but then we had that heavy rainfall, and the water level rose to the point where I was driven out into the open. I ran over to a friend's house, and he hid me in his attic. It turns out that the coppers had been visiting all my anarchist friends — somebody ratted me out, and not just about this job, but about a lot of past ones, too." His brow clouded over. "When I find out who, they're *really* going to have something to put me in jail for."

"Who would rat Rick out?" Hastings said thoughtfully. No one knew anyone who would.

"I don't know either, but I'd had a lot of interesting dealings with a lot of people in the period just before that. There were some rich Germans who claimed to be anarchists, and they wanted me to come and work with them. I told those wankers to get stuffed. There were a few bands I gigged with, a few parties I went to.

Sometimes I run my mouth off too much after a couple of beers. Everybody in the fucking country seems to know who I am now. So I decided to lay real low for a while. But one day, while I'm in that friend's attic, the pigs come again to harass him — gave him a mild concussion, actually. So I told him I was leaving, because there was no way I was going to put him in danger. They let those bastards carry guns."

"Why didn't you come to me, you stupid shit?" Brock roared. "They'd never take me alive!"

"I'm getting to it, damn you. I decided that I couldn't risk being seen by anyone, or of putting the police on to any of my pals, so I went to the East End."

Parts of the East End had become so decrepit in the 1960s that most inhabitants simply moved away, leaving a crumbling ghost town — even St. Paul's had fallen into disrepair. Underground service to the area had stopped, and increased suburbanization of the middle classes kept it largely empty.

"I thought no one would ever find me there. I moved into an abandoned old house in Mile End, the worst part of town, which still had some furniture and an old bed. There were lots of other people hiding out in the area, far worse people than me, that's for sure: rapists, murderers, psychopaths, you name it. It was depressing. I went out by night to a small shop for food while I still had money. I don't know how that shop manages to stay open. I never saw anyone in there but the old French fellow who runs it. After a while, even he started looking at me funny, so I had to find food other ways. You don't want to hear those details." He sat down again and wearily ran a hand through his greasy hair.

"It was rough, I can tell you, living like a scavenging animal in that wasteland. Even for me. I wouldn't recommend it. But it came to an end soon enough. Either someone saw me and recognized me, or more likely one of the sleazy types living around me was a copper's plant. I'll never know, but I woke up one night to find the house surrounded by police cars and spotlights. They had a megaphone, and they told me if I came out and surrendered, they wouldn't shoot me. The fuckers! No one's ever been physically hurt by anything I've done, and they wanted to shoot me. Well, I wasn't going to stand for that. They tear-gassed the place when I told them to fuck off, and then they took a couple of shots at the windows. I shot back, though I hate bloody guns. After a couple of days cooped up like that, I got pissed off and decided to fool the motherfuckers, like I've done so many times before. I dug through the cellar wall, which was crumbling, into the sewers, my home away from home, and escaped. I got away to Kent, where I lived under a hedge and ate blackberries for a couple of weeks. When fall came, I snuck back into town to my little hideout again. Just today, I was driven out by this damned rain again, and I ran into Steve Took, who told me that everyone had been looking for me to give me some kind of important news — but I already heard about Guy.

"Steve said there was a party going on here, so I came by for some nosh and booze, and to find out why the hell all of you were trying so hard to find me. And you didn't do a very good job, I must fucking say. So what's up?"

Hastings laughed. "We don't usually go poking around the sewers, you know. There's alligators down there, somebody told me. We're glad to see you in one piece, but not on account of the coppers. There's something even more sinister going on. You haven't by chance seen Ed Barrett, have you?" He led Farren off to the kitchen to fill him in over some kale dip and a smoke.

Mallorn leaned back in his chair. "This certainly is fortunate. Now we just have to find Ed."

Marty looked at him sharply. "And what if we do? What if he's still alive? That won't end it. There's still a professional assassin out there looking to kill us. I'm not going to recommend that we hide out or anything. I'm just hoping that this bloke doesn't become desperate to carry out his commission in any way possible. I don't want to lose anyone else."

A silence fell over the group.

"The Uncaring Mother" by Hunter L. Burlington,
from *Life/Death and other Short Stories*
(Dilettante Press, 1965)

If
In a flash
The air was chilled
The juice was squeezed from our lemon sun
The nearest candle stars blown out
Would the universe cry in pain?
Would it cry as a mother torn by loss?
Would she weep for us?
The children of her fecund womb
Our lives plucked like fruit from the bough
Left to rot on barren ground

No
She has no need for us now
She has countless children

SEVENTEEN

The next day, the band held its last rehearsal for the gig. They played for two hours, going over the contents of the set twice to make sure they would at least be competent. As they played, Hastings reflected on his discussion with Mallorn the night before. Was he really comfortable with the aggressive cast of new lyrics in songs like "The Misanthrope"?

If the population grows
And the world is clearly finite
Where did all these apes come from?
I know isn't right
You say I'm no better than you
You say we're all born the same
But good is good and bad is bad
And I know who to blame!

Of course, that was one of the few that could possibly been seen as advocating violence, which had not been his intent in writing it — at least, he didn't think so. It was more of a satire, a form of humor that most people never seemed to understand. The other sets of lyrics were simply less abstract than his lyrics had been before, and much more negative or resigned in tone, like the song he was most proud of amongst the batch, "Further Up, Further In":

You stumble through the streets
Drenched in rain
The shock resounds, explodes in your brain

Somewhere far away
The sun is setting fast
Some time years away
You think about the past

Sung with Teresa's breathy voice accompanying, the song was as chillingly beautiful as anything he had written with Guy. Ferris wanted to release it as a single from the album they were due to begin recording. The forthcoming record had already inspired a great deal of interest due to his tireless promotion, and he had more than earned his percentage of the door from the upcoming gig.

As the afternoon wore on and everyone else took naps, Hastings lay awake. He was starting to feel nervous. He hadn't played in front of a crowd since the night of his horrendous acid trip, and he knew that a great deal would be expected of him. The wild (but mostly true) rumors that were circulating about how Guy Calvert had been assassinated to prevent him spreading his anarchic message meant that the rise of Astronomy from the ashes of The Spheres would be an occasion of grave symbolism. They would have to give it their all.

After tossing and turning for a couple of hours, he deemed his attempt to sleep useless and rose, slowly so as not to wake Teresa, who was snoring beside him. He fetched himself a sandwich from the refrigerator and went over to the front window. Looking out, he was startled. Was that a shadow slipping into a doorway on the other side of the street? He stared but saw nothing but blowing leaves. Shivering, he wondered again how long he would have to live as a marked man.

The sky was still thickly overcast, but now the clouds possessed a nasty greenish tint. It was almost dark as night. Hastings had seen clouds like these when the band had taken a holiday to the southern Virginias, close to the Spanish Zone. There, it usually meant a severe storm, even a tornado, could be imminent. It seemed like a disturbing portent of evil to come.

He sighed and picked up his brand-new orange Gibson, which he had just got back from being set up. Tentatively, he began to pick out the chords of an old Spheres tune from the first album, another of his many musings on the cycle of life and death. He inadvertently slowed the tune down to a funereal dirge pace, and his voice fell muffled in the room's dusty confines.

We depend on one another
So the wisdom goes
But have you ever wondered why
It's so easy to forget someone
When they're gone?

A face you've known all your life
A voice you loved in time
Still haunts your brightest dreams
But you awake to find it slipped away
When they're gone

And when at last I pass away
My voice soon lost forever
Lay me down in an open field
Whisper my name to the driving wind
And let me go

For the first time since his friend's death, he felt a real weeping fit coming on, and he didn't fight it. Where had Guy gone? Where had his mother gone? And where would he, Simon Hastings, at the end of a life wracked by cynicism and doubt, go when his turn came? Why could he not reconcile himself to living in the darkness of the world, eternally damned to know nothing was ever certain, lost in a vacuum where our only realities were the myths we created to comfort ourselves?

Hearing a sound, he saw Teresa approaching him from across the room. She also had tears in her eyes. She sat down and put her arms around him as the darkness deepened another shade.

*

At eleven thirty, Hastings stood beside the stage, watching openers the Sonic Assassins as they closed their set, as always, with their most popular number, "Brainbox Pollution." The Assassins sound, which they called "space-rock," was driven, like The Spheres' had been, by an innovative use of modern electronics and synthesizers, in addition to traditional rock n' roll instrumentation. Their songs were much heavier and simpler in structure, almost primitive-sounding, and their aim seemed more to overwhelm the audience with the sheer size of their sound rather than soothe and cajole them. Their latest album, *The Space Ritual*, was somewhere in the Imperial Top Twenty at the time. Hastings considered them to be most enlightening musical experience going, but a little hard on the ears after an hour.

Listening to his friends' music had set him more at ease, and now, after a couple of joints and a vial of Alpine Mist (a stimulant and another Kässel Pharma product), he now felt much more himself, whoever that might be. It would be his first performance as a lead vocalist. Teresa and Marty were engaged in a cheerful argument about current men's fashion styles, yelling in each other's ears over the noise, and they seemed to be perfectly calm. Only Basil Baker looked nervous. He was banging his sticks on a wooden tabletop, and although it wasn't audible over the roar of the Assassins' "oscillators," the sight of it was threatening to damage Hastings' newfound calm.

He walked over to the drummer, who had never been in a real band before and whose emaciated-looking face was sweating profusely, and laid a hand on his shoulder. "Don't worry, lad," he yelled into the young man's ear. "We know you're good enough.

We wouldn't have brought you in otherwise."

Basil broke into a grin and stopped pounding. "Thanks," he mouthed.

The final cacophony of "Brainbox Pollution" ended suddenly, degenerating into a chorus of raucous shouts and cursing.

"—I wear a little mascara myself, but not enough for the chaps to — oh…" Marty's voice blared into the split second of silence before the stunned audience could recover enough from the sonic attack to applaud. "Er — well, time to play, eh?" He walked over to his bass stand, hissing at Hastings as he went by. "If you tell anyone I said that, I'll kill you." He picked up the bass, pulled his aviator's goggles over his eyes, and waved toward the short staircase leading to the stage. "Those about to die salute you!"

The Sonic Assassins came piling down the stairs as he spoke, their faces lit by broad grins. Stick Turner's bearded face was red from nonstop puffing into his saxophone.

"Warmed 'em up a bit for you, lads," he rasped, collapsing on a table.

Brock shook Hastings' hand. "We're going out front to watch, old son. Do the Grove proud tonight."

As they stepped out onto the stage, they were greeted by a roar from the thousand-strong attendees. Hastings had to smile, but he wasted no time strapping on his Gibson and launching into the opening chords of "The Misanthrope's Blues," a simple boogie-style riff. The drums and bass kicked in with a thump. As always, the surge of intoxicating electricity almost threatened to freeze him to the spot. Controlling his excitement, he managed to start singing the first verse on key:

Here comes the arrogant ape
Mother Nature's fatal mistake
Each group wants the others dead
Atrocities they love to make
They strip the earth of all that's good

Always too blind to see
Their evil sets my blood to boil
So I'll let this fire consume me

This tribute to the misanthropic anarchy of Rick Farren and his ilk was something of a dangerous artistic move for a new group. There was little doubt that the VBC would ban the song if it were ever released as a single, which was why Franklin, whose mind was still focused on the business, was opposed to it being performed at all. Flower Power was in style, and the public, he claimed, had no time for cynical dismissals of the entire human species and its purpose. Hastings didn't care; he was determined to finally express the negativity he felt about the world in more direct terms.

This crowd, at any rate, seemed responsive. In fact, it was only on rare occasions like this that he felt such intensity in a room. The trancelike expressions he usually saw on the faces of the dancers had changed to hard, set looks of comprehension. These people were well aware of how radically their view of life differed from that of the society in which they were forced to live. Their dance and his music were statements that individual lives, beauty, and fellowship still lived on, despite the endless pursuit of material gain and power that swirled around them.

As he went into his solo, his spine twisted into an unnatural shape by the strength of the vibe in the hall, he could feel the vibrations of Marty's bass improvising an unplanned solo along with his and shaking the floor. The drumming was relentless, and Teresa's organ drifted over the top of the mix like a fog over a tempestuous sea. There was no doubt about it, this band could be the most fulfilling thing that ever happened to him. He shot her a smile as he wound up his solo.

Glancing back into the audience, he felt a sudden shock. Had he caught a glimpse of Ramón Rosas in the audience? He stared again at the spot as he sang but saw nothing. Rosas was starting to haunt every glance from the corner of his eyes. Not wanting to lose his concentration, he put that evil out of his mind as the song ended. This was no time to be morbid.

The cheers of the crowd seemed louder than the band had been in the first song. They were engulfed in the adulation to the point where the emotion was almost too much. Hastings felt tears pricking at his eyes, and, looking over at Marty, he saw matching diamonds glittering in his. Then Basil counted in their second song, "Further Up, Further In," which featured a repetitive and hypnotic rhythm part. Basil's pattern on the snare and toms was the backdrop across which Marty spattered notes from his bass, and Hastings used his array of guitar effects to the fullest, casually floating long, sustained chords drenched in reverb into the mix. Teresa's voice, which she deployed in her first gig without a trace of nerves, was beautiful. Hastings allowed her to start the verses alone and joined in with harmonies (something The Spheres hadn't paid much attention to) on the chorus:

Somewhere ahead, you foretell your end
Stars as they fall,
Lead you further up and further in

And so the set went on, the audience's enthusiasm mounting with each piece and cresting during the second encore, which was a souped-up version of the old Spheres song "Judgment Day," the song Guy had been singing when he met his demise. This was a symbolic act that would not be wasted on the press and which pointedly began a new era in Hastings' career. Who knows what promise Guy might have fulfilled if he lived? The ghosts of Guy Calvert, Hunter Burlington, Miguel Gonzalez, and the shadow of Ramón Rosas were temporarily banished, along with Billy Prestwick, Electron Z, the Hammer, and all the rest of the people left behind in Virginia that he might never see again.

I was in town for this gig (it was considered too important to miss), and I still regard it as the single most transcendent rock show I have ever attended. I have never seen a group of musicians and an audience meld like Astronomy did with the crowd at UFO that night. I myself had tears in my jaded eyes as the last majestic chords of "Judgment Day" echoed from the walls of a room that was suddenly, strangely, silent in an unplanned moment of respect. Then the place exploded with ricocheting cheers and screams until we were all deafened.

The members of the band were drenched in sweat as, after shaking hands with and hugging the front row of the audience, they regretfully left the stage. They plainly did not want to leave, and we did not want them to go.

Their friends were waiting backstage. Bottles were cracked and vials were opened. Basil Baker's eyes showed he was still far away as he toweled off his drenched hair. Marty embraced Hastings as they stood together in the center of the room.

"Well, we've done it, eh?"

"We've *done* it, you bastard! I've never been so relieved."

Teresa walked over to the table in the corner and stat down heavily on the rickety wooden chair. She idly scooped up a piece of notepaper that had floated to the floor during the excitement.

Hastings and Marty were already talking about planning a full tour of the island and possibly the intact and relatively radiation-free zones of Europe when she interrupted.

"Uh, Simon?"

"Yes, dearie?"

"I think you better look at this." Her face was taut as she handed him the soiled scrap of paper.

Hastings' jaw dropped as he read. "Shit."

"What! What?" Marty grabbed the paper. It contained one line of typed text: *Dear Simon: I've left a surprise for you at your home. I'm sorry. Ed.*

"Ed? What the hell? Is this a joke?"

Hastings' face was grim as he rummaged in his gig bag for his gun. "Ed's in trouble. He wouldn't have written a note like this. I wouldn't be surprised if it's something to do with our goddamned friend the assassin."

"It says home. Does that mean our home?"

"We'd better go see. I'm expecting the worst. Damn us! We should have found him."

Marty and Hastings quickly corralled Steve Brock to give them a ride to Ladbroke Grove in the Sonic Assassins' battered old van. It was another night of wind and freezing rain as the threatened storm hit furiously. Hastings shivered in the back seat as he pondered what could have been done to Ed Barrett. Any way you looked at it, it wasn't good. *I'm sorry.*

When they pulled up in front of the house, they could see through the rain that the front door was open, and a light was on in the parlor. Once again, the door was blowing violently in the gusts. Hastings jumped out first and ran to the entrance, his weapon in hand in his pocket. When he reached it, he fell back, his face twisted. Marty rushed by him.

"No!"

Ed Barrett was sitting in a chair, staring glassily at them. His black, curly hair was wet, as were his clothes, as if he had been carried or dragged through the rain. A long scratch disfigured the muddy side of his face, on which there was a dull, emotionless expression. Brock walked cautiously up to him.

"Ed? Can you hear me?" He waved his hand in front of Ed's face, but there was no change.

"He's dead." Hastings still stood by the door, leaning on the frame. A great ennui had fallen over him. "Look at him. Don't bother touching him. He's bloody well dead."

EIGHTEEN

The scene in the house was nightmarishly familiar. Two bobbies had shown up, friendly chaps on the surface but just as disbelieving as their New York counterparts. An ambulance had also come, which was at least an improvement.

The paramedics examined Ed's body then shook their heads. "Looks like massive toxic shock," said one. She held up an empty package with the Colombian Cartels logo on it. "Maybe mixed some homebrew product with this, which is a safe product, as long as you follow the directions. We see this sort of thing all the time."

She looked disdainfully around the room, as if expecting to see dirty drug-taking paraphernalia littered everywhere. Hastings actually kept the room painstakingly well organized. He bit back an angry retort and spoke to the police officers instead.

"Listen, Constables..."

"DC MacSweeney."

"DC Khan."

The two clean-cut officers looked exactly the same in every regard, with the same short cut under their caps, not a hair out of place, clean-shaven and buttoned-up. They looked like they belonged in the army, not the constabulary.

"I'd like to have a word with you about this matter."

"Certainly, sir," DC Khan said. "But this appears to be a clear-cut case. The message you've shown us looks like an obvious suicide note."

"But why would it show up at a gig I was playing? Did his ghost fly over and put it there?"

Khan sighed. "It could have been placed there before, sir."

"Anyway, that's not the point I wanted to raise." Hastings

told them briefly about the New York murders and some of his subsequent experiences. Khan took sparse notes in a small notebook, shaking his head in disbelief.

When he had finished, MacSweeney raised an eyebrow. "You really expect us to believe this?"

"Take a look for yourself! You'll find that the circumstances of Guy Calvert and Hunter Burlington's deaths were very similar. You'll also find out that I was indeed in Colombia for the period I've stated."

"Hmm. Of course, we'll try to check these things out. You seem like a level-headed enough fellow for someone of your sort, Mr. Hastings, but as a straight-living teetotaler, I have to wonder whether you dreamed all this up during some kind of trip."

"Listen, you—"

"Ah-ah, none of that, sir! None of that!" MacSweeney seemed to be enjoying himself. Even Khan rolled his eyes a little at his colleague's self-righteous tone.

Marty was arguing with the paramedic, and Brock had retreated outside. He stood on the porch, smoking ferociously, his brows knitted.

"Listen, sir," MacSweeney said, puffed up, adjusting the peak of his cap and twirling his baton, "I've already investigated three stabbings and one shooting tonight. The London Police Force investigates any suspicious deaths in the metropolitan area with equal thoroughness, regardless of economic standing, race, or ... hair length. This case will be no exception. We will contact the New York police and compare the cases. But since you have no real evidence of foul play here to back up your word—"

"Why don't you contact the Colombian authorities? I spoke to the bloody minister of the environment!"

The officers exchanged looks that made plain their agreement on Hastings' mental state. "Ahem, well, Mr. Hastings, yes, absolutely, we'll have someone talk to th ... um ... Colombian authorities and the consulate there. Absolutely. Now," Khan said officiously, seeing the paramedics removing Ed's body. "I believe we've taken all of your statements. I'm sorry about your friend. Good evening."

Hastings didn't answer, just stared after the officers as they briskly exited. Brock stuck out a leg to try to trip MacSweeney as he descended the porch stairs, but the officer nimbly leapt over his leg and disappeared into the heavily armored police car without so much as a backward glance.

Hastings couldn't believe what had happened. It was obvious that Rosas had sent him a message, and the message was: *You're next.* He could now see that their unspoken hope Rosas would simply give up on fulfilling his task had been feeble. This man was a professional thug who probably enjoyed his work a great deal. He had engineered the murders to appear as overdoses or suicides, knowing full well what the police would fall for it without question. But if there were no authorities to appeal to, and the killer was as crafty as he seemed, how could they ever hope to defend themselves?

*

Another hasty conference was called the next day, this time in the front room of the band's house. Hastings meant business, and he kept a tight rein on the proceedings. All of the same people were there (with the additions of Ferris, Baker, and Rick Farren, the latter having reluctantly agreed to briefly join them from his sewer dwelling), but the adventurous atmosphere and black humor of their previous meeting was replaced by a gloomy pall that matched the omnipresent cloud of tobacco smoke.

"All right." Hastings cast his gaze over the assembly. "Obviously, we're dealing with a crisis. There's a hired killer running around, and no less than four of us are still on his list. Who knows whether he might go for some bonus pay and knock off some more?" Steve Brock's face blanched a little. "We all know that the authorities won't help us, here or anywhere. What shall we do?" He brandished a copy of the day's paper, which contained a tiny news item.

Popular Singer Found Dead
LONDON (Reuters) Singer Ed Barrett, formerly with psychedelic pop band "The Peuce Frank," was found dead of an apparent overdose at a friend's house. Police contacts said that Barrett had a history of illegal substance addiction and that an investigation would not be forthcoming. There is also some unconfirmed rumor of a suicide note. The Minister of Justice was quoted as saying that this "should be warning to those unfortunate thrill-seekers who are tempted to go beyond the Empire's already lax laws concerning recreational pharmaceuticals into the shady world of the underground drug trade."

"Look," Farren said, "this arse is having no problem tracking us down, is he? While we sit here like cowards shaking in our boots. It's time we made him run."

"But how?" Daevid Mallorn was as relaxed as ever, lounging in a long purple robe with matching slippers.

"Well, he's been hired to find us, hasn't he? It's time to hire someone just as nasty to find *him*, and I don't mean some hippie sage or mage or whatever crazy old Mallorn over there tried to hire. What happened to your pal, eh? Was he absorbed back into the ether? Did some little green teapot men come down and take him away?" He leered over at Mallorn, who showed his offense only through a slight frown.

Hastings rubbed his chin. "Even though he's obviously trying to pick a fight, Farren may be making a valid point. I realized a long time ago that if ever want to beat this bastard, we'll need to beat him at his own game. I just wouldn't admit it to myself. This means that if we have to play dirty, that's what we'll do. And we'll have to leave our qualms behind."

"Count me out of hiring any hit men," Mallorn said. "I won't try to stop you, but I'd rather be killed myself than participate in something like that."

"Wimp," Farren muttered under his breath.

"Caveman," Mallorn responded.

Hastings shrugged. "Suit yourself. Just remember that he's after you too, and if he can't get you the crafty way, he may resort to direct violence."

"Yes, Daeve, stay out of dark alleys for a while." Marty smiled. "We don't want to be attending your memorial. Stay home and brew up some good vibes for us."

"That I can do," said Mallorn.

"So, Rick, I assume you have someone in mind?"

Farren's gaze was shifty. "I might know someone for the job. But if he completes the assignment, it might cost us a few quid."

"Whatever it takes, man," Marty said. "This situation's a real downer." He wasn't pleased with the limitations being a marked man was putting on his free-swinging lifestyle.

"Well, then. I'll report back to you when I've confirmed my ... friend's ... participation." Farren's eyes swept the room darkly. "And this doesn't leave this room. Any squealing and we could be in serious trouble."

Mo Wyatt, who had been quietly smoking a hash pipe, suddenly let out a bitter laugh. "This becomes more outlandish by the second. A bunch of pacifists taking out a hit on someone most of us haven't even seen."

"No, it's not funny, Mo. Not funny at all." Hastings strode stiffly from the room, the now-familiar weight of tragedy beating down on his shoulders.

*

The hit man hired by Farren turned out to be no less than one of the feared Brennan Boys, Seamus to be exact. Hastings' meeting with the burly Irishman sent chills down his spine. Seamus Brennan's heavy, ruddy face registered no expression at all as he agreed to his assignment and his fee, but his eyes, which were a bizarre shade of purply blue that clashed with his vulgar, plain face and crew cut, lit up with unmistakable pleasure in anticipation of the chase and the kill. He calmly informed Hastings that he was familiar with seven different varieties of choke hold, a few karate moves, and was a crack shot with both pistol and throwing knife. How he came to learn those things, Hastings did not inquire. It was rumored that Seamus had once, as revenge in a dispute over a girl, beaten a neighbor to death back home in County Kerry.

Rick explained that Brennan wasn't exactly a pal; he had met him a few years back at Cheeky Murphy's Pub in Clapham through a mutual acquaintance, Ronny Gallagher the blues guitarist, and though he didn't approve of organized crime as a rule (it was, like capitalism, a parasite that fed on the weakness of the proletariat), they had occasionally been useful to one another. Hastings was forced to see his wisdom when he said, "If you want to kill a snake, you don't enlist a bleedin' hedgehog. You get a man with an axe." The advance was steep, but considering that they had no idea of the current whereabouts of the Irish killer's target, it seemed reasonable.

But despite the hiring of Seamus Brennan, another uneventful fortnight passed. The band continued to rehearse and record. The sessions went well, with Marty and Hastings coproducing at cavernous Opiate Sound Studios in Soho. They took their time, coming up with innovative new sounds and processing techniques that they were sure no one had committed to vinyl before. The only setback was Baker's sudden attack of nerves at facing the recording environment. The moment the "record" button was pushed, he would drop a stick, knock over a cymbal stand, or start a song wildly off rhythm. Hastings well remembered how nervous he had been when he, Guy, and Marty had made their first recordings in his parents' basement and how thrilled he had been when he first heard his guitar played back to him over the speakers, so he tried to have patience.

Two weeks after the meeting, the band played its second gig, this time at the more restrained venue of The Royal Edward Auditorium, across the river in Battersea near the massive new nuclear power station. This old theater was now primarily a rock and roll venue, although substance consumption was banned within its decaying walls, and music hall revues were sometimes still held there for the benefit of the older set.

It retained something of its nineteenth-century elegance, but it had fallen into some disrepair; someone had gone right through one of the rotting floors of the former royal boxes earlier that year. They Wylde Flowers were the openers and had brought a four-piece horn section. Hastings had taken the opportunity provided by playing in a slightly more posh, seated venue to invite his father and brother, partially to get them on speaking terms again, if only through their mutual disdain for his profession, and partly because of a childish need, which he barely admitted to himself, for the approval of his family. Even Henry.

Surprisingly, both his father and brother agreed to come. Although the sight of Seamus Brennan skulking around the hallways and through the audience in a sharp suit and a flat cap set him a bit on edge, he did his best to put his heart and soul into the performance for the benefit of the packed house. Word of the band's prowess had spread quickly around town, aided by a live performance on Radio Catherine, the East End pirate station. After the show, his father said the music was "all right, I suppose, a bit loud," and added that it wasn't very ladylike for Teresa to be playing in a rock band and showing most of her shins. He had nonetheless given Hastings a pat on the back.

Henry didn't mention the show at all; he had just attained a new position, Head of Marketing and Promotion for KässelPharma UK. The company had been expanding with branch plants in many countries as it made a push for market dominance. Henry claimed he had never touched pharmaceuticals, saying they clouded a fellow's decision-making abilities, but he was a man of absolutely no scruples where a fat salary was concerned. As the family members enjoyed some tea at a local late-night café, he had spent about an hour crowing about what he would do with his enormous paychecks, while his father dozed off and Teresa and Simon stared glassily at the small drifts of dirty snow gathered under the streetlamps.

Everyone had kept their eyes peeled during the course of the evening, but there was no sign of Ramón Rosas.

About a week later, as they were finishing the mixing of the record and were almost ready to pass the master tapes on to Groovy Melon Records, they received a report from Brennan that he had tailed a man matching Rosas' description for several blocks the previous night. The man was himself following a very drunk Rick Farren, whom Brennan had decided to survey for the day, to his hideout from Scruffy Flaherty's, where Farren spent the night drinking with his anarchist friends. There had been another mild snowstorm at the time, and Brennan lost sight of the man around a corner. When he reached the manhole cover, he had found Farren enjoying some sausages roasted on a stick over a small fire in the hideout, but no trace of the Colombian, not even footprints. Nonetheless, much to Farren's dismay, Brennan had informed him that his hiding place was most likely compromised and that he had better find a new one. Farren then moved into Steve Brock's house.

A few days later, Brennan disappeared without a trace.

Astronomy

Beyond the Sky (Groovy Melon Records)

Starred review in *New Musical Tribune*, December 15, 1968

by Rodney Blair

After the tragic death of Guy Calvert this fall, many wondered if we had heard the last of the members of his previous band, The Spheres, and the songwriting team of Simon Hastings and Martin Sharpe-Thornton. I am pleased to announce their return with this wonderful independent release, which, with all due respect to my late friend, I was surprised to find an advancement over anything the prior band recorded. If anything, it charts the direction Calvert himself might have taken had he lived. They have recruited a powerhouse drummer whose rhythmic abilities far outstrip those of Ed "The Hammer" Bentham, now a member of reviled Virginian primitive rock combo The Muttonchop Killers. The sound effects and brilliant instrumental work for which The Spheres were justly renowned have been preserved by the magnificent find of first-time band member Teresa Cappadocia. The tragedy that members have suffered has influenced the sound as well as the tenor of the lyrics. "The Misanthrope's Blues" is a hard-edged satire of human folly, but the new sonic toughness also carries over into the more typical Hastings mysticism on numbers such as "Further Up, Further In," sung beautifully with Ms. Cappadocia, the lengthy Eastern stylings of "Kalpas," "Ashoka," and "Ring in the New Age," an eloquent condemnation of modern materialism. All clothed in the spacious psychedelic trappings of mysterious sounds, languid chord progressions, and layered harmonies.

This album is a stirring reaffirmation of the former Spheres' commitment to change, now a little wiser and less naïve, but still willing to fight the intellectual battle on behalf of their generation.

NINETEEN

Time was crawling on toward the big record release. Two weeks had gone by without any further reports from the hulking Irishman. Farren warned that the Brennan family was starting to ask questions, and someone was going to pay if Seamus didn't show up soon. He hadn't been seen at any of his favorite watering holes and had failed to report to Fiachra, the boss of the crime family, on any of the aspects of the business with which he had been entrusted.

Farren showed up one day at the band house, limping and with a bloody nose. He said that the Brennan Boys had taken him from a pub to the family compound somewhere in the north end for a "little chat." They had seemed to believe him when he said he had no idea what happened to "Little Seamus," but they'd roughed him up in case he ever got any ideas about crossing the family.

"It's unlike one of the Brennans not to report to the boss," he said glumly, holding a handkerchief to his nose. "We have to assume the worst."

"You mean he's dead?" Teresa said.

Farren shrugged. "Well, I can tell you that Seamus Brennan is one of the craftiest deviants in London. There's no way he'd just disappear like this — unless, I suppose, he's chased after your pal somewhere. But the Brennans don't like to leave the city under any circumstances; it's their natural environment."

Hastings shivered. "If Rosas isn't afraid to do away with one of the Brennan boys, then we'd better all go and hide somewhere quick."

The next day, the news they had feared appeared in the *Times*.

"Bloody hell!" Marty spat, jumping up and nearly spilling tea on himself. He had been enjoying the front-page section, clucking at the international news.

"What?"

"Read this!"

Hastings grabbed the paper. He already knew what to expect.

Underworld Figure Found Dead

Foul play ruled out in Seamus Brennan's death

Police report today the discovery of the body of notorious underworld crime henchman Seamus Brennan, of the infamous Brennan family. Police Commissioner Ronald Fotheringham told the Times this morning that Brennan's body was found in his sister's house in Clapham, where he had apparently been living. Family members detected a strange smell emanating from a locked and disused upstairs room. When they entered, they found the body upright in a state of decomposition, sitting in a chair. What Brennan was doing in that particular room will likely remain a mystery. There were no signs of trauma on the body, and the police are currently awaiting the results of the coroner's report. Despite the family's insistence that Brennan never touched either legal or illegal pharmaceuticals, Commissioner Fotheringham stated that foul play is currently being ruled out, as the family has long been suspected of being involved in the trafficking of illegal substances. Further investigation of this angle will be forthcoming.

"Christ!" Marty said. "Some street thug gets examined by the coroner, but they wouldn't touch Ed or Guy."

"Well, we know exactly what they'll find in this corpse," Hastings said. "But we also know what conclusion they'll come to. They'll just be glad to get one of the Brennans out of their hair for good, and it'll end there. How the hell did Rosas get to him?" He lit a smoke with shaking hands. "What are we into here? We'll have to go into hiding."

"And destroy our career?" Marty was incredulous. "Simon, you know how important this time is! We're about to release our first record, and if we drop out now, all the momentum will be lost."

"I know, I know." Hastings had gone into the kitchen to fetch himself a stiff whiskey, which he didn't usually drink.

"What I don't understand," Teresa said, "is why, if he's so damn good at offing people and getting away with it, he hasn't killed us all by now."

Hastings remembered his discussion with Ricardo Alvarez in Colombia. "It's obvious that Rosas is very patient, and he's probably under orders to leave no traces. If he were to be captured and he were to talk, it could be catastrophic for his employer, whoever that is. There's big money at stake here. But rest assured, he'll try to get us all. And he seems to be enjoying taunting me too."

"Well, what the fuck are we going to do?"

"Okay, let's use our heads." Hastings got up and paced. "Marty here, in his wisdom, has expressed that he'd rather die than take a break and disappear to throw a ruthless assassin off our scent. Very well." He paused. "Here's what we'll do. We're going to put on a tour together, our band, The Flying Teapots, and The Wylde Flowers. This will cover all the people remaining on the hit list, although who's to say Rosas might not kill a few extra for fun? Or he might follow us, but that's the risk of insisting on being in the public eye. We'll hide Farren in a packing case or something, seeing as he's probably banned from just about every European country.

"We'll get Franklin to book the dates, then we'll all go, in disguise if necessary, across to France. It'll be difficult to get our gear across without anyone noticing, but we can rent a lot of it in Paris. About a week after we arrive, Franklin will release the details of the tour to the press. We'll play a different town each night, with the gigs being announced only a day or two in advance. We'll watch like hawks to see if he catches up to us. This way, we'll still be visible, but we'll all be together, making a little money, and we can defend ourselves. We can stay out for months if necessary. What do you think? It's not perfect, but it will buy some time. What happens when we get back is another story."

Marty got up and hugged him. "You're a genius, Si. He can't get us if we're all together."

Teresa spoke up, frowning. "Genius? Are you guys crazy? He'll find a way to kill you if he wants to. You idiots aren't fighters or spies. And what about after this tour? What can a bunch of crazy hippies do against someone like that?"

Marty waved her off. "We'll hire security, and we'll all stay in the same place. We won't let anything happen."

"We'll see about that." She sighed. "I guess my job will be to keep an eye on all of you."

*

Since the tickets for the album release had already been sold, Marty and Hastings decided there was no alternative but to go on with the show. They kicked The Fairport Convention off the bill with apologies but no explanation and added The Wylde Flowers. They also hired some tough Cockney security guards, products of the decrepit East End, and arranged a flight for good old Jerzy the roadie from New York. He had tried to warn them when they were first approached by Rosas at the Elysian Fields, and his surly suspiciousness would be useful on the tour. He was also pretty handy at keeping guitars in tune.

The members of the other bands saw the sense of the tour as a stopgap measure and made arrangements to cancel their engagements in London. All except Daevid Mallorn, who naturally preferred to flee to India to stay at the ashram of his personal guru. He was talked out of this with some difficulty. Franklin Ferris was able to book three weeks' worth of shows, starting in Paris then moving on to New Paris (formerly Brussels), Amsterdam, Düsseldorf, Bonn, Stuttgart, and Munich. This would be followed by Prague (which was somewhat dangerous due to the high levels of radiation there but had recently been declared safe by League of Nations scientists), and a swing through the Mediterranean, including a couple of cities in Italy, where psychedelic music was popular, France, Lisbon, and ending after a long flight with gigs in Dublin and Belfast.

The would have to bypass the harsh totalitarian regime in Spain, which had banned all visits by foreigners and had just expelled or massacred its entire Moorish population. Ferris told them that news of the band had reached the continent, where The Spheres had been reasonably popular, particularly in countries where adolescents were actually allowed to buy their records, and he had been able to ask enough for each gig that the tour would break even and perhaps even make everyone a few quid on merch.

In the meantime, they all walked cautiously through the chilly streets, glancing frequently over their shoulders. Some had even taken to carrying weapons. Maurice Wyatt had availed himself of an army pistol (supplied by Farren), which he had painted in psychedelic colors and referred to as his "love gun," although he said that he sincerely hoped he would never have occasion to use it. They all tried to be alone as little as possible. Rehearsals for the show went forward normally.

Thanks to a little extra funding from Shorty Mackintosh of Groovy Melon Records (no one knew where the mysterious Jamaican actually got his money), they hired a state-of-the-art liquid light crew, who would work during all three sets. The Flying Teapots would be the headliners, but each band would be supplied with their own customized light show. Mallorn and his friends had never agreed with the indignities headliners commonly inflicted on the support such as denying them a color light show, turning their volume down and raising their own, giving them a smaller beer rider, and cutting their sets short. As far as Mallorn, Hastings, and Marty were concerned, competition had absolutely nothing to do with music-making. They had always tried to befriend the musicians they played with and had gained many friends and few enemies on the London and New York scenes as a result. It made their current dilemma even harder to bear as their friends saw them withdrawing from their usual social circles without much explanation.

The Wylde Flowers had chosen to use a lot of dry ice and multicolored lighting in an attempt to reflect the jazzy, rhythmic intensity of their set. Astronomy preferred appropriate projected backdrops of stars, galaxies, nebulae, etc., and a lot of cold white lighting, with a touch of dry ice for effect. For the Teapots' set, Mallorn had instructed the lighting and effects crew to prepare nothing but to do whatever they felt, emotionally and spiritually, in reaction to the music.

Mallorn also did not believe in planning, saying that since most of the events that befall a person happen randomly, no matter how much scheming and worrying is done, it is better to accept the fate the universe has designed for you. He attempted to conduct his own life by this random principle and was, therefore, the only marked man on Rosas' list who was walking around perfectly content, completely accepting whatever the future might bring. He refused to listen to all warnings but had agreed to bring his band on the tour because he hadn't visited the continent in a while and said he'd enjoy meditating against a few different backdrops. In the past, he had traveled through almost every nation in the world. Mallorn was at least seven or eight years older than any of his friends and had done a great deal of soul-searching in his life, which was why he was looked up to as something of a guru, except in the subject of medicine. Too many of his friends had been subjected to the tender mercies of Ms. Moonstone.

The first run of the Astronomy record, which was to be titled *Beyond the Sky,* had just come back from the manufacturer: LPs, eight-tracks, and a hundred copies in the new computerized "Compact Disk" format, of which Hastings was quite skeptical, seeing as the stereo component used to play them was selling for three hundred pounds (it has not gone down much since). Nevertheless, he considered it prudent at least to make a mild effort at keeping up with technology. There was no sense in being a Luddite; that wouldn't get you anywhere.

The artwork had been created by Acid Reflux design studios of Chelsea, which was creating some of the most remarkable sleeve designs at that time. It had a gatefold (Marty said it was shameful to release a record without a gatefold), and the cover featured a photo of a streaking comet, in keeping with the old Spheres tradition, but the inner gatefold was a psychedelic collage of images taken from the band's first two stage shows, interspersed with seemingly random images such as a cow grazing in a meadow, a child on a roundabout, a close-up of a cat's eyes, and the peak of Snowdon in the sun. Mallorn said was "very Zen," which they assumed was a compliment. It would be released to record shops the day after the show, and old Shorty and his staff of two had been busily packing and shipping throughout the week. Radio stations had, however, received advance singles. There were some that had played The Spheres' Aureola releases in heavy rotation but would not play the new one due to its independent status and low marketing profile; still, many stations had already made a much-requested hit out of "Further Up, Further In." *NMT* had even requested a solo interview with Teresa, the "mystery woman" with the beautiful voice.

The musicians were still living in fear, but as December arrived with more snow and unusually chilly temperatures and the week of the show began, their excitement began to overcome the tension. They still kept together and made no journeys alone, not even to a public toilet.

If they were to die soon, and if Mallorn was right, perhaps what was meant to be would be regardless. Hastings was determined to go out with a bang. The upcoming UFO show would be his greatest moment, as well as a declaration to the employer of Rosas that the new music and the messages it carried would never go away, no matter who they silenced.

TWENTY

The afternoon of the big concert, Hastings, Teresa, and Marty relaxed in their front room, enjoying some stiff drinks. All were in decent spirits. Hastings was idly playing with the little hair-dryer gun in his coat pocket, a nervous habit he had acquired. Basil Baker was off buying new heavy-duty drumsticks. To promote the gig, Ferris had arranged for the band to play at a lunchtime anti-fur protest outside the Pelt Complex in Bromley, a massive shop that sold only animal skins imported from the Canadas, incidentally located in the area where all of the major record companies and PR companies had their offices. They had played a fifteen-minute set from the back of a platform truck until the police tried to shut them down. It had delighted Ferris to see some of his old corporate masters looking down in surprise from their windows. Hastings had even written a new song for the occasion, "Wearing Death," and Marty had appeared looking dashing in a silky red faux fur coat. Teresa had shown her usual lack of humor and declined to dress up, sticking with a drab set of surplus army clothes. They had made their escape from the angry, violent mob and a line of riot-gear clad policemen that formed as they played. Rick Farren, who accompanied them disguised as a French waiter, set off a smoke bomb under the truck, which had then driven away through the clouds.

"Wonder if the police'll show up here," Marty said lazily, reclining on an old sofa.

Hastings shrugged. "They hate us, but not enough to bother coming all the way out here to slap us with a fine or arrest us so we can do community service sweeping out the gutters."

"They've done their job by getting us out of the view of the money-makers," Teresa said. "Now they can go back to pretending that people like us don't exist."

Marty smiled evilly. "Except that they might be so unlucky as to have a teenager at home who likes our records. Then we'll be inside their heads forever!" He cackled.

Hastings had fallen into one of his studies. "They don't notice, though, do they? I mean, maybe all of this is for nothing. Maybe their kids will grow up, forget they ever listened to us, ever were curious to pick up a book by Hunter Burlington or Mort Moorhen, and become just like their parents."

"That doesn't mean we shouldn't try, Mr. Mopey," Teresa said. "If the way people think isn't changed, a tiny percentage of wealthy people like those skyscraper carnivores will continue stockpiling money while the poor and starving waste away all over the world. Not to mention the ecological destruction caused by the acts of these monsters. We have to keep speaking out."

Hastings nodded but stayed quiet while the others continued jawing. *But why?* he thought miserably. History just rolled on, and the actions of all these billions of people meant nothing. Why, even the corporations themselves were merely self-perpetuating profit-making machines. The people who ran them and worked for them were expendable, but the growth of the company was paramount. Its life extended well beyond those of the people who comprised its lifeblood; they could all be replaced overnight, and the gigantic nonentities would continue on as if nothing had happened, completely indifferent to the suffering they caused. Could a few people speaking out ever affect the future of a species when no one had a clue about how to seize control of its destiny? Not a few; it would need to be tens of millions, even more. And what did it matter in the end, since everyone was destined to die anyway? Could people like Henry Hastings be right? Should everyone focus exclusively on their own well-being, since it didn't matter one way or the other?

Basil Baker came loping through the front door, brandishing

his new sticks. "'ello all," he said.

"Feeling good about tonight, Bas?" Marty said.

"You bet, mate." Basil looked calmer than usual. He always looked like he had fallen into a snowdrift. His clothes were covered in tiny, shining ice crystals.

"Well, Simie, time to stop moping!" Teresa said loudly, jolting Hastings back to reality. "Whether it means something or not, we've got a show to play."

Marty stuck a fresh needle in his arm for a little No-Catch Cocaine pick-me-up. "We should have a little rehearsal before tea. That new song is great! The anti-fur one. We should play that tonight, but it wasn't very tight earlier today."

"All right, but not too much. We'll screw up our voices."

They decided on a ten-song set, including "Wearing Death," "Further Up, Further In," "Judgment Day," "The Misanthrope's Blues," another rocker from the album, "Dualistic Stomp," and a cover of "Brainbox Pollution" in tribute to the Sonic Assassins. The lighting crew was already at the hall setting up, and Franklin Ferris was having a meeting with Shorty about promo.

The rehearsal went well, with everyone relaxed and a couple even happy; this night would hopefully be the exorcism of Guy's ghost, and they hoped it would be a fitting send-off. They all tried not to think about the assassin, still loose somewhere. An extra five strapping bouncers had been hired to guard the backstage. If they made it through the night, they would be leaving the country two days after the show.

The rehearsal over, the band headed over to the Mountain Grill for a quick tea with Mallorn and Shakti. Jerzy the roadie picked them up in their van, and they were on their way to sound check at UFO. The day had been unusually warm in light of the weather they had been experiencing, and even as evening fell, the snow was still melting a little. Hopefully, Hastings thought, it would melt the foreboding that was clogging his mind. There was no time for morbid philosophizing or worry. This evening was about the reason he had started playing music as a teenager, making a statement about who he was and the things he believed in. The rest of the world could go to hell if it didn't want to listen.

*

Everyone was already at the club; many of their friends had shown up just to watch the sound checks and hang out. Steve Brock was entertaining a table by trying to roll the world's fattest joint, which barely fit into his mouth. When he lit it up, he took one large puff and fell off his chair, coughing, to laughter and applause.

Hastings walked over to Shorty and shook his hand. "I want to thank you for what you've done for us. It feels much better than being with you instead of some faceless hit machine."

Shorty beamed broadly. "Eh, no worries, mon. I'm just going Jah's work, you know? You're Jah's kind of people, Simon Hastings."

Hastings was touched. "Thanks, Shorty. That means a lot. Hopefully, the record will make up the money you've put into it and then some."

Shorty waved a hand. "I don't do this for money, my friend. Though it's nice when it's a-comin' in, eh? I do a favor for some good people is all." He wandered off, chuckling.

When The Wylde Flowers started noisily sound checking, sounding even more uncontrolled than usual, Hastings went backstage. Daevid Mallorn was leading a few people, including a blissful-looking Basil Baker, in a meditation session on the cold concrete floor. Jerzy and the other hired help looked on with disdainful amusement.

"Eh, Simon, look at this nonsense!"

Hastings patted Jerzy on the arm. "To each his own. And you have to admit that you've never seen anyone more at peace than our Daeve."

One of the Cockney bouncers, who was standing in an

aggressive stance with his muscles bulging, spluttered noisily. "I wouldn't trade for all the peace in the bleedin' world to be an unnatural fuckin' poofter."

The silence in the already quiet room deepened a shade. Hastings walked up to the man and into his face. "You're sacked, mate," was all he said. Out of the corner of his eye, he could see Jerzy uncoiling his own massive arms, preparing to dole out one of his infamous beatings.

The man shrugged. "That's what I was fishin' for." He leered, grabbed his bomber jacket, and strolled casually out the back entrance, spitting on the ground near Mallorn as he went.

"My, who hired that fellow?" Mallorn opened one eye and grinned. "Oh well, takes all types to make a world, even the nasty ones! Worse things happen at sea." He returned to his trance.

*

That incident was the only blot on the evening. The sound checks went smoothly; that was the good thing about gigging with friends. No one argued about the small things, and everyone got equal time. At about nine thirty, everyone who was playing got together backstage to enjoy The Wylde Flowers, whose set started with five minutes of lights and a seemingly endless drum beat, before the rest of the band even got on stage. That wasn't planned; Herb Hopper and Mitchell Ratledge were so involved in a discussion about pataphysics that they never even noticed the set had begun. Mo Wyatt never even dropped a beat; he just launched into an incredibly complicated drum solo that had Basil whistling between his teeth in amazement. When the others finally joined in and the horn section kicked into a blaring fanfare, the roar of the sound was more powerful than any high. The first tune was "Why Am I So Short?" a humorous number about Wyatt's diminutive stature, but he seemed to have forgotten that he was supposed to sing, and the piece was transformed into an instrumental.

And so the set went on, as one piece metamorphosed into another without any breaks. The musicians were tireless, and the audience matched their energy by adapting their free-form steps to suit the rapid changes in the rhythms. It could have gone on forever, which would have suited everyone in the room. Even morbid Hastings found himself grooving in a hypnotic state, his arm linked with Teresa's. When he looked over at her, he saw that her eyes were closed and a tranquil smile had settled on her usually quizzical face. A moment of sadness as well as tenderness came over him as he thought of how few people were willing to open themselves to such simple and pure experiences as these. Only their children, for a few brief years, would enjoy such freedom, thence to pass on to the decades of dull tiredness and drudgery that succeeded the years of discovery.

The set did, of course, eventually end. The Wylde Flowers came offstage looking sated. Hopper and Ratledge resumed their former pataphysical discussion as though nothing had intervened. Marty had grown tired of his aviator's gear and, inspired by Teresa's army drabs, now wore a navy officer's uniform, complete with stiff-visored cap and fake medals. Hastings had always stuck with the same ragged but stylish dark clothes, but this night he had also put on an old tweed blazer he had inherited from his grandfather so that he could keep the gun handy. After all, anything could happen.

The response as they took the stage was rapturous. Hastings felt it proper to say a few dignified words before they played. The audience listened in respectful silence. "Good evening, ladies and gentlemen. This is an important night for us. Not only are we releasing our new record, but, as you've probably heard, we've lost some friends lately. I don't want to speak too much about that, because this evening is about the future. No matter what happens, we'll always continue making music for you, to reflect the way you view this world, not the images forced on you by society."

The answering cheer almost completely drowned out his first chords.

The set was flawless. The crowd, which should have been tired out by this point, seemed to recover its energy. The band responded by adding several longer improvisatory passages, during which the songs would threaten to disintegrate entirely, only to come back together magically, as if Teresa, Basil, and Marty and Hastings were bound for this time by a deep psychic connection.

The ghost of Guy Calvert, he now realized, would never fully be exorcised as long as they all lived. Even if the quest for vengeance had been fulfilled, the spirit of this man who had died before he could even properly bestow his gifts upon the world would continue to haunt the places and the people that had been his passion. Hastings could always take refuge in his music to feel reunited with the memories of his lost friends.

They ended with their raucous cover of "Brainbox Pollution," and Hastings could see Brock and Turner grinning as though their faces would split at the sight of their friends finally giving their all in a metallic performance that caused the light fixtures to vibrate. Hastings did not know it, but that night he looked like the spirit of Calvert reborn, and he sang like a man possessed. Audiences have not had the privilege to hear a performance of such power and beauty since that time. The subsequent events to be described in this narrative, in my opinion, finally broke what was left of Simon Hastings' belief in the power of change, and he never again attained quite the visionary, messianic power onstage that he achieved in those early Astronomy shows. It was a sad loss even before his death.

When the band was finally allowed to leave the stage (after several encores), they all agreed that they had never been more exhausted, but also never more content with a performance. They slumped down out of the way backstage, under the dour, unappreciative gaze of their hired guards.

"Well, we did it," Marty said.

"It's good to see you guys back on your feet again," Teresa said.

"I owe it to you," Hastings said quietly, returning her smile. It was true. Teresa's uninhibited exuberance had lifted him out of many dark hours.

They talked quietly until the sound of Shakti Yoni's patented singing style, the "space whisper," heralded the beginning of The Flying Teapots' revolutionary stage show. This singing style consisted of a mixture of whispers and high, airy shrieks with lots of reverb in the mix that sent chills down the spines of her admirers. The Teapots' music was similar in many ways to The Wylde Flowers', but it featured more concise songs, with thematic lyrics based around a fictional planet. The metaphorical lyrics illustrated various principles of Eastern philosophy, and the unpredictable, jerky music, powered by Mallorn's glissando guitar and the virtuosic saxophone playing of blissed-out Frenchman Count Bloomdido, seemed designed to pull the audience quite rudely into a stage of enlightenment. The Teapots, whose music the public seemed unwilling to wholly embrace, were nonetheless a legendary live band and had acquired a diehard following that followed them wherever they went on tour.

Hastings was enjoying their set immensely, but halfway through their second number, "The Pot Head Pixies," another wave of weariness fell upon him, and the smoky atmosphere suddenly seemed unbearably stuffy. Teresa and Marty had gone to the side of the stairs leading up to the stage, so he decided to seize the moment and step outside for some air. It was foolish, considering the potential danger, but he simply couldn't stand to spend another moment in there.

"Just popping out for a moment," he said to the guard nearest the door.

"Yer the boss." The man shrugged carelessly and turned away.

Cold, clean night air greeted Hastings as the door swung open. He almost fell through the doorframe in relief and leaned up against the brick wall. The sky was clear for once, and what few stars could be seen fought the electric glow of the city for dominance. Unfortunately, the city always won. The rear of the club had a small parking area on an alley and a tiny vacant lot covered with dirt and scraggly weeds that was mostly filled with rubbish. Other buildings rose up all around the secluded area.

He heaved a sigh and crouched. Perhaps he had not yet completely recovered from the strain of the past two months; he let his head droop.

At that moment, a shadow loomed over him, and before his weary mind had time to react, a hand suddenly clamped down on his shoulder and a blade was at his throat.

"Simon Hastings," the shadow hissed, "at last I have you."

"The Murtherer" from
Thee Courte of Lucyfer or
An horribul revell of ye cityzens of Helle
by Sir Francis Roundtree (1574)

The Murtherer's aboute by dai and nyte.
He killeth for fee ande also for spyte.
Wot nobel harte can nott forbere
To look upon hym as he rendeth and tere?

To kyll is butt hys one intente,
To evyl deeds hys wyll be bente.
In Satans service he doth perform,
From Goddes love forev'r torne.

Staie by thy harthe, straie nev'r oute,
Unlesse ye harte be strong ande stoute,
Or drag ye he mote downe to the mudde,
Ande mak hys feaste on your harte's bludde.

TWENTY-ONE

All he could hear was the rapid, excited breathing of the shadow standing over him. The cold steel bit into his neck, and he could feel a small thread of blood trickling into his collar.

"Get up," Rosas said. "Get up, damn you, or you die now!" His hoarse whisper was urgent.

Hastings had no choice but to follow along and wait for the unlikely opportunity to reach into his pocket. He realized that he was being led toward the band's own van, the back door of which was open. Rosas shoved him in, shining a torch after him. He then climbed in himself, still brandishing the knife, which was as long as a machete.

"Lie on the floor and do not move a muscle," Rosas commanded. Hastings could see his sallow, thin face, which glowed a jaundiced yellow in the torchlight. The narrow eyes were lit with fury. *What reason does he have to hate someone like me?* Rosas wore a black suit, which was ragged and torn. It didn't look like he'd had an easy time of it during his stay in London. Rosas sat on the spare tire, still panting, and again held the knife to Hastings' neck. With his free hand he fumbled in a bag, the same bag from which he had pulled his wares at the Elysian Fields what felt like ages ago. "You and your dirty friends have made my job very difficult. But you could only stay together for so long. Did you really think that sending some beer-swilling thug after me would keep me from my work? I am going to separate you one by one, and there is nothing you can do about it. I have spent far too long on this job."

Though his face was pressed onto the freezing metal of the floor, Hastings managed to croak out a few words. "Why? Who are you working for?" He was trying to move his left arm, inch by inch, closer to his coat pocket. He desperately hoped that the handle of the gun was close to the mouth of the pocket.

The assassin let out a wooden chuckle. "The thought of that has no doubt been tormenting you. Thinking of that has given me some pleasure. Why? Why indeed. I do not think I will tell you." He had pulled out a syringe containing a dark liquid. "No, I am sure I will not. It will give my employer great pleasure to know that you died in an agony of uncertainty." His eyes glowed in the half-light.

The joyous sounds of The Flying Teapots' music could be clearly heard emanating from the club. Ironically, the song they were playing was titled "You Can't Kill Me," an energetic ode to the immortality of the soul. Hastings wondered whether he had been missed yet. But he had only been gone a few minutes; they would assume he was stuck on the toilet.

"Now I am going to kill you the way I killed your other friends, with the same poisons you use on yourselves every day, with some slight alterations. No one will ever believe that you did anything but overdose, or, I hope, perhaps they will finally decide that my former employers in Colombia are responsible through their negligence. The evidence, the Cartels' packaging, will be right here beside you. Then I will move on your other idiot friends." Once again, the dry, humorless chuckle.

The pressure of the knife lessened slightly, and Hastings felt a prick on his neck as Rosas searched for the vein. He used all of his strength to roll away, receiving a wild slash on the arm as a reward. At the same time, he plunged his hand into his pocket, which luckily gripped the handle of the gun. He brought it up, remembering suddenly, vividly, Alvarez's instructions, and aimed it at Rosas' head, pulling the trigger. A burst of bassy sound like a malfunctioning woofer was followed by a groan from Rosas. Hastings flung himself away toward the door, holding his arm and bashing his head on the roof in the process. Rosas seemed to recover for a moment and advanced again, still holding the knife, but his eyes clouded over with alarming speed, and he fell to his knees. The knife dropped from his suddenly lifeless hand, and he fell on his side, convulsing, blood streaming from his ear.

Hastings took one step closer to him and dropped to his knees. He grabbed Rosas roughly by the face. The man was rapidly slipping away. He stared at Hastings as though he was looking through to another world, and his pupils were so large that they seemed to occupy his whole eye.

"Who!" Hastings yelled. "Who, you fucking bastard! It doesn't make any difference now. Tell me!"

Lost in the pain of his death, Rosas seemed to have forgotten his earlier refusal. His lips puckered as he said, "Schmidt."

"What? What the hell are you talking about?"

"Schmidt ... Kässel."

Did he mean Helga Schmidt? The CEO of KässelPharma, manufacturer of most of Hastings' favorite recreationals?

"*Why?*"

Rosas' head lolled over.

*

In a daze, he stumbled back into the building. The security guards had turned out to be completely undependable; there were none left backstage. Marty was the only person in the room, watching the set from the stairs and grooving awkwardly.

Hastings stumbled up to him. "Marty..."

Marty turned and gasped. Hastings had a shallow slice on his neck that was still bleeding and a cut on his arm. His face was white as a sheet. "What the hell happened to you?"

Hastings pulled him away from the stage door. "Marty, where's Teresa?"

"In the loo, I think. What's wrong?"

"Come with me and see."

He led Marty out to the van. Marty blanched when he saw the

corpse lying contorted. "It's him!"

"He attacked me, but I got him instead."

Marty shook his head in admiration then stared at Hastings with a mix of respect and dismay. "Jesus, Simon, you're quite the superhero."

Hastings slumped down on the rear bumper. "What are we going to do with him?"

Marty rubbed his chin. "You're right. We can't have that kind of trouble. The police would love to take us down."

"But they don't even know who Rosas is. I'm sure he's here with a false passport or something."

After scanning the vacant lot for a few moments, Marty brightened. "Let's just chuck him through that manhole there. He'll never be found that way. He'll go straight to the river, and if he's found, it'll be ruled a drowning."

This seemed to be the only quick and convenient way to dispose of the evidence, so they found a piece of old, rusting metal in the rubbish pile near the back door and pried the grate off the drain.

Hastings felt like vomiting as they dragged the inert corpse with its still-open eyes across the winter-hardened ground, onto the pavement, and tossed it with some difficulty down the hole, followed by Rosas' bag. Well, there it was. He had known that one day he would have to come face-to-face with the assassin, and one of them would likely die. Simon Hastings now had a death, albeit the death of a thoroughly unpleasant person, on his conscience.

"Marty, he told me who he was working for."

Marty jumped about a foot directly in the air. "Really? Bloody hell!"

Hastings looked wildly around him, as though expecting to be confronted at any moment by a German contract killer. "Come back inside. I don't think we should tell anyone about this until we figure out what to do about it."

Hastings visited the toilet to get some paper to wipe his wounds. When he washed it his neck, he found that it didn't look too severe, resembling a bad cat-scratch. He turned his collar up, put on a different jacket, and returned to Marty, who was giving himself a quick hit of Harmless Heroin to calm himself down.

He sat down beside Marty and lit up a Dunhill. He pulled in the smoke so deeply that he was overcome briefly by lightheadedness, something that hadn't happened to him since he was a schoolboy. "You're not going to believe this."

Marty looked like he was going to burst. "What the fuck did he say?"

"The last things he said were 'Kässel' and 'Schmidt.' You know who that means."

"KässelPharma? Helga Schmidt?"

Hastings shrugged. "It appears Rosas was paid by Schmidt to kill us. Or so he claimed."

"But why?"

Hastings searched his mind for what he knew of the reclusive CEO. Helga Schmidt had been hired as chief executive officer of KässelPharma about ten years before, after she had begun the building of the Rauchstern Food Products empire, which controlled most of the supermarkets in the German-speaking world. That company had taken a hit when most of its Eastern European holdings were vaporized in the nuclear wars. Schmidt had wisely left the company and its rebuilding process for Kässel, which had been a mainstream producer of painkillers and other prescription drugs. When recreational drugs were legalized in Germany in 1959, she had immediately recognized the opportunity for growth and had in ten short years built up the largest line of recreationals in the industry. She had also engineered a buyout with a group of investors that made her the *de facto* controlling owner.

An unmarried recluse, she lived in a sixteenth century castle near Augsburg and had moved the company's headquarters and manufacturing center onto the same grounds. She had not been seen in public for several years, leading to widespread speculation about the soundness of her physical and mental condition. She was known to be eccentric and romantically inclined, with a passionate hatred for the modern world and its accompanying openness and "loose morals." Schmidt had supported the anti-Jewish New Reich movement of Göring that had almost started another Europe-wide war but had escaped the jailer in the aftermath with the aid of massive bribes. She had also opposed the giving of aid to her war-ravaged neighbors after the terrible atomic strikes and had tried to have a law passed to restrict immigration from Germany's former African colonies; she was rumored to espouse some bizarre racial theories. However, as she aged, she had participated less and less in the country's political life and had concentrated on running her company with an iron fist.

The monumental irony of an old-fashioned conservative supplying the youth of the world with inexpensive, safe highs was not lost on the observant, and she had been the object of much ridicule outside of Germany. But there had never been a word of response or protest to the hecklers as profits grew steadily with each quarterly report.

The famous businesswoman's sanity had obviously at long last cracked for good, and she was playing angel of death. They had rid themselves of her agent, but who was to say that this mad person, with her limitless financial resources, would not send someone else after them? She would have to be brought down.

Not only did pondering all of this make Hastings doubly incensed, but he also became angry with himself and his own hypocrisy for buying so many Kässel products over the years, blithely ignoring just who his money was benefiting.

"Well, it buggers me," Marty said, still shaking his head in astonishment. The Teapots were now well into their encore, the "Eat that Phonebook Coda." Teresa still had not returned and was no doubt enjoying the conclusion of the show from the audience's perspective.

"We need evidence," Hastings said. "We're going on tour

and stopping in Germany. We'll have to think of something. The authorities here, and in Germany too, won't believe us, we know that. There's no point in asking for assistance without evidence."

"Aye, that's for sure." Marty was glum. "I don't see what we can do."

But Hastings had already come to a sort of conclusion. If their problems, which had suddenly grown even more menacing, were going to be solved, he would have to do it.

"I don't think we should tell anyone about this, not even Teresa. I'll tell her when I think it's appropriate. We have too many hot-headed friends who might do something stupid. For now, keep it under your hat, and try not to look too relieved. Rosas is dead, but the threat isn't. We've just got some breathing room."

"All right, whatever you say, boss." Marty broke into a sudden rueful grin as the Teapots came clattering cheerfully down the stage stairs. "We've got a pantry full of Helga's products. The first thing I'll do when we get home is flush them."

Hastings had to laugh at that.

TWENTY-TWO

After all the gear had been packed up and the hall was deserted once more, a huge gang of revelers retired to the band house, which had become the epicenter of their large group of friends. Everyone seemed in higher spirits than they had been in a long time. Hastings was glad that they had not told anyone, especially Teresa, who was looking quite radiant after what was the finest night of rock music anyone had ever experienced. He wished he could share in that joy. He had explained away the long, shallow cuts on his neck and arm, saying he had slipped in a puddle of beer and got the scratches on the side of a table; he had, however, been very careful to sterilize his wounds with peroxide in the lavatory. Rosas' knife could have been in all sorts of nasty places.

At around quarter to five in the morning, when the crowds had finally dispersed or fallen asleep (aside from a few raucous stalwarts determined to welcome in the morning in at least a semiconscious state), Hastings slipped out onto the front steps to ponder the matter further. He was bone-tired, but there was little time to waste on rest. During the course of the festivities, he had tried to formulate a coherent plan but had been constantly interrupted by well-wishers. Now, a strange clear-headedness, possibly brought about by the crisp early dawn air and residual adrenaline, allowed him to identify his options.

He had remembered with an uncomfortable shock at one point in the evening that his own brother had been boasting about obtaining a situation with none other than KässelPharma at their Empire office in London. Henry might possess some inside information about the security of the company's location and other tidbits of gossip about Schmidt. It was even possible that he had visited it by now and would know his way around; whether he would divulge any information was another topic. As loathsome as the prospect of spending even five minutes in his brother's company had become to him, it was too coincidental an opportunity to miss, despite the remoteness of the likelihood that Henry had ever even met the reclusive Schmidt.

Another, even more unlikely possibility had also occurred to him, which presented moral difficulties. There was only one person Hastings had ever met who was equipped to offer him tangible aid or advice in the area of corporate espionage: Ricardo Alvarez, director of security for the Colombian Cartels. The opportunity to strike a blow against one of his company's chief rivals would no doubt be too tempting to pass up for the ruthless Alvarez. The thought of trying to reach such a powerful man seemed daunting until he remembered that Alvarez, before putting him on a plane for Britain, had written his private telephone number on a scrap of paper and told him to use it if he ever needed help, an offer Hastings had not wanted to accept. He was not sure exactly what kind of aid Alvarez might offer, and he was still not sure he'd take it.

Hastings, though intensely reflective, was also a very practical man who liked to see himself as a straight-talker and a clear thinker. He recognized (as he thought any truly intelligent person must) that human moral systems, in all their diversity, really have no objective rational basis beyond our tiny planet and the survival needs of our species, unless an all-powerful deity should someday reveal itself, but he had found principles like honor and compassion to be of much solace, despite their irrationality; and besides, he couldn't help himself. He was raised that way. He still felt, although his actions had been entirely in self-defense, guilty and shocked by the death of Rosas, and a sense of responsibility for the death of Gonzalez, as well as a strong desire to see the deaths of Guy, Ed, and Hunter Burlington avenged. If it took making a deal with the devil to assuage his guilt and his need to see justice done, then so be it. He had no desire to die any time soon.

That difficult decision out of the way, he retreated to the bedroom, where a very drunk Teresa was snoring loudly and grinding her teeth. He fell into a deep, fortunately dreamless sleep.

*

He slept much later than planned; it was eleven thirty by the time he rose and dragged himself to the bathroom to try to soak himself into wakefulness. Nevertheless, it was past twelve thirty, several cups of coffee and half a pack of Silk Cuts before he was able to bring himself to ring Henry at his new office and arrange a dinner meeting. Henry was curious and as rude as always, but Hastings revealed nothing of his motives. Teresa and Marty were not in the house, most likely helping Franklin tie up loose sends for the tour. Basil was still lying passed out in a pile of heavily breathing limbs on the floor. Hastings checked the telephone book for the time difference between London and Medellín and found that he would have to wait several hours before attempting the call. Alvarez had, in common with many beasts of prey, looked like a man who enjoyed his rest. Hastings decided he might as well get some more sleep himself.

When he woke again, it was four thirty, and he felt much more alive. The house was now completely empty. He put his hair back in a ponytail and searched the room for some conservative clothing. The best he could do was a pair of trousers of questionable vintage and another old tweed jacket. Wearing a white shirt belonging to Marty, he still looked a bit rumpled, but he was entering Henry's territory, where he was likely to be stared at anyway. Being treated like an alien invader could become quite tiresome.

Hastings locked up the house and set out for the Underground, forgetting until he was on a southbound Victoria Line train that as far as Teresa knew, Rosas was still on the loose, and no one was supposed to go around by themselves. He would catch hell for this later.

The restaurant Henry had suggested was Chez Philippe, an upscale bistro in Bromley that catered to the business class. As he entered the plush, tastefully dim interior, Hastings quickly realized that his attempt to dress to fit in had been futile; the other patrons were dolled up to the nines in the latest business style, suits of dark cloth, pastel-colored waistcoats, and shiny fob-watches. There were, as far as he could see, only a couple of jewel-armored women dining there, and he garnered the usual bewildered stares and upturned noses as a disdainful waiter led him to Henry's table. The man himself was, of course, the paragon of current good taste in a dirt-brown silk suit with a bright lemon-yellow waistcoat and a huge gold watch on a thick chain, which he was pretending to inspect as Hastings pulled out his chair to sit down.

"Oh, hello, Simon," he said, looking up over his monocle. "Must say, this is a surprise, although I suppose not an entirely unpleasant one. I recommend the duck; it's scrumptious." He leaned forward to pour Simon a glass of white wine. "So, to what do I owe this fraternal pleasure?" He grinned, showing bleached white teeth.

Concealing a shudder, Simon realized with astonishment that he had not bothered to make up a story. He was not on his game at all these days. "Um ... it's business-related."

Henry unleashed his laugh, a loud, rich, melodious but very affected noise. "Business! Business! Ha! Thought that was a profanity to you, Simon! Have you finally run out of money, or do you need a bigger flophouse budget?"

Simon felt himself flushing and fought down his ire. "No," he said humbly as an idea for drawing out information from his odious sibling occurred to him. "I remembered your new situation with Kässel—"

"Yes indeed! In fact, I'm working on some new—"

"We're thinking about adding corporate sponsorship to our upcoming tour," Simon broke in hurriedly. "You know, that's the latest thing in the music business. Del Morris and the Hi-Tops made a killing that way last summer. We were thinking, since our demographic is by far the largest consumer of Kässel's products, that perhaps your company might be interested." Del Morris and the Hi-Tops were definitely not cool any more and hadn't been for some time, but it was at least a band Henry might have heard of, and their last tour for the forty-something set had indeed been sponsored by Good Fortune Cola, a United Chinese Chemical subsidiary.

Henry tossed back his head and laughed even louder, which drew some hostile glares from neighboring tables. "You've got to be joking, right? I mean, don't you even read the newspapers?"

Simon feigned ignorance. "What do you mean?" While Henry continued to splutter, the waiter returned. Simon ordered some crêpes while the man raised a waxed eyebrow at Henry. He was relieved that his mannerless sibling was attracting more attention than himself; still, he had never hated Henry more than he did now, and he was having a great deal of trouble keeping himself under control.

"Surely you know that our esteemed CEO, Helga Schmidt, hates rock and roll with a passion! She even tried to get some of her barmy old friends from the Reichstag to set mandatory hair-length levels, with punishment of imprisonment! She'd have my head if I suggested something like that, wouldn't she?"

"Oh. I see." He pretended to be embarrassed. "Well, that's that, I suppose."

"Yes. Nice try, though. About time you and your commie friends got some financial sense. There's a huge youth market out there waiting for you to exploit, isn't there? Why, we work with some image consultants that could—"

Simon pretended to choke on a piece of bread, feeling that a change of subject was badly in order. There was only so much talk of Henry's business dealings that he could stand, and he had endured a lifetime's worth already. Henry had first started swindling the neighborhood kids more than twenty years ago.

After a feigned recovery, he made a play for information. "So, have you ever met this Schmidt? Ever been to the mysterious headquarters?"

Henry nodded. "Augsburg? Yes. For my final of five interviews, I mean. Not to the castle, though. Hardly anyone ever gets in there. Never comes out, just stays up there listening to her Mozart records all day long or something. The company's really run day-to-day by the VP, Himmler. Word is that the old hag is completely barmy. Had my interview in the main office building."

"Are they close together, these buildings?"

Henry frowned. "Why?"

"I was just thinking that a modern office complex and a medieval castle can't be a very attractive combination."

"Always the bloody aesthete, eh, you little poofter? Actually, the castle is on top of a hill, pretty far from the rest of the complex. Big lawn around it. Looks really menacing and artsy-fartsy, not to my taste. More to yours, eh? No, they'd never throw in their lot with the likes of you, and I can't say I blame them." Henry shifted his weight to a more comfortable position, and his face took on a condescendingly sage expression. "Now, since you're here, I've been meaning to have a chat with you, haven't I?"

"About what?" Hastings was sure his own face must be scarlet with suppressed violence.

"Think it's time you straightened out a bit. You've had your fun, but you're giving the family a bad name. You're tainting my own reputation by association. And that's all Dad needs too, in addition the rest of his problems. I'm getting tired of telling people who inquire that my brother's a hippie muso with no career and no prospects."

"*You're* ashamed? *You're* ashamed of *me*? Dad almost has a heart attack every time he talks to you. You're a fucking hypocrite." Hastings could hear his voice rising, but he knew his self-control and patience had vanished for good where Henry was concerned.

"You don't believe in drugs, but you work for the largest drug-maker in the world—"

"They're called recreational pharmaceuticals, and it's just an administrative position. I don't care what—"

"That's just it. You don't give a damn about anything but yourself, your fucking career, and your fucking image. You don't care about Dad at all. Mum and Dad raised us to care more about what happens to people. People like you are the reason most of the world lives in misery. You're complete fucking rubbish!"

Henry sighed. "I've heard all this shit before from your fellow juvenile bleeding hearts, Simon. Your ideals and hostility won't get you very far, and being pissed off at successful people like me won't either, will it? If the average man had my work ethic, he'd be better off. Lives in misery? What's the big fuss? Someone has to. We can't all be well-off. Life is about hard work to get places. That's what Dad taught us. And if we all got there, how would a man enjoy his success compared with others? Do you want us to end up like Dad, working in a bloody factory? Look at me! Look at where I am now. Where will you be in ten years? Living in a bloody cardboard box with the rest of those who expect society to provide them with something for nothing, I daresay. As if I'll help you out then! Lazy tosser."

This fight, in one form or another, had been repeated during their youth a thousand times.

Simon stared coldly across the table at his brother, his food still untouched. Then he stood up and took a few banknotes from his pocket. "Here's what I think, Henry. I think you should stay away from our family altogether. Dad doesn't need you or want your help. And you won't be hearing from me again, either. Just because we're blood-related doesn't mean we owe each other anything. Not even courtesy. You're just not the kind of person I want to know."

"Suit yourself, you little prick. You don't deserve to spend time in decent company anyway." Henry turned his eyes down to his duck and did not look up again as Simon strode from the restaurant, much to the staff's relief.

As he walked to the Underground, he was surprised to find that he felt very little regret at this final, irreversible parting of ways. He only wished that his brother had not turned out be such a horrible person. Since he had, what was there to do? Henry's Krupp-Benz stood glittering under the streetlights in a row of similar luxury autos, the perfect symbol of stylized wealth, and he was tempted briefly to run his keys down the side, but he decided not to relinquish even the slightest bit of the moral edge he possessed over his self-serving, ignorant brother.

They never set eyes on one another again during the remainder of Simon Hastings' short life.

From the annual report and official
press release of KässelPharma GmbH
(English-language edition), released May 1968

KässelPharma, the world's premier manufacturer of recreational pharmaceuticals, as well as traditional therapeutics, anti-radiation defenses, and front-line medical technologies, is pleased to announce our highest ever annual gain, including a fourth-quarter profit that has eclipsed all known records for a multinational of our size. This good news is not the result of luck, but rather, we believe, of a combination of product quality and customer service unparalleled in ours or any industry.

Under the leadership of our Chief Executive Officer, Helga Schmidt, and our long-serving board of directors, KässelPharma has achieved a competitive edge and an international standing that is a source of pride and a symbol of modern prosperity to all Germans, and we wish to state our renewed commitment to our retailers and consumers that we will continue to endeavor to put out the best quality and safest recreationals on the market today. And all of our products are, naturally, guaranteed 100% nonaddictive.

We would also like to take this opportunity to announce our excitement at the expansion of our British plant and offices, in order to better serve our customers within the British Empire. A search is currently on for a dynamic executive staff member to aid in spearheading our growth into the next decade and beyond.

Heinz Schlossel,
Head of Public Relations

TWENTY-THREE

When he arrived home, Hastings decided it would be best not to waste any more time dwelling on the overdue demise of his family unit and snuck into his bedroom to make the unfortunately necessary telephone call. The others were in the kitchen, loudly preparing their own dinners. He had not touched his food at the curtailed meal with Henry, and his stomach was growling like an angry skinhead, but Hastings knew he wouldn't be able to settle down properly or rest up for the next day's departure until he'd heard what Alvarez would say.

The ring on the line was faint and the connection crackled and echoed, but the call was picked up by a male secretary who at first refused to put through the call to Alvarez's office. But when Hastings told him angrily that the call involved a tip that could break one of the Cartels' biggest rivals, the man reluctantly connected him.

Alvarez's silky, sinuous voice cut through the static, sounding even more sinister in the trans-Atlantic echo. "Mr. Simon Hastings! What a pleasant surprise to hear from you this fine afternoon. Do you have some news for me about our mutual acquaintance, Mr. Rosas?"

"Yes," Hastings said flatly. "I killed him."

"Ah-ha! Smashing, is that not what you Brits say? I knew he would turn up, and you'd have the stomach for it. Did you enjoy it? You see, it was not very hard, was it? How did the gun fare? The international arms trade is another area we are anxious to exploit, but hand-held sonic weaponry is something of a new field. Hard to concentrate the killing power into a small package."

Hastings sensed that Alvarez was trying to bait him, so he

decided not to give the director of "security" an answer concerning the weapon's performance; besides, a long-distance call was not cheap, and he was not about to waste his money on exchanging pleasantries with a crime boss. "Look, Alvarez, do you want to know what I'm phoning about or not?"

"Mmm, you are still a testy one, I see. By the way, I hear you have a new record. My daughter is quite anxious to obtain a copy. She reads the *Musick Maker*, you know."

"I'll send you an autographed one." It wasn't the kid's fault, and if Alvarez was to be of any assistance, Hastings had better stop being quite so surly.

"Really? That would be so kind. Now—" The voice became abruptly harder and more businesslike. "Your information."

"I know who was paying Rosas."

There was a moment's silence. "Good, Mr. Hastings, good. Always make sure you obtain the required information before finishing off your subject. You really ought to come and work for me."

Hastings ignored this. "It was Helga Schmidt of KässelPharma. I'm not totally clear on it; it may just be her own initiative, without any knowledge of anyone else in the company."

A much longer silence. "*What?*" The voice was almost a whisper.

"You heard me. Or so he said. We don't know for certain, of course."

There was a loud thump from the other end of the line and the sound of scattering papers. Alvarez cut loose with a string of Spanish curses. "I should have known. That bitch! That cunning Teutonic swine. Hiring my operative to kill a bunch of hippies and trying to pin the blame on us and our products! This is exactly her style. If your police forces had not been too lazy to make the obvious connection into which she was thrusting their noses, our public relations department might have had a shit storm on its hands today. This is dirty, dirty business."

"Well, what are you going to do about it?" The reaction had been most gratifying, listening to one unscrupulous ultra-capitalist angrily denouncing another as dirty. A most delightful irony.

"What am I going to do about it? I will tell you! I am going to bring that dog and her company to their knees, that is what I'm going to do."

"How?"

Alvarez sighed. "I need time to come up with a strategy. Even I, Hastings, cannot devise a foolproof scheme on the spot. I will contact you when I know what can be done to remove this blight from the Earth. You may be of assistance again."

"I'm going to be on tour in Europe for a month or so. Very hard to reach." The last thing he wanted was to be drawn further into the Cartel's web of organized crime; if he was going to attempt anything, it would be on his own.

"Oh, do not be concerned with that. We will find you. And do not tell anyone about this. I tell you this because you have helped create a conflict between two of the largest powers in the world, and my intention is that only one of us will survive. You are involved, whether you like it or not."

"Mum's the word."

"Ha! Very good. But tell even your mother nothing." Alvarez's insincere good humor had suddenly returned. "Well, I will not keep you. You have done the right thing in bringing me this information, and I believe that vengeance for your comrades will be satisfied. Goodbye."

Hastings hung up gladly. He sincerely hoped he'd never have the opportunity to speak to Ricardo Alvarez ever again.

*

The rest of the evening went by quickly. After they had admonished him sternly for his disappearance, Marty and Teresa informed him that all of the arrangements for the tour were finalized (no thanks to him), and the van had been packed. They were to meet with the others at 6:00 a.m. to start the journey to France.

Hastings had become a bit excited about the prospect of the tour, especially now that they seemed to be out of immediate danger; it would take Schmidt time to realize that her operative was no more.

The Spheres had toured Europe only twice, once as an unknown beat group called Hadrian's Wall when they were just out of their teenage years, and again after their first album was released many years later. Around the time Guy died, they had been planning to launch a worldwide tour, at least of radiation-free areas, including their first-ever trip to Tasman's Land/New Wales, the giant island continent and British colony in the South Pacific. During their last tour, the Hammer had been arrested for disorderly conduct in New Paris, Hamburg, and Rome, and they had seriously considered sacking him. Hastings had also lost his prized Rick Booker fourteen-string guitar. Nonetheless, he retained fond memories of the continent. The cities were still mostly small and had kept something of their ancient flavor, but most of the societies there were more open in their approach to modern culture, and the band had received a hero's welcome in the towns they had visited. It was certainly preferable to touring the garish new neon conurbations of Virginia or the dreary, crumbling mill towns of England's north.

Germany, Vienna, and northern Italy could, however also be extremely depressing to visit. In addition to a permanently thick cloud cover that had still not quite cleared up, the fallout from the Eastern European nuclear war had left many of the inhabitants and refugees with disturbing and grotesque medical conditions. This pathetic group was mostly made up of those who had refused to be evacuated to the giant refugee camps in Normandy and Cornwall during the war and were now paying the price for their obstinance. But there was little sympathy to be found for these people in their own countries, and little had been done by their governments to provide for their needs. However, the land was now reinhabited by mostly healthy occupants and was considered safe for travel. There was no reason to discriminate against the people of those regions because they had suffered past misfortune, as long as the discerning, health-conscious traveller ate only in newer establishments offering imported food and bottled water.

They spent the rest of the night resting to save energy for the long journey and turned in early, all except Marty the night owl, who went to sit up on the balcony, smoke a joint, and gaze at the cloud formations and the few visible stars.

Hastings was troubled by a vivid dream from which he could not wake, no matter how desperately he tried to wrench himself back to consciousness. He was lost on a battlefield, the turf torn and mauled beyond recognition into an endless waste of mud stretching from one horizon to the other. Corpses, some with olive skin and some pale northern European white, were strewn around in the thousands, though none showed any sign of serious trauma. They lay quite at peace, each with a red mark, a puncture standing out on their arm. Suddenly, this misty dream landscape was illuminated by a flash off to his right, followed by a huge, blossoming mushroom cloud. In the blinding light, he saw that the nearest corpses were those of Guy Calvert, Hunter Burlington, Ed Barrett, Ramón Rosas, and Miguel Gonzalez. As he looked at each in turn, the dead faces broke out into sickening grins, but the bodies stayed inert. He turned away and began to run, but after a few paces he found himself caught in the center of a raging hand-to-hand battle between Zoot-suited Colombians and stone-faced Teutons. Both sides wielded the dreaded sonic gun and a small amplifier that played the latest bubblegum pop hits. As a giant Aryan lunged at him, he saw the gun brought up to the level of his head, and he woke with a scream.

He sat up, shaking and sweating profusely. Teresa hadn't stirred at his wail; she still lay snoring beside him like a jackhammer (this had taken some getting used to at the beginning). After a couple of minutes, he lay back down to try to resume sleeping, but he was too upset. He got up and went to the medicine cabinet for a sleeping pill. He flipped the cap off the bottle and was about to pop a bright blue tablet into his mouth when he caught sight of the label: *A product of KässelPharma UK.*

Disgusted, he tossed the half-full bottle in the rubbish and went upstairs to look for Marty. No matter what further tragedies occurred, it was unlikely he'd ever recapture the peace of mind he had once been so close to attaining, only a few months before.

TWENTY-FOUR

After an early and very grumpy start in the chill morning air, the vans left in a modern nomadic caravan for the coast. None of the vehicles were in very good shape — each was cramped, uncomfortable, and at least ten years old — but they should at least last the length of the tour. Three hours later, Hastings' van rumbled out of the mouth of the Calais-Dover Tunnel (which, it bears pointing out, since it seems to have been forgotten, was built by legions of Indian and Algerian laborers in the 1950s who suffered a fifty percent mortality rate on the job) and onto the roads of France. The three bands had attempted to follow one another in a cordon when they left that morning, but Teresa's aggressive Virginian driving had quickly left the others in the dust. The long vehicle was crowded, with Hastings, Marty, Basil, Jerzy, and Farren all taking turns on the seats; the others perched on pieces of equipment and luggage in the rear. They had hidden Farren under a seat when passing the border checkpoint at the entrance to the tunnel, and he had nearly been crushed by Jerzy's weight positioned like a mountain on the cushions above him. However, the border check was uneventful, with the guards cheerily waving them through. This was at least a heartening sign that not everyone in Britain found the sight of a busload of longhairs repulsive.

All through the journey to Paris, the van's inhabitants were in good spirits, aside from a few fights over which cassettes would be played on the van's unreliable player. Basil and Rick indulged heavily in various kinds of recreational drugs, much to the displeasure of Teresa and the big Pole. Hastings and Marty would normally have joined in with abandon, but ever since learning the identity of their would-be murderer, neither of them had felt the slightest appetite for any kind of chemical stimulation. They had naively purchased products of massive corporations for years, never bothering to consider who was manufacturing them or how they ran their businesses. Now they had discovered that one of their favorite suppliers was run by oligarchs who employed thugs and assassins to terrorize their own people, and the other by a maniac who wanted them dead for no good reason. They could have resorted to some Chinese Chemical products, but the chances seemed pretty good that the third competitor was no more ethical in running its affairs.

They confided sheepishly in each other that they actually felt physically better than they had in years, more clear-headed and in control of their actions. Though recreational pharmaceuticals were supposedly tested for their capacity to cause physical addiction, there was nothing that could be done about the inevitability of a user developing a psychological dependency to the respite from cold, harsh reality that the drugs provided. Almost all of The Spheres' music had been produced under the influence of one chemical or another, and there is no doubt that not as much of their creative output would have emerged from their minds or have been quite the same without the aid of drugs.

But those days were over. As far as Hastings was concerned, no organization designed for the sole purpose of profit could be trusted; you could only put faith in people you knew personally. Big record companies, drug companies, governments, they had all betrayed the trust of the people who looked to them for enlightenment in what had been heralded as a brand new age of freedom. In the shadows behind all of them lurked the leering face of base human instincts, the desire for power, money, and control.

Teresa was very happy with Hastings' new cleaner lifestyle. Though she did not side with those who demanded recreational pharmaceuticals be banned again, she scorned them as artificial props that did more to block a person's thinking than inspire it;

drugs were the tools of lesser people. When she asked him why he suddenly decided to stop using, he told her that his experiences in Colombia had convinced him that you never knew who your supplier was or what they were like, and he thought it best to stop supporting the industry. It wasn't a lie, after all. She accepted this in her frank, open way, which caused him a pang of guilt.

They finally reached Paris in the afternoon. The drive had been a peaceful one through soothing farmland of timeless meadows and quaint stone houses. Only the sight of tractors in the fields spewing black exhaust, cars racing down the motorway, and the endless ropes of power lines gave evidence that they had not travelled back to the nineteenth century. The transition between country and city was sudden. Paris, unlike London, is of course no longer the industrial and financial center of its nation; that is currently located in Lyon, and the endless, thoughtless expansion that has permanently defaced London has not occurred there. Paris retains an old-world charm and a relatively small population, and it is home to a thriving bohemian community. The Spheres had been through Paris twice on tour and had always been received well in this old center of the arts, home of the Impressionists, Expressionists, Primitivists, and the infamous Scatologists of the thirties, who employed human and animal fecal matter as their painting materials. The hostility that faced them in most of London was nowhere to be found; France is on the whole a more culturally open-minded place.

Nevertheless, there is of course a great sense of natural friendliness and brotherhood between these two Imperial powers and longtime allies: we can only speculate how different the world would be today if France and Britain had indeed united their empires in one world super-state, as was recommend by M. Gabriel Yacoub, the French premier, after the First Great War. This empire would today cover more than half of the globe. It was pride that killed this possibility, and perhaps it is for the best. As we have already seen, large structures rarely remain free from the vagaries of corruption and the lust for power.

The band reunited with their friends at Club Jump, where Daevid Mallorn had once played a two-week solo stand during his happy time spent living in the city. His van was an hour late for the rendezvous; he had stopped at several farms along the way to ask if he could halt and "reflect" on the property for a while to gather up nature's vibes, and he had (he claimed) been turned away only once. His group had bought several baskets of fruit and a dozen bottles of wine along the way and drunk half of them.

The British all-star triple bill caused a sensation, and the club filled quickly, even though the show was only announced the day before. Hastings was astonished at the French audience's fervor. They clustered around the stage, waving their hands. They seemed to know the words to many songs, not bad for an album that had been released only a few days before. All three sets were ecstatically received, and they were even asked for autographs afterward. Because of Mallorn's former residency in the city, The Flying Teapots headlined and were treated like returning heroes by the audience, with whom he amiably exchanged French wisecracks. The only blot on the evening's vibes was Rick Farren's first experience with absinthe, which caused him to go into something of a fit in which he declared himself the Angel of Death and tried to jump several unsuspecting Parisians whose hair was too short for his liking. He was restrained with some difficulty before passing out.

They left Paris with regret after sleeping in the club's dirty guest quarters and hit the road again in a fine drizzle at midmorning for Nouveau Paris. Farren was fortunately sleeping off an experience that he had called "fantastic" but which had been a nightmare for everyone else, so they were all able to sleep as well. He had laid in a supply of several more bottles of absinthe, so there would be rocky times ahead.

The uncharacteristic quiet in the van gave Hastings, who was driving, a chance to think about what he would do when the tour reached Germany. Nothing would probably be the prudent thing to do, since one man could do very little against such a power. He knew, however, that he would have to make something happen soon. It was too much of a coincidence that the tour should be scheduled to pass so close to the home of their nemesis. He did not want, for the sake of their safety, to ask for the assistance of his friends, and besides, there was little they could do as a group except be beaten up and/or captured by the security forces he had seen in his nightmare (which recurred nightly) and which no doubt existed in the real world. There was really only one proper response to the situation, and once more it was like something from a thriller film: he, Simon Hastings, armed with fully loaded sonic gun, would attempt an act of espionage. He would try to gain entry to the castle and find evidence, if he could, of Schmidt's plan for the assassination of his friends.

It was a slim chance, but there had been no further word from Alvarez, who was untrustworthy anyway. He toyed briefly with the fanciful idea of trying to hire some kind of mercenary group to combat Schmidt openly, but that was ridiculous. Where would he find one? And what would happen if the German government got involved?

He sighed and looked over at Teresa, who grinned back sleepily, mistaking his hangdog expression for someone jonesing for a hit.

"Don't worry, sweetie, it won't be long before you forget you ever took that nasty stuff."

He took out a cigarette (those he still allowed himself) and steeled himself for the task ahead. There was no more point in debating it. This business would have to be taken care of, and he was, once more, the only one in a position to do it.

"The Ruined City" by Astronomy
Lyrics by Simon Hastings

Black rain invades through broken windows
It washes some more of the paint away
A mound of earth covers all the signs
Of the countless lives spent in this place
They are gone now

A murder of crows wheels across gray sky
They've never seen anything move on two legs
They perch on the steeples of our arrogance
We cast the gods in our image, such folly
They are gone now

The road, though broken, still wanders
Leading nowhere, it fades into tall grass
The forests stretch on unharmed and unrazed
No one to take and to hate and to hurt
To destroy everything

They are gone now
The earth reclaims what they stole from it
The earth has forgotten they ever lived here
They are gone now

TWENTY-FIVE

Another hard day of driving brought them to the old Belgian capital of Nouveau Paris, from which the former Belgian empire's African possessions had been governed. Visitors to this small lowland province were surprised that a peaceful idyll of polite, quiet people and moist, emerald-hued meadows could be the same land that held the entire west coast of Africa in thrall under the most brutal oppression for a century, until the peaceful annexation of Belgium by France in 1948. There is, however, even in this land of traditionally conservative, suspicious people, a small bohemian counterculture centered in the oldest quarter of Nouveau Paris, which is ignored and tolerated by the city government as inconsequential, although there is no doubt that it would react quickly against any dangerous, widespread movement should it arise. Nevertheless, there were enough fans in the city to justify a visit by the tour.

Like Paris, Nouveau Paris retains a wonderful flavor of old Brussels, with its cobblestones, tiny churches, and legions of rusty bicycles. Great strides have been taken in racial relations as well, and the city's population of African immigrants, though most must unfairly work in menial occupations, coexists peacefully with the town's stolid French and Flemish citizens.

Though the show they played at the Château de Rock, a new club, in no way equaled the Paris set, the smaller audience was enthused. All went well until halfway through Astronomy's closing set. They had just begun the final chorus of "The Misanthrope" when the power was suddenly shut off. A group of black-clad policemen armed with nightsticks burst in and violently cleared the room, telling the musicians only that the timing of the show had gone well past the city's curfew. The bands knew full well that this early closing was meant as a warning to the citizens. There was nothing they could do about it, so, forfeiting their pay, they bundled into their vans and drove on in the middle of the night to Amsterdam.

They had all been looking forward to this stage of the tour; the city is one of the finest and most beautiful in Europe. Ever since the socialist government had been elected in the 1940s and granted independence to most of the imperial possessions, the Netherlands had been the subject of intense international bureaucratic disapproval, even economic and diplomatic sanctions, from other nations throughout the continent. The city of Amsterdam was renowned as a meeting place for bohemians and anarchists from around the world long before the scenes in London and Paris developed. Even before they had ever played there, Guy, Marty, and Hastings had spent many a pleasant weekend trip exploring the city's delights.

In Amsterdam, they were again received like old friends, and indeed, the members of all three of the bands had friends in the city. Rick Farren disappeared, absinthe in hand, with a group of anarchist associates from Siberia, no doubt to plot a statue theft or three in London or Petrograd.

The show at the Royal Concert Hall was even taped for state television and was to be broadcast on the radio the following week. This was the largest venue the band had played since its formation, and it was nearly sold out. Though he almost choked on the massive clouds of pot smoke that filled the room like the pall of a giant forest fire, Hastings greatly enjoyed the party atmosphere of the gig, which was attended not only by the city's colorfully dressed bohemians, but also by the town's thirty-something deputy mayor, who came up to shake his hand (Hastings couldn't believe it). Franklin Ferris, who had been traveling in the Teapots' van, reported after meeting with the Dutch distributor of the record that they had already sold more copies of the record per capita in the Netherlands than anywhere else. Teresa advised that they really ought to consider, for the sake of their mental and financial health, a permanent move to the country, the current climate at home being so unfriendly.

Thus far, there had been little discussion of the shadow that had hung over their heads, and as far as almost all of them were concerned, still did. Only Hastings and Marty knew the truth, and it caused them sharp pricks of conscience to see their friends occasionally glancing nervously over their shoulders as they exited the vans. On the way to Germany, they talked about the situation again. They were sitting behind the seats in the van on their amplifiers. Hastings was reading the latest Moorhen, *The Golden Void*, and The Fairport Convention's version of a bawdy traditional song, "Fly Up My Cock," was droning on the tape player.

"Well, we're in bloody Germany now, aren't we?" Marty said quietly. They had been through the border crossing a half hour before.

"You retain a shocking gift for recognizing the obvious." Hastings rubbed the new creases on his forehead. He felt he had aged about twenty years in the last couple of months.

"Any more bright ideas?"

He stared at Marty for a moment before answering. Could he confide his plan in his free-swinging, loose-lipped pal? There was no doubt that Marty would insist on going with him. He didn't like to play second fiddle where there was drama to be had. But clandestine activity wasn't exactly Marty's forte, and allowing him to come on a mission of espionage could be fatal for both of them. "We're not going to do anything," he said finally.

Marty's mouth fell open. "What?"

"Well, what can we do? You want to go to the gates and ask if they could surrender Fräu Schmidt to our custody, pretty please?"

"We have to do *something*!"

Hastings (partially) feigned exasperation. "Look, we'll figure it out when we get back. We can't spoil the tour for everyone by getting into trouble."

Marty looked very confused. "You're very prudent all of a sudden. Aren't you the chap who jetted off to Colombia on the spur of the moment? But you're probably right. I suppose we're not in any more danger — yet."

*

The first stop in Germany was Düsseldorf, an industrial city, where they observed a street battle between anarchist and skinhead gangs. This was a regular occurrence in central Germany, an area of political ferment and the historical home of the legendary Engels. The nation's twenty-year-old democracy was still experiencing growing pains, and street fights between political factions were one obvious sign of it. Düsseldorf was not as prosperous as Bonn and Frankfurt and was home to much of the country's intellectual counterculture outside of Berlin. The situation in the downtown core was much like that in London, with a large bohemian population constantly being forced to defend itself against attacks by groups of right-wing thugs, mostly young men from poor backgrounds. Rick Farren was naturally in his element and went to participate in the fight, getting a nasty cut on his arm in the process. The pain from his wound served to keep him quiet for much of the southbound trip.

The bands stayed over an extra night in the city to catch their friends Aluminum Can playing a gig at the Rockpalast, the largest club in town. They felt right at home, both with the band's hypnotically rhythmic music (they were known for their pioneering use of electronics as well) and with the crowd of local freaks, some of whom were wearing only black clothing and had a strange, jerky way of dancing. It was explained to Hastings that these were members of a new religious cult based in the industrial cradle of central Germany's Rhineland that worshipped machines as the future rulers of the Earth and believed that rock and roll was the sacred music of this evolving master species. When computers were finished their evolution, they would miniaturize into hand-held devices, take over the minds of men and women, and establish a new world order. The cult members' dance was a tribute to their future masters, with whom they hoped to gain favor. The whole thing sounded crackers.

He avoided taking any drugs, but Marty had now fallen back into his old habits, buying a large vial of Peking Sunrise and consuming the whole thing over the course of the evenings; at least it was a legit product that wouldn't kill him. Farren and Mo Wyatt split the two remaining bottles of absinthe and disappeared until the next morning, when they were discovered by two members of the local constabulary asleep in the alley behind the club. The two musicians had no idea where they were, so the unusually jocular *polizei* drove them back to the hotel.

A short drive the next day through miles of industrial parks and belching smokestacks brought them to Bonn, which had been almost destroyed by aerial bombing during the Great War and then completely rebuilt. The architectural firm that was responsible for the erection of the Bogota dome had also done much of the rebuilding here, so miniature versions of that construction were popular as greenhouses and garden sheds to shut out the palpable pall of smog. The local affection for glass exteriors had created a city that could be seen gleaming from miles away, a forest of glinting skyscrapers; even the opera house was roofed with shingles of clear Plexiglas.

The city looked like an exotic, mysterious vision from a science fiction novel, but the truth is more prosaic; Bonn is the business center of Germany, and the population is primarily made up of one class: the financial office worker. The Spheres possessed only a small following in that strange, shining, soulless epitome of the future city, so the gig took place in a small club, even smaller than the hall in Nouveau Paris. The audience of a hundred or so watched the set dispassionately, sipping schnapps and beer in cushioned seats, then clapped politely but half-heartedly at the end of each number. It was something of a mystery why these people bothered to come at all.

When they stopped in the next city, Stuttgart, an unremarkable commercial metropolis also built on Great War ruins, Hastings quietly popped into the local mega-department store to buy supplies for his mission. He picked up a length of rope, which he stowed in the tire compartment of the van. He also bought a change of black clothing and a black balaclava. A small bag that could be worn around the waist under his clothes and a sharp hunting knife would complete the ensemble. He asked the wide-eyed clerk if he had heard of the impending reign of the machines, and if he was ready for it. That kept the lad's questions at bay. He already had his deadly sonic hairdryer, which he sincerely hoped he would not have to use again — not even on Schmidt.

In Stuttgart they saw for the first time on this tour the refugees of the atomic wars. A group of young people aged well beyond their years, dressed in the rags of once-respectable clothing, lay shivering listlessly on the pavement of Palace Square, their faces sunken and pale, marked by tragedy and a lack of care about whether they lived or died. When Hastings stopped to offer them a little money, they told in cracked voices and broken English of the horrors they had witnessed, of the black marks on the ruined buildings that showed where a person had once stood, of the radiation-wasted corpses lying by the thousands covered in their own vomit in the ruins of Sofia, of wandering through a wasteland where no houses stood, where the trees were blasted into charcoal, where no birds sang and the voices of children playing were silenced forever. The comfortable modern burghers of Stuttgart paid little heed to the refugees, who would soon continue their laborious journey northward, their only goal getting as far away as possible from the hell that was their former home before they died.

The musicians were all glad to leave this characterless town and head for the hills and peaks of Bavaria, except for Hastings and Marty. Their apprehension grew with every mile that brought them closer to their nemesis.

Munich was to be the last stop in Germany before the tour moved on to Italy and then to Vienna. The city was actually farther than Augsburg, which they would narrowly pass on their southward journey, but Hastings thought it would be wise not to make his break if they stopped there; Marty would realize right away what had happened, and the others would come after him, thus ruining his plan and quite possibly putting all their lives in jeopardy. Instead, he would wait until after the Munich show to disappear and make his way northward by train or coach. A phone call to the bus station in Munich confirmed that an overnight coach leaving the terminal at eleven thirty would take him to Augsburg within a couple of hours.

His friends noticed his unusual silence but attributed it to road-weariness and left him alone. The landscape was becoming quite hilly, and there was some snow on the ground. The scenery possessed a Gothic quality, with the crags and ominous castles clinging to the hillsides, looming over the villages as a grim reminder of the peasants' former overlords. The sky had been overcast for days; the London weather seemed to be following them as they went farther into the heart of the continent. Hastings found himself wishing that their tour had focused instead on the Riviera and Southern Italy.

In the afternoon, he awoke groggily in the back of the van, flipping his body-heat-warmed blanket away from his face. His back was sore and stiff from the van's poor suspension and the bumps of the autobahn. Marty had been pulling the overnight driving shift, and Hastings went forward to visit him.

"Near Augsburg," Marty said, rubbing a reddened eye with one hand.

"Hmmm," Hastings answered sleepily. *Not far now.* "Why don't you go and get some sleep in the back? I'll take over. We'll stop for some food when some more of us are up."

Marty grinned. "All right, then."

"Shut the hell up!" Teresa growled from where she reclined awkwardly in the seat behind them.

Marty pulled gently over to the shoulder, and they exchanged places. He too was soon snoring away by the back doors with his feet stuck in Basil's face. Hastings had an excellent view of the historic town of Augsburg in the few golden rays that penetrated cracks in the gloom. This ancient town had been transformed over the previous decade into the model of the twenty-first-century corporate city, devoted almost entirely to the activities of KässelPharma. The company's childless founder, Bernhard Kässel, had originally based the company in Munich, but after her takeover, Schmidt had preferred the isolation of the hills and refused to move the headquarters somewhere more convenient to the world's business community.

The actual company headquarters were outside the town proper, a typical small European city of stone houses and old churches, and, as Henry had described, the company property was a heavily guarded community unto itself. Kässel provided schooling, shops, and basic social services, so that a worker and his family could hypothetically spend their entire lives within the gates without wanting for any of the basic amenities or comforts of life. This new system of absolute corporate governance of employees' lives caused people like Hastings to shudder, but the idea had become very popular and has unfortunately become even more so over the last few years. Hastings' personal theory was that the state would eventually become so impotent, it would wither away, but not to be replaced with a people's republic like Engels, the prophet of socialism, had predicted. The rulers of the future would be the oligarchical spawn of an unholy union between capital and government, with eternal expansion the only goal of the state. Corporations already possessed such economic power in theory, which transcended all borders, that governments were powerless to stop them from doing whatever they wanted or effectively regulating their activities. Humanity would become enslaved again, tranquilized by recreational pharmaceuticals and television while the Earth's rulers, corporations like Kässel, Common Motor Vehicles, and the Microware Corporation fought larger-than-life battles over market territory with no regard for the human or ecological cost.

And Kässel was to a great extent the very prototype of this sort of arrangement.

Hastings could see the compound in the distance, built mostly of shining glass and white brick low-rises in elaborate, curvy, but utilitarian modern styles, dozens of buildings, dwellings, and warehouses, its acres surrounded by a fence, which he hoped was not electrified. The pharma companies guarded their secrets jealously.

The castle where Helga Schmidt resided poked out like a sore thumb in the middle of this scene, a sixteenth-century leviathan of pointed spires and wind-worn brown stone built onto the side of a small hill. It was said that she now never left the castle for any reason and that many of her chief executives had not so much as glimpsed her face in years. Well, she might be receiving a new visitor very soon, he thought grimly. An unhappy visitor — and a very frightened one too.

TWENTY-SIX

Hastings was a fast driver, and they pulled into Munich within half an hour of his taking over the wheel. The others had slept through the rest of the journey while he chain-smoked and pondered his impossible task. When he pulled into Ludwigstrasse near the club they were booked into, he roused the van's bedraggled inhabitants and bundled the groggy sleepers into the nearest café. As always, there were no signs of the other two vans, which would likely arrive a few hours later.

After checking into the cheap hotel, they spent the rest of the day exploring the city, as they usually did. Hastings and Teresa enjoyed visiting historic sites, but Farren, Marty, and Basil preferred to spend the day sampling the city's bars and beer gardens, so they split into two groups.

The city's beauty had sustained very little bombing during the Great War, but it was still at that time filled with a shocking amount of atomic refugees who had entered illegally via the Austria-Hungary border. They saw dozens huddled begging on street corners, hiding in alleys or shuffling across streets, men, women, and a few children in rags of formerly respectable clothing. Most were grotesquely thin and deathly pale, some hairless and constantly coughing as radiation sickness slowly consumed them. The citizens ignored them with a determination born of discomfort and pity; there were so many refugees that they could not all be assisted, a sight to pain anyone with the slightest amount of compassion. So much for the League of Nations, which in several years had done little to alleviate the suffering caused by the wars.

Despite his near-suicidal plan for that night and the pathetic presence of these exiles, Hastings spent with Teresa what he later remembered as his last happy day. The shadow of Rosas seemed far from her mind as they strode along the cobblestone byways, talking carelessly of their future. Until a couple of months before, though neither of them had been with another person, there had been no declarations of fidelity or permanence. Teresa had never seemed like a very permanent woman, likely to suddenly decide upon waking up one morning that she was off to join the freedom fighters of Mexico, and no one could stop her when she made a decision. But the tragedies that had befallen them had brought them closer, and she now spoke only about the things that they would do together. And after that evening, he realized there was a good chance she would never see him again.

He was strongly tempted to tell her the truth about what had happened and what was to come, but he knew that, like Marty, she would want to participate, and there was no way he was going to put her in danger. He also briefly considered giving up, running as far away from KässelPharma as possible, taking Teresa away to some isolated Arctic cabin where no assassin could ever find them. But no. For too long he had hollowly preached the language of revolution while actually doing very little about the issues that angered him. He had been directly confronted with a real evil, and he must now react as an equal force; he would bring down Helga Schmidt, at the price of his life.

And he already had two deaths on his conscience. Why not another? The inevitability of someone not making it out of this alive was starting to feel palpable.

*

The rest of the day and evening went by in a blur. Hastings sleepwalked his way through the gig at a dingy church hall, although no one seemed to notice that he wasn't mentally quite there. Astronomy played the first set, which they hadn't done yet on the tour. He had suggested it earlier that day, saying it was not really democratic for the amiably pliant Wylde Flowers to be taking the first spot all the time. This meant his own set would end at ten thirty, giving him ample time to retrieve his supplies from the van and make his way to the bus station before he was missed. He hoped that when the others found out he was gone, Marty wouldn't clue in immediately what his destination was. They would probably assume he'd been kidnapped. It was painful to think of their suffering, but there was no alternative. He would contact them as soon as he could.

When it was all over, he slipped away through the backstage door and into the night. Retrieving his supplies and placing them in his bag, he hailed a taxi and asked in his halting German to be taken to the station.

Once on the bus, which was only half full of mostly sleeping people, he pulled his hat down low and pretended to be dozing for the rest of the journey. It would not do to be recognized anywhere in the close orbit of Helga Schmidt. He wondered what had become of Ricardo Alvarez's hint of assistance; he had kept his eyes open for suspicious characters but had been approached by no one. Perhaps the Cartels' reach was not as far-ranging as the security director would have had him believe. He saw nothing through the window of the bus as he sat alone with his fears, his hands shaking slightly.

At twelve fifteen, the bus pulled into Augsburg's high street. Hastings looked around him warily as he disembarked. He had only a rough sense of direction, but there were plenty of signs pointing the way to KässelPharma, the pride of the town. For a Saturday night, the streets were remarkably quiet, the only sounds faint laughter and clattering from the pubs, the barking of distant dogs, and the whistle of the wind through the eaves of darkened buildings. A fine layer of new snow covered the ground, and it lay largely undisturbed.

Hastings made his way through the sloping side streets for about fifteen minutes until he came to the edge of the old town.

Off to his left he could see a large, spotlit main gate dominated by a guard tower. There were about fifty meters of snow-covered lawn between him and the fence, which stretched toward him and off into the distance on his right. The fence was roughly ten feet high and was illuminated by spotlights every few meters. It would be risky to try to scale the fence at any point, and he had no idea how well the area was patrolled.

On the other side of the fence across from him were athletic grounds, with football goalposts and a track. A large, low building, which might have been a school, stood nearby. Beyond that were the lights of other larger buildings, presumably office blocks or the apartments that housed the workers. To his left, he could see shining luminescent in the mist a large dome, possibly a greenhouse and presumably made of the same material as the amazing Bogotá Dome. A faint outline peppered by sparse lights in the distance showed where the dark castle and its mastermind brooded over their dominion. He decided to move a healthy distance away from the main gate before attempting to scale the fence, on which he had noticed a hazardous climb lay ahead. There were also no warning signs except *Betreten verboten!* placards posted at even intervals.

Hastings kept to the road for a few minutes but had to jump behind a bush when a large lorry lumbered toward him. It went through the gates, which were now far in the distance. When he felt he had put sufficient distance between himself and the gate, he moved toward the fence, brushing his footprints away as best he could as he walked. He had picked a fortunate spot. The only building close to the fence was what looked like a power station. It had no windows and only one light burning on it. The sound of humming turbines drifted toward him. He put out a tentative hand, touching the fence as lightly as possible, half-expecting to be thrown back by a massive shock, but nothing happened.

After a quick glance around him, he took the short length of climber's rope out of his bag and made a noose at the end. He awkwardly threw it upward, catching on one of the top spikes on the first go. After a few agonizing seconds of inept but determined climbing, he was on top, using the bag for cushioning against the spikes. The links in the fence were very small and had afforded his toes very little space for footholds. Rubbing his hands, which were slightly rope-burned, he ran into the shadow of the building. Just in time; a few seconds later, footsteps crunched in the snow across the field. A guard came into view, trudging slowly along the length of the fence. Hastings cursed himself, looking over at the fresh boot prints he had neglected to wipe away. He drew his sonic gun. However, when the man, who was heavy-set and wearing a military-style uniform, lumbered by, he seemed to be half asleep and did not even pause as he walked over the tracks. Hastings waited several minutes after he passed then ran for the nearest clump of trees, thinking it would have been in the best spy-film style to have killed the guard and donned his uniform as a disguise. But he still wanted to get out of this mess with as little blood on his hands as possible.

He made his way gradually toward the castle, moving from landmark to landmark, running across roads and ducking behind fences. He wondered whether the castle was the best destination; perhaps better intel could be found in some kind of office building. But he had no idea what each building was for, and his German was not good enough to translate the longer text on signs he came across.

The area looked a lot like a Virginian suburb, with orderly, prefabricated houses jostling one another along the wide, treeless avenues. He saw few people or vehicles, all in the distance. There was an air of unnerving tranquility about the place, almost like the hushed, anticipatory stillness of Christmas Eve.

At last, he passed over a final road and stepped onto another field. This one stretched for about half a mile to the foot of the oddly placed hill on which a prudent sixteenth-century nobleman had built his fortress. Standing under a scrubby tree and sticking close to the trunk for cover, Hastings looked up at the castle. It certainly was impressive, with towers and gables sticking out all over, capped by the typical Bavarian spires. The walls loomed dark in the mist, dotted by the odd light in the windows. He wondered how many people lived in the castle with Schmidt. His heart sank when he saw that there was only one entrance, reached via a road that ran up a concrete ramp. One guard at least could be plainly seen slouching under the massive archway of the gate. There would be no way of gaining entrance without killing the guard, who would see him coming anyway and would have plenty of time to raise the alarm. All he could do was walk around the base of the hill, looking for a window low enough to reach, an unlikely chance; the castle had obviously not been built to allow an easy, undetected entry.

The cold was beginning to numb his feet and hands, and Hastings was starting to feel quite miserable. It had been a madcap scheme right from the start. Perhaps it had all been inspired more by boredom than revenge. But was too late for self-recrimination. With a quick glance up at the few stars visible through ragged tears in the cloud, and a made-up prayer to any higher power that might be listening, he began to circumnavigate the castle grounds.

After walking only a few hundred feet, Hastings had occasion to give thanks to the gods. On the west side, well away from the gate, was a peculiar series of low, very small windows, only about fifteen feet above the slope of the hill. Why they had been placed there is something an amateur historian might wish to research, but Hastings had no time for speculation. He ran up the steep floodlit slope until he was directly under one of the windows, which was unlit. The wall was smooth, but the rough rock around the window sill looked uneven. He made a small loop at the end of the rope and tossed it up without much hope. It fell back uselessly. On the fifth attempt, it finally caught on something. He wrapped his shaking hands around the rope and began to pull himself up. The rope held.

Dragging himself with much effort onto the wide sill, Hastings was surprised to see that the outer pane of the window was broken. His rope had caught on the jagged, thick glass and ragged iron that remained in the frame. During his climb, the glass had cut into the rope so that it was now held together by a few strands.

He sighed in relief, managed to find the catch to open the window, which only squeaked a little on opening, and pulled the remaining length of rope up behind him, then gingerly lifted himself over edge, dropping down into the pitch-black room. Striking a match, he saw in the flickering light that the room was empty, except for a portrait on the wall of an aristocrat in early nineteenth-century garb, glaring down at him over a huge walrus mustache. An thick layer of dust covered the floor, the sill, and the picture frame, and he stifled a sneeze. Letting the match go out, he made his way to the massive wooden door and tried the handle, perhaps unused for decades. His luck held again; the door was not locked from the outside, and the handle turned smoothly, with only a small protest.

He peered out into a hallway, shielding his eyes from the sudden glare of electric light. There was no one around in what he took to be a servant's passageway. A deathly silence reigned over the building. The entire castle was quite likely inhabited by fewer than twenty people: the unmarried Schmidt, her servants, and bodyguards.

Hastings made his way to a wide spiral staircase at the end of the hall. There was no dust in the hall or on the staircase, which was a sure sign that this wing of the castle must be used for something. He assumed that the inhabited quarters would be on the upper floors, where he had seen most of the lights. Coming to a landing, he found himself at the entrance to a large, well-lit hall, the former banquet hall of the castle. Ducking behind a headless statue, he saw that a stout female servant was moving around the room, straightening the portraits and switching on the lamps that ringed the walls. He slipped noiselessly around the statue and continued his climb, hugging the right-hand wall in case he should hear someone descending; he gripped his gun tightly.

On the next landing, hallways stretched out on either side. This area of the castle was well decorated and obviously used. The deep red carpet would muffle his footsteps. A door at the end of the left-hand hall was slightly ajar, and bright electric light poured from it. He avoided it and started checking the other doors, keeping an eye on the lighted doorway. All of the doors were locked, but the one nearest to the danger opened. Praying that the room would be unoccupied, he slipped in and, hearing no sounds, fumbled for a match.

He could not believe his luck. The room was clearly an office. A large desk filled half of it, with papers organized in stacks. A modern portrait of a middle-aged woman with steely eyes and gray-blonde hair was on the wall. The rest of the décor appeared to be ancient weaponry or instruments of torture. A well-oiled iron maiden, which he recognized from a book he had read as a child, took up one corner, and maces and battleaxes hung from the walls. At least, he thought, there would be no shortage of primitive weapons if he needed them. Family heirlooms, perhaps, or a bizarre collecting hobby. He shivered in the presence of the evidence of such sadism and cruelty. This could be Helga Schmidt's own personal domain, or someone close to her in her business. A door joined the room to the lit one beside it. He pressed his ear to the wood but heard nothing.

He walked over to the desk, switched on a small lamp, and began scanning the documents on the desk. They seemed to be internal company memos and held nothing of interest. If he were to find any evidence of assassin-hiring or anything else he could use against Schmidt, he doubted it would it would be left on display, where the servants might find it and potentially use it for blackmail. He had to admit he had no idea what he was doing.

Nonetheless, he turned his attention to the two filing cabinets under the portrait, which seemed to be glowering in disapproval as he started opening the unlocked drawers. He was just pulling out the first folder when he heard a soft click from behind him. Too late, he spun around, pointing his weapon.

"Drop it!" There were five men in uniform crowding in, pointing weapons at him, and the door to the adjoining room was open.

He let the gun drop, and Helga Schmidt entered.

TWENTY-SEVEN

She looked exactly like the woman in the portrait, but several years older. The now completely gray hair was scraped back into a severe bun, and she was dressed in a prim pink dressing gown not unlike one Hastings' mother had owned. She strode up to Hastings and stared into his eyes. She nodded once with a look that told him what was in store for him.

He knew the game was up; he had been insane to try this. All he could do now was die with some dignity. Strangely, under the fear and despair, he detected something that could only be described as relief.

Schmidt's unblinking gray eyes continued to hold his. She would have been very beautiful once, with sharp but symmetrical features and a lean, robust body, and was still severely handsome. A genuine Teutonic warrior queen.

"Well," she said in an even, low voice, "what have we here? This is Mr. Simon Hastings, I believe." She had a melodious accent and the voice of a much younger woman. "I would not have expected you to walk right into my hands." She took a seat behind the desk and did not invite him to join her. The men continued to train their guns unwaveringly on him, expressionless.

"I think I know why you are here. I have been following your activities for a very long time."

"Why?" he croaked.

"*Why?* Why have I been following your life with such interest? Or do you mean, why do I so fervently wish to end it? I suppose I am willing to answer, although I owe *schwein* like you no explanation of my motives, no waste of precious breath. You are lower than dirt." He eyes flashed passionately as her façade cracked.

"My father, as you may have heard, was once conductor of the Berlin Philharmonic, amongst his many other achievements." He did not know that but said nothing, gazing steadily in front of him, trying to look as brave as possible while his knees threatened to knock together.

"From birth, he imparted in several values to me. Love of great, heroic music was one, particularly the music of our Fatherland. Discipline and ambition were others. And God and country were a third. A desire to see an orderly world spring up from the ashes of history."

She got up and perched on the desk. "Yes, my father was a great man, and he taught me these virtues. Though I was a woman, I was determined to become whatever I wanted to shape the modern world. I have to some extent attained this goal, you will agree. They call me 'The Iron Lady.'" She smiled. "My first wish was to play the cello, an instrument of surpassing beauty, as even an animal of your sort must agree."

"A lovely sound," he muttered.

"Yes. However, I found myself without a talent for music. It is the greatest tragedy of my life. Not possessing the desire to take up any other instrument, I applied myself to the world of business. Myself and others like me, we rebuilt the world's economy after the Great War. We built the great companies that employ the people, we made the laws stronger to regain order and discipline. We worked with the government to ensure that our industries were stocked with all the labor we needed to maintain strong economies. We allowed culture to thrive—"

"*Your* culture!" Despite his fear, Hastings was becoming very angry at the old reactionary's rhetoric. The knowledge that his father, an intelligent man but one of low birth, had been forced to work in a factory by a world that didn't care what he actually had to offer, had always filled him with rage. Now he was faced with one of the people who had fashioned such an unfair world.

Schmidt smiled thinly and dismissed three of the guards.

The other two stood stiffly at attention in the corner. "Yes, *my* culture. You see me as regressive, do you not? And yet when the governments decided it was time to relax social controls and allow the average citizen a little more freedom, did I protest? No, though I knew in my heart it might be disastrous in the end. I expanded my own stake into the pharmaceutical industry that has given people, even wastrels like you, such pleasure. We have also lengthened lifespans and fought disease. I gave in to the times. I had cause to regret it.

"What have I received in return? A generation of youth that is beyond control and reason, that scorns the values we established, that spits on industry, that lives for laziness, rolling in its own filth, listening to jungle music devoid of beauty, complexity, or form! That revels in consorting with the inferior races of foreign lands. No matter how much freedom you are given, you always want more and different, more rights for different groups of freaks, until you tear up the seeds I have sown! You are swine!" Her eyes were now blazing, though her tone remained even.

She suddenly slapped him across the face, hard, and he could feel blood dripping from his mouth. He was left speechless.

She sat down and regained her composure. "The world should have been as orderly as a Bach concerto, as well constructed as Beethoven's symphonies. Instead, the chaos of *your* music is, it would seem, the most powerful symbol of a future I fear will soon come to pass. Well, I decided not to let you have your endless party without feeling some of the grief and pain I have felt. I took the time to find out who the leading makers of this noise where. I knew I could do what was necessary; and it would be even enjoyable. Removing the leaders may not stop a movement, but it can wound it deeply and slow it. Silence some of those poisonous sounds. And I am not finished. Ramón Rosas' incompetence as an assassin is what gave you the clues, not your own intelligence. This mistake will not be repeated. I have enjoyed it too much. Soon, after I am finished perfecting my methods through your friends, I will move on to other activists. No one will suspect KässelPharma could be in any way involved."

"The Cartels know."

She shrugged. "What can they do? It is not as though they even sympathize with your plight. They and we are cut from the same cloth. And while the power of those brown-skinned savages may equal mine, their intellect does not. These deaths cannot be traced to me. What will they do? I am well protected here. And besides, the one aspect of my plan that has not worked well thus far is that, since these 'crimes' have not been investigated at all, the Cartels have not yet been suspected, as I had hoped. A small wrinkle. No pressure has been put on them as yet. They have no reason to be hostile. I will have to make that connection more obvious in the future."

Hastings wanted to make some great speech in rebuttal, for sake of Guy, Ed, and all their friends, before he died. He wanted to tell Schmidt that she would never win, that freedom of culture and of choice and celebration of diversity were values that could never be stamped out. That every person deserved to realize their own potential, not only the people ruthless, calculating, and fortunate by birth and position. That governments belong to the people by right, not to corporations, and should exist to benefit and take care of them, not to collude with the rich to rule heavy-handedly. But his tongue was frozen by the memories of how the police on two continents had refused to listen to him and laughed in his face. He was tired and had been for a long time, and now his own death was imminent. There was no point in railing against it. He could only hope that the fight would go on.

Schmidt had been lost in a reverie of her own for a few moments, but she broke out of it with a snarl. "Well, I have an experience in store for you. As I killed your friends by means of the very drugs that fueled their deviance, I will do to you also. I pondered what to do with you when you were spotted climbing the gates. I did not know who you were then, but I am very grateful that you have delivered yourself into my hands. What did you expect, that I would leave evidence of my transactions lying around like a schoolgirl's diary? No. You are more intelligent than that. You were here to kill me with that little weapon of yours, were you not? You will pay a heavy price, Herr Hastings.

"*Führt ihn ins Nebenzimmer*," she said to the guards.

The game was up. Now was the time to show some spine. He had always wondered what lay beyond this life and had written plenty of sad songs about it. Whatever she had planned for him, it could not be worse than living another minute with the knowledge of his failure.

TWENTY-EIGHT

The punishment that Schmidt had devised was indeed the product of a diseased mind. After a preliminary beating that seemed more for the benefit of the guards and likely left his nose and some ribs broken, Hastings was taken to the room next door, which seemed to be her own quarters. It was sparsely furnished, the only decoration being an old, yellowed photograph of a sickly-looking bearded man in early twentieth-century evening dress. Presumably the esteemed father. On another wall, a chain had been embedded in the wall. Hastings was shackled to it by the guards and placed in a wooden chair.

Schmidt explained calmly what was about to happen. He would be killed the same way as Guy and Ed, but over a week's time. A cocktail of Kässel products, mixed with trace amounts of deadly poison, would be administered twice a day for a week, or until he was dead. Schmidt would be able to view his agonies whenever she cared to. The "treatment" would begin the next day.

Hastings spent the night curled up in a ball on the floor, watched by a guard. Schmidt did not sleep in the chamber. The next morning, he was awakened from a surprisingly deep sleep by kicks from his guard. A few minutes later, a small, nervous-looking gray-haired man in a white coat entered the room, carrying a black physician's bag. He pulled out a small syringe filled with a blood-colored liquid, avoiding making even the slightest eye contact. Hastings tried to fight, but the burly guard restrained him in an iron grip while the "doctor" rolled back his sleeve, and, without even bothering to carefully locate a vein, plunged in the needle. Hastings howled, but the man depressed the plunger then left the room in a hurry, sweating noticeably.

Hastings felt no effects for about an hour, then a feeling of strange euphoria came over him, which he recognized as the high induced by the Cognitive Enhancer, but amplified tenfold. His thoughts became scattered, and he was unable to focus his mind on any topic or his eyes on any object. His arms and legs began to move of their own accord, and he writhed around on the floor, watching his twitching limbs almost with disinterest.

Later in the day, just as the spasms were dying down, the man returned and administered another dose. Hastings didn't have the strength to try to fight him off. This time the reaction was faster and was accompanied by a dull pain that gradually increased in intensity. The pain originated in his lower back and traveled up to his head. Soon he was moaning in agony as his guard looked on. Schmidt entered shortly after and sat watching, smoking, and drinking a glass of red wine, not speaking but watching him with quiet enjoyment.

Desperate to lose consciousness, Hastings closed his eyes and tried to relax his body, but the pain and loss of motor function could not be stopped. He had little doubt he had soiled himself at least once that day. Eventually, Schmidt dismissed the guard and prepared for bed. She went about her toilette, going modestly behind a screen and emerging in another nightdress, a deceptively virginal white garment embroidered with tiny edelweiss. Leaving a lamp on, she lay in bed and did not move for the rest of the evening, although he could see her eyes watching him, glinting for a while in the darkness until gentle snoring finally filled the room. He wanted to shout out and disturb her, but all he could produce were a few croaks that fell uselessly into the silence.

Throughout the night, his head cleared slightly and the pain lessened, but he was tormented by visions similar to those that had afflicted him during his bad trip. They primarily centered around his friends. He saw Teresa put in his place in this room, contorted by spasms of pain. He saw Marty screaming under assault by a hundred sonic guns. Ladbroke Grove was razed by an army of tanks and bulldozers led by his brother in a khaki Krupp-Benz, while Schmidt rode on a palfrey placed atop the fancy automobile. An airplane piloted by Schmidt dropped an atomic bomb on New York, and she cackled with glee as the city was vaporized. Hastings had never before been tormented by such powerfully clear, realistic visions, not even on his worst acid trips. He realized that a concentrated hallucinogenic had been included in the cocktail, and throughout the night he fought desperately to keep the visions at bay. This internal fight raged until dawn, when the drugs again began to subside. He was so weak that he could not move at all, and he was covered in a layer of cold, stale sweat.

Shortly after sunrise, Schmidt rose and left, patting him on the head. The guard dragged him to a washroom to allow him to relieve himself, and he was force-fed some kind of tasteless stew, most of which he defiantly spat out. The "doctor" returned and administered another dose, again refusing to meet his eyes and ignoring his mumbled pleas. Despite his best efforts, Hastings was slowly being reduced to a drooling mass of flesh that had only one goal left: to die and have the suffering end.

*

This went on for three more days, and he knew he would soon expire. Through all this time, Schmidt sat for long periods in her upholstered antique chair, saying little but watching him rave and fight off his invisible demons. When she spoke, it was only to ramble on calmly but insanely in the same fashion as she had when he was first captured. During his brief periods of lucidity, he would return her gaze glassily but mockingly to show he was still unconquered. Late at night, when the dosage would wear off a little, he reflected on the futility of the life he had lived. He had never taken the time to try to be content, his philosophical bent being his perpetual downfall. He had never learned to enjoy life for the moments of joy it presented and had rarely managed to generate any of his own. He had thrown himself, craving an optimistic meaning and goal, into a movement that now appeared pointless, its objectives unattainable and ill-defined. His was not the generation that would bring about utopia; they would fail their ideals.

At least he had always been able to immerse himself in the beautiful solace of music to remind himself that there may be other worlds beyond this prosaic, brutal one we are cursed to inhabit, even if, at the same time, his rational faculties denied it. If only he could have ignored the ugliness of the modern world and found a way to enjoy his small place in it, to "live in the world but be not of it," as Mallorn was fond of saying.

But by the fourth evening, it had become obvious that his life was fast trickling away. He had refused to eat in an effort to speed things along and allow his oppressor as little pleasure as possible, but they had force-fed him twice. He could no longer move at all, but his eyes were still fixed on Schmidt from where he lay with a hateful intensity that matched her own. The sun was setting, and the room was suffused with an orange glow that, for a few moments, convinced him he was now truly dying and being welcomed into the very same afterlife he had never believed in. But though the glow remained for a while, his surroundings remained the same, and Schmidt loomed above him, framed in the light like an avenging angel, nudging him with the toe of her slipper.

Her voice rolled into the silence, breaking the spell. "You are fading fast. I had hoped to see more resilience from you, Herr Hastings. No matter. I have enjoyed this time with you. I will now stay at your side until you die, which will give me the greatest joy. Then, rest assured, I will do the same with to all that you love, cleansing the world.

"But first, let me enlighten you somewhat concerning your errors. After all, though I do hate you, I recognize that you are merely misguided, a product of your environment and upbringing, as we all are, to an extent. You no doubt like to shroud your degenerate nature in mysticism, with illusions such as the supposed equality of all living things, a concept borrowed from the barbarians of the East."

She twirled an unlit cigarette in her fingers. "I realized early on, with my father's assistance, that there is only one reason for human existence, and a rage-filled God designed the rules: survival. A man or woman exists only to procreate and to struggle with others for supremacy, to prove their worth. To decide how others will live and die, and thus reach a god-hood of their own. It is a harsh reality there is no point in fleeing. In fact, it must be embraced. And our race is the one best positioned to rule; do we not already rule the world?

"I found out early in life that I had no taste for domestic life. I do not dispute that bearing and rearing healthy babies is the woman's natural role and proper place, but surely an exception must be made for women of genius! I was possessed of great intelligence, and I could defeat the male on his own terms. I did so, and I have conquered. You too, Herr Hastings, could have been a leader. I can tell by looking at the nobility of your face. But you turned your back on your own destiny to embrace these dreams of equality, for the mass of people who possess no more intelligence than dumb animals. Why? You see where that blind affection for the rabble has taken you?"

She walked over to a small, old-fashioned gramophone in the corner and put on a record. "I love music which can only be appreciated and understood by the chosen few, with arcane harmonies that speak only to the elite, those capable of understanding power and order. You know the work of Gregorovich? Court composer to the king of Prussia, where I was born. Something of a revolutionary in his youth, but he fortunately acquired greater wisdom from mixing with society's rulers at court."

The room filled with the hushed tones of a string quartet

playing a mournful but sickly sweet melody. Hastings found a trace of humor left, thinking that stuff like this still wasn't his scene, but it wasn't that bad either. Guy had been right in a sense; the emotion in this music was so indirect, almost false and stylized, like an overwrought tragedy, created to be acted out for the pleasure of a debauched, shallow noble and his court.

Well, it didn't matter now. What kind of music would they play in heaven, in the unlikely event such a dimension existed?

This last return to analytic thought was interrupted by a cracking sound from far away. It sounded like a gunshot. Schmidt sat bolt upright then jumped to her feet and lifted up the stylus. There were more muffled retorts, seemingly from the lower floors. She flung the door open, her already stretched skin taut with concern.

"*Verdammit nochmal, was ist denn hier los?*"

The guard shook his head. "*Verkündige dich.*"

He scurried off down the hallway. Schmidt turned back toward Hastings. "Broken plates in the scullery, no doubt. Not enough to distract us from our time together."

But the musty silence was punctuated by yet another shot, and another; there was no doubt what they were.

"*Scheisse!*" she hissed through clenched teeth, opening a drawer and pulling out a pistol. She swung around to Hastings, her eyes alight. "If someone has come to rescue you, they will not find you alive!" She trained the gun on his head, her arm twitching with the slightest tremor, as though her mask of icy self-control was finally slipping for good.

The shots continued for a few seconds, until slow, dragging footsteps could be heard close by in the hall. Schmidt's hand shook a little more as she swung her gun arm toward the door. "Halt!" The guard that she had sent to investigate the noise appeared in the doorway, his formerly beer-ruddy Bavarian face white as a sheet.

Then he fell to the floor, squirming a little, bleeding from his ears, his gasping face only a couple of feet from where Hastings lay. Hastings shuddered at the memory of Rosas, even as his spirit leapt with hope. This could only mean one thing.

The man managed to croak a little before he went limp.

Schmidt finally snapped. "So you have rescuers after all," she shrieked. "You are a worthless insect, but you have more wiles than I thought. No matter. They will not dare to touch me, but they will find you dead!" She swung the gun up again.

Hastings made a wild kick upward with all that was left of his failing strength, connecting with her thigh and knocking her aside. Her gun fell to the floor. He dived for it, but his chain wasn't long enough. Schmidt reached to recover her weapon, cackling madly, spittle dripping from her chin. She brought the gun up a third and final time, and Hastings fixed his eyes on hers.

At that moment, a dark hand reached down and plucked the gun neatly away. She gasped and fell backward. Ricardo Alvarez stood nonchalantly in the doorway, dressed in a dapper gray pinstripe suit and black fedora, looking like he was out for a leisurely stroll. He held one of the sonic weapons in his hand. Several men, dressed in black clothing and sunglasses like characters from a spy film, brandishing more conventional weapons, stood behind him.

Alvarez flashed Hastings his toothy smile. "*Guten tag,* Fräu Schmidt. And hello again, Mr. Hastings. I am glad to find you alive. It only improves what has already been a very successful day."

Suddenly, without warning, he moved forward like a pouncing cat, grabbed Schmidt savagely by the head, and squeezed the trigger near her ear.

Hastings closed his eyes and stayed that way for several seconds. But never again would he be able drive the images of death from his mind.

AFTERWORD

An odd story indeed. And yet my conversations with Simon's friends corroborate much of what has been recounted here. The truth about the death of my good friends Guy and Ed, as well as the mysterious murder of Helga Schmidt, an event that mystified the entire world, has finally been revealed.

The rest of the story is as follows: Hastings was released by Alvarez, but not before he had signed at friendly gunpoint a nondisclosure agreement (in triplicate), which required him to keep silent about all that happened. Hastings was tired of being pursued by killers. He was exhausted and sick in both mind and body, near death in fact, so he signed.

He kept silent, as have his friends, fearing for the life of this dear man — until now. Now that he is himself dead, there is no obligation to maintain the cloak of silence over these events, and I, as the one entrusted with the story, am morally obliged, despite the consequences, to tell it to the world as a warning and an alarm about what is going on behind the closed doors of boardrooms, factories, and mansions of the developed world. I alone have had exclusive access to these facts, and I have related them truthfully. If there are consequences for my own safety, I will accept them. Simon's story has convinced me that I too must choose a side and take a stand to prevent a horrible future instead of standing by on the sidelines, commenting dryly on what I see.

After a brief stay in a Munich hospital as an overdose patient while he healed, Hastings returned to England to rejoin his friends, who had naturally cancelled the remaining dates of the tour and waited with fading hope for news of him. The following article appeared in the *London Times* two days after the secret assault on the Kässel fortress:

Kässel CEO Murdered in Bizarre Incident

Terrorists take responsibility for assassination

The headquarters of KässelPharma in Augsburg, Germany, were raided just after nightfall two days ago, seemingly by a large group of armed men. All of the guards in the castle inhabited by the company's CEO, Helga Schmidt, and her servants, were killed, along with the businesswoman herself. The manner of her death has not been disclosed.

A terrorist group calling itself FreiBayern (A Free Bavaria) later telephoned the local police station and claimed responsibility for the raid, calling the deceased "an enemy of the free Bavarian state." There is no such militant group on record.

The crime contains many baffling aspects. The guards at the gates of the heavily patrolled compound were also found dead of gunshot wounds, and no alarms were sounded. The perpetrators were never seen by any Kässel staff, and the bodies were found by maintenance workers the next morning. However, German police report that forensic evidence suggests several gunmen were present, some bearing weapons of a highly unusual function. Whoever designed this raid would have considerable resources and planning abilities. The authorities are not releasing further information until their investigation is complete.

KässelPharma AG is the largest producer of recreational pharmaceuticals in the world. Telegrams of sympathy have been sent by the British government, as well as the firm's main competitors, United Chinese Chemical and the Colombian Cartels. It is unclear what the company's leadership succession plan will be.

Of course, the investigation revealed nothing, and the crime remained unsolved. The Colombians did their work well. Although Simon Hastings was never troubled by Ricardo Alvarez again, he fell soon after into a deep depression from which he never really emerged for any length of time. Astronomy broke up, going their separate ways. Basil Baker and Marty Sharpe-Thornton founded the Time and Space Collective, which has released several fine albums on Groovy Melon Records. Hastings made one solo album two years, ago, *Barren Land*, a desolate acoustic album that wrenches the soul.

It did not sell well but is still worth seeking out as a singular artistic expression.

Teresa took him on several trips around the world to try to lift him out of the darkness that enshrouded him, but to no avail. She did stay with him until his death.

A year ago, in December 1972, during an unseasonably cold early winter like that in which this story took place, Hastings stepped out onto Holland Park Avenue and was hit by a speeding motorist. He survived into the night, but the memory of the deaths he had witnessed had already destroyed his will to live. The press unashamedly and unfoundedly speculated that his death was a suicide.

It is my fervent wish that this book will at last give the public insight into the reasons for his decline, rehabilitate his reputation as an artist and a man, and preserve the memory of his bravery. I hope that you will remember my friend, Simon Hastings.

—Rodney Blair

APPENDIX: SONGS

THE MISANTHROPE'S BLUES
by Astronomy

Here comes the arrogant ape
Mother Nature's fatal mistake
Each group wants the others dead
Atrocities they love to make

They strip the earth of all that's good
Always too blind to see
Their evil sets my blood to boil
So I'll let this fire consume me

They clog up the streets
They block out the sky
They cut down the trees
They tunnel in the mines
Somehow they think they own what they find

If the population grows
And the world is clearly finite
Where did all these apes come from?
I know isn't right

You say I'm no better than you
You say we're all born the same
But good is good and bad is bad
And I know who to blame!

They clog up the streets
They block out the sky

They cut down the trees
They tunnel in the mines
Somehow they think they own what they find

I wish that I could tell you
The gods of tech will save you
Instead you'll choke and drown
On chemical fumes and metals

You say that I'm no better than anyone else
But I hate no one more than I hate myself

They've gone into space
They've put up a flag
They're just monkeys dressed in divine drag
How many of their own kind
Have died trying to earn those rags?

JUDGMENT DAY
by The Spheres

I knew a man
Who suddenly went insane
He ran away
Out into lonely meadows
In the lands beyond
Where the subway ends

He lay alone
Watching the grass grow
In a field
Near a winding river
Above his head

Not a cloud in the sky

He reflected
But his mind was full of TV
He screamed aloud
Life's become too easy
I don't want to die
I'm not even living

Then the sky opened up
And rained stars down upon him
The flowers cried
In the presence of their maker

He returned to town
And all the people ran away
A beam of light
Was searing from his eyes
They couldn't look
The brightness burned their souls

Then the sky opened up
And rained fire down upon them
There was nowhere to hide
From the passing of the judgment

BARREN PLANET
by The Spheres

The sands have run down the glass
The long day fades into sunset
The wind blew all they had built away
When they decided not to pay their debts

They never found their way home
The barren planet mourns alone

They were like animals trapped in a cage
And they grinned at death like mannequins
While those who foresaw the future wept
They knew too much, they'd worn too thin

They never found their way home
The barren planet mourns alone

They'll never return
They threw it away
They watched it burn
And danced in the flames
And laughed in their pain

Who will watch now in the withered land
As deserts engulf the city streets
Who will mourn now for a finite world
And laugh in the face of the fate
That he must meet

They never found their way home
The barren planet mourns alone

THE SHINING SEA
by The Spheres

The light takes so long to reach us
From the distant galaxies
And all our lives are but seconds long
I know I'll never see that far

But there's a reason beyond the awe
This smallness that I feel
And in the light we create together
A beauty is revealed

I make this vow to you
I will live this life for you

The only thing that we really own
Is the love that we share
We're just drops in the shining sea
It knows no joy or despair.

I make this vow to you
I will face this fate with you

FURTHER UP, FURTHER IN
by Astronomy

You stumble through the streets, drenched in rain
To find a way to ease this mortal pain
Somewhere far away, the sun is setting fast
Sometime years away, you think about the past

Somewhere far away, she looks down on you alone
Living out your life on this tiny stone

Melancholy minds pass you by in darkness
They're empty souls with no sins to confess
Somewhere inside them a spark is still glowing
Somewhere inside them a love may be growing

Light years away, a star implodes in silence

If we could see it, the mysteries might make some sense

Somewhere ahead, you foretell your end
Stars, as they fall, lead you further up and further in

Now comes a message from another world
From the mind of a lonely girl
Somewhere outside she felt you calling
Somehow she knew that you were falling

Sometime far ahead, you witness a birth
and you're finally glad that you graced this Earth

Somewhere ahead, you foretell your end
Stars, as they fall, lead you further up and further in

BARREN LAND
by Simon Hastings

Barren land, desolation
Pale sun pushes at the clouds
Dry river cuts the land like a scar
Broken buildings, jagged teeth
The skeleton of our society

Barren land, nothing left
Rust and bones and silence
Sobbing souls trapped in concrete
All sorrows, all regrets
They're gone, there's nothing left

Barren land, desolation
The final sum of all we were

All arrogance, all hubris
Now scattered, dust on a dry breeze
The failure of an entire species

Barren land

ACKNOWLEDGMENTS

I would like to thank my family, a few friends, musical or otherwise (who should know who they are), Laura Boyle for the fine cover, Samantha for the proofread, and Michael Moorcock, Hawkwind/Robert Calvert, and Daevid Allen for their profound influence on my way of thinking.

Allister Thompson has been a professional book editor since the late 1990s and a musician since his mother ordered him to take up an instrument, a long time before that. He was a member of several rock bands during his youth, including glam rockers Crash Kelly, and is now prolific in releasing a shocking amount of music from his home in North Bay, Ontario, Canada.

Visit *thegatelessgate.bandcamp.com* for more info, and listen to the Music of the Spheres playlist, featuring the very songs described in this book:

https://tinyurl.com/jmsjmr8k

YouTube:
https://tinyurl.com/pz5wjhw8

You can also visit Allister at *@gatelessgate1* on Twitter. And if you enjoyed this book — please tell someone!